THE MOON IS A GOOD PLACE TO DIE

A <u>LIQUID COOL</u> CYBERPUNK
DETECTIVE NOVEL

Book Eight

AUSTIN DRAGON

WELL-TAILORED BOOKS

Published by Well-Tailored Books, California

The Moon Is a Good Place to Die
(Liquid Cool, Book 8)

978-1-946590-75-6 (paperback)
978-1-946590-71-8 (ebook)

http://www.austindragon.com

Book cover design by Leslie K.

Printed in the United States of America

CONTENTS

Introduction

No introduction here. I've been arrested by Metro PD! I've been in Metropolis solving cases and surviving gun battles and have never been arrested once—until now. Sure, I came close. I'm a working street detective. But never for real. So, no time for games, witty banter, or any gripping stories. I've been arrested, my vehicle has been impounded, and the police have their paws on my prized omega-gun. This is bad, very bad. I've been framed hard by a pro—all bases covered, planted evidence conveniently laid out for the police detectives, incriminating photos and vids, and worse still, phony witnesses. I've been wrapped up with a big red bow for the authorities. This bad guy must be smiling from ear to ear thinking he's some kind of criminal mastermind genius. He's obviously never spoken to the Guy Who Scratched My Vehicle. He should have spoken to the lobotomized Red Rabbit, the late NeuroDancer, the later Mr. Viper, the late Mr. Vega, the later Ripper, the late Mr. Diagram, and plenty more. How does the saying go? "Don't make me angry. You won't like me when I'm angry." I know who you are, you skell bastard. The second I get out on bail, I'm coming for you, Mr. Three-Armed Man! Run, run. I don't care where you go; I'm going to get you. Leads or no, I'm going to get you. In fact, I may already know where you are.

Yes, _**The Moon Is a Good Place to Die!**_ (The bad guys, not me!)

PART ONE

The Arrest

CHAPTER 1

Metro PD

Though my home district of Rabbit City was far from being an upscale neighborhood, lately I had to remind myself it wasn't the dumps like Free City. We were working class. My residential megatower, known by all as the Concrete Mama, was an architecturally uninspiring chunk of granite that looked like it was set down on Earth from space, but it was home. Its residents were all legacy babies like I used to be—laborers. With free housing for life, our only needs were to make a meager living to cover basic incidentals, and nothing more. But now that I was a "famous" detective, I had inspired a revival of the monolith tower. Just because the Concrete Mama could withstand a planetary shockwave from a nuclear blast or an asteroid crash, didn't mean that inside needed to look so ugly. We had a solid daytime doorman—thanks to me—and he brought our solid nighttime doorman-security guard. We residents were transforming The Concrete Mama from the mundane to the classy.

Why was I thinking of such things? I had lived there for more than fifteen years—my apartment willed to me from my maternal grandparents. Well, before I only had a vehicle and a cool hat. Then a wife, a son, a vehicle and a cool hat. Now, we'd added a new daughter to the Cruz family. Kat had arrived!

It was a work morning, but I wasn't at work yet. I had wrapped up a call in my home office. The wife had left for work early. I could hear running around outside my closed door in the apartment. At least he was running rather than flying around in his hoverchair, which thankfully was too small for him these days. I told him he was getting "big boned" instead of "fat" so as not to hurt his feelings. He was playing Cops and Robbers with his toys.

I had finished my video-call and opened the door to see what Kat was up to. Besides being a "famous for real" fashionista at Metropolis's premiere hair and beauty salon, Eye Candy, my wife had channeled her interior design abilities into our apartment home on the 150th floor of the Concrete Mama. I was always seeing something new.

Cruz Jr. ran by laughing with a toy hovercar in one hand and a toy police cruiser in the other; and he was gone. The boy ran a full marathon every day in the place. I could hear whispering in the living room. I tiptoed in to see what they were plotting.

My head slowly peeked around the corner to look into the living room but my parents were sitting together on one of the couches watching me.

"I hope you're better at skulking after people on the street than this," my pops said to me.

"How did you hear me?" I asked.

My ma never wore much make-up, but had a perfect complexion, and her black hair was always pulled back in a braided ponytail. My pops had a graying mustache and beard, but his hair was all black. He had started wearing fedoras too that looked suspiciously like my own, but his hat was elsewhere. He sat with a mobile computer on his lap, and my ma sat with Kat, bundled up in a blanket, on hers. My daughter was a bundle of cuteness with big bright eyes. She looked like an angel. However, my parents looked guilty of something. I smiled. They smiled.

"Kat, what are your grandparents doing over there?" I asked my daughter. She giggled, though she had no clue as to what I was saying.

"Tell him: taking care of his kids," my pops said.

We heard Cruz Jr. run by again through the apartment and disappear.

I strolled over to them. My ma handed me a plastic paper flyer. She had a stack of them on the couch next to her.

"What's this?" I asked.

"What does it say?" my pops asked, in a challenging tone.

The flyer's text was in Spanish.

"'*De la gente que te dio Cruz el famosa detective.*' I know what the last part means. 'Cruz, the famous detective.' I'm very glad to see you acknowledge my stature in this supercity. '*De.*' That's a nonsense word like in French; skip it." I could hear my pops groaning. I looked to see my ma shaking her head. "I'm not finished. '*La gente.*' That's 'people.' '*Que te.*' Don't know. '*Dio.*' Isn't that 'day?'

"Cruz, day is '*dia.*'"

"*Dio*? Hmm."

"Cruz, '*Dar.*' To give."

"Oh. Give. 'The people who give you...' 'From the people who gave you Cruz, the famous detective.'"

I burst out laughing.

"'From the people who gave you Cruz, the famous detective.' You're my parents. Not people,' I said.

"Aren't we the people who gave the world you?"

I was laughing and because I was, Kat started laughing.

"You can build a—"

"Don't say it," I interjected.

"—a hovercar in our basement. But can't you learn another language?" my pops chastised.

"I know the language of the streets," I said with a smile. "That's why I'm famous." I held up their flyer. "Here. You said so yourself."

I looked at the rest of the flyer. "Wait. What is this?" I tried to piece together the other words. "Is this daycare? You're starting a daycare center and using my good name for publicity!"

Now my parents were laughing.

"Your good name?" my pops said and chuckled some more, with Kat laughing with them.

"Kat, get control of your grandparents."

The doorbell rang and we heard the rumble, then the blur of Cruz, Jr. flashing by us to the door.

"Cruz Jr.! Leave that door alone!" I yelled. "Only adults answer the door."

The human rocket—aka my son—came back the other way.

"Cruz Control, however many cups of coffee you're drinking, cut your intake by at least 80 percent," I said after him.

I strolled down our main hallway to the front door. The doorbell rang again. I reached it and I stopped at the video monitor. I slowly opened it.

In the hallway outside my door were several police officers. The sight of Metropolis police could always make your heart skip a beat, even the hardened gangster—they could kill you in an instant, if you did the wrong thing. But the police were my friends. Six police officers stood there in their silver-and-black body-armored uniforms, with the word "PEACE" in big bold white letters on their chests, wearing visored half-helmets. The lead officer had "DETECTIVE" on the chest.

"Mr. Cruz," the detective said.

"That's me."

"We're here to place you under arrest."

"What? Whatcha talking about?" I asked.

Cruz Jr. appeared next to me on his new toy hoverbike and sprayed the detective in the nuts with his water rifle. The policemen were not amused.

Now, you might be saying, from all my exploits to date, that my son was constantly trying to get a gun, had a gun, or had a gun being taken from him. Well, your thinking would be wrong.

Cruz Jr. is not a gun-o-maniac. He's a toddler who is simply developing his tactile skills by grabbing all kinds of objects. He is not drawn to guns. And even though my wife is yelling at me in the background that I'm lying, I'm going to ignore her and tell my story. Because this is my story. She can write her own story, on her own time. Our son is not a gun maniac.

I repeated my question to the detective, "Whatcha talking about?"

"Your son greets visitors by shooting them?"

"He's a kid. Kids play. And it's spraying water, not shooting. The adults greet visitors at this house all the time and we don't shoot anyone. Who are you? I don't know you, Detective."

"Get your slicker and that hat you wear. You're under arrest and we're taking you downtown."

CHAPTER 2

Detective Dent

My pops joined me at the door with such a sour expression; he wasn't happy. I had him take charge of Cruz Jr. My ma also appeared, with Kat in her arms.

"Tell Dot what happened," I said to my parents as I grabbed my tan slicker and fedora from the coatrack near the front door.

"What's going on?" he asked me, then looked at the detectives.

"I'll be at Metro PD." As I put on my slicker and hat, I looked at the detective. "We should give G. Jr. a call too."

The detective smirked. "None of your friends will be able to help you this time," he said.

"Not Chief Hub?"

"Not him either," the detective said.

As I said goodbyes to my family, I stepped out and closed the door behind me. The detective led the way to the elevators, with me right behind him, then the six other officers. The detective was unfamiliar to me, and so were the officers, and I knew all the officers who worked my district and all the surrounding ones.

Wilford G. Jr. was the head of the Metropolis Police Union. Hub was the chief of police. Metro PD, with its half million officers, was the largest police force in the world. G. Jr. was a good friend. The chief was a sometimes-friend but never gave me a raw deal. But my name-dropping had no effect on this bunch as they led me out of the elevator, through the main lobby, past the Concrete Mama's doorkeep, Mr. Post, and outside to *two* waiting police cruisers. At least I wasn't in handcuffs.

However, the question remained. Why was I being arrested?

The Concrete Mama may have looked like a granite fortress in Rabbit City, but in Downtown Metro, Metro Police Central was the real thing. Police One was the building's official name, and it stood at the opposite end of the avenue from City Hall. It was rumored to be the deepest building in the world, burrowing endless levels into the ground—a holdover of those ancient days when nuclear annihilation and civil unrest of a biblical proportion was the daily fear of government bureaucrats. That was long before the mega-cities and supercities of today, and the rain.

When the two police cruisers landed, the detective got out first and waited with the three officers. The three officers of my cruiser got out then let me out. Cruisers landed and departed all around in the police parking bay. The detective took the lead again to the elevators and down we went to ground level. I'd interned there back when I was a kid in high school. But like most Metro citizens, I had no idea how many levels there really were—nor should I. I was a civilian, not true law enforcement, though being a private detective was definitely more dangerous than being a cop—a factoid I made sure not to share with the wife.

We exited and made our way down a private hallway. Even so, we still had to go through security. Security at Central was formidable—armed police guards, security cameras, armed sentries, and scanning archways—all for anyone entering. For exiting, there were no checks.

I could hear people on the other side of the wall to the right. The outer waiting room was nothing but a proverbial zoo. Hundreds of people waiting to make a police report or for their appointment with an officer or detective. We walked through the inner waiting room with benches every few yards in the hallway. I saw the bull pen of dual cubicles where the street police sat and worked when not on the beat. Beyond them were the offices for the higher-ups. However, we weren't headed to any of that. We headed to another area of the police station that I'd also visited many times before.

I saw him. A glimpse of Hub—the chief of police. He saw me but was walking away, as if intentionally. He was a six-foot-tall, muscle-bound, veteran officer. Dark hair, thick mustache, and dark green eyes. I still felt uneasy because I'd never seen the detective and these officers with me before. I certainly couldn't know all five hundred thousand police personnel in Metropolis, but they all knew me. My "escort crew" didn't know me, as if they were new to Metro PD. And now the chief was scurrying away as if I had the plague.

What was going on?

There were two types of interrogation rooms at Metro PD. The nice ones with the white walls, ceilings, and floors, decent tables, nice lighting. Then there were the grungy, nasty ones, where you were afraid to touch or sit on anything. Lucky me, they put me in a nice one, alone, closed the door, and I heard it lock. The locking of the door was what they did for those people they put in the grungy interrogation rooms. I didn't like it. It meant this was *not* going to be a friendly "conversation" at all.

I waited twenty minutes. The same detective came in. He closed the door and sat down across from me at the table. I always sat with my back to the wall and facing the door. He had a small recorder in his hand.

He was an average-looking man. Dark hair, dark complexion. Nothing stood out about him, though I instinctively knew I didn't like him. He set his recorder on the table and pressed play. It was kind of a game because the room had both video and audio recording from the moment a person was brought in.

"I'm Detective Dent," he said. "Please state your name for the record."

"You know who I am."

He stared at me. I did the same.

"Mr. Cruz, are you going to be a cooperating suspect?"

"What am I being arrested for? You said I was being arrested."

"You are being questioned."

"No," I said. "You're not the only one who has recording equipment. The video monitors at the front door of my apartment also record. I have your voice recorded, pal. You said I was being arrested, so I'll ask again. Why?"

"Mr. Cruz, you know the routine very well. You haven't been arrested—yet. However, we can stop and go back outside and do a real arrest—photos, you holding a big number in front of your face, front and side, fingerprint, DNA. Is that what you want?"

"Why am I here?"

"You're being questioned."

"I want to talk to Chief Hub."

"Why? The chief has better things to do than talk with you. I told you already. No one's here to help you this time."

"Who are you? I've never seen you before."

"Let's start the interrogation."

"Listen to me, Detective. I'm not answering a thing until you tell me why I'm here."

"We're starting the interrogation."

I pushed my chair from the table and started singing "la-la-la-la-la" over and over again. Dent didn't like it. I'd done it to Cruz Jr. too when he misbehaved. The technique worked. Dent got up from his chair and headed for the door. I stopped my childish singing.

"I'll get my boss. You two have had some history, I heard."

"History with who? Who's your boss?"

"You two can chat. Then, I'll officially book you."

"Book me for what? I haven't done anything."

"You're going down hard, Cruz, for this one. You showboat detectives think you can make up your own rules, break whatever laws you want. I can't do that. My officers can't do that. Why should lowlife detectives be able to?"

"I didn't do anything."

"After you're officially arrested, then you're going before a judge. You won't get bail, so then it's off to jail. I've heard you're responsible for the incarceration of quite a few of its residents. Your own fan club. They'll be happy to reacquaint themselves because you'll be spending a lot of time in there until your trial. Imagine the press. The rise and fall of the famous Detective Cruz of the Liquid Cool Detective Agency."

I wanted to smack that smirk right off his face.

"You're not going to see that family of yours for a very long time, Mr. Cruz. Your new daughter might be in college before she sees dear ol' dad again."

I stood from my chair in a menacing stance, glaring at him. Dent waited.

"You want something? I'm right here," he said.

"Why don't you turn off the cameras and recorders?" I said.

"Then what, tough guy? I know all about you. You like to shoot people too, like your baby son. Only you use fancy, Up-Top weapons. Without them, you're nothing. I beat up people like you on a regular basis." He cracked the knuckles of his right, then left fist. "I could beat you to death with my pinkie. I'll get my boss so we can get your nightmare started."

He left and I heard the door lock again.

CHAPTER 3

Captain Monitor

I was on fire! I was so mad that it was a good thing they left me in there over an hour. First, I was pacing the room, then I tried to sit awhile, but was too wound up. I was pacing again when I heard the door unlock.

Police rank-and-file used to call him Detective Do-Little. Captain Monitor was from a wealthy family and born on the fast track. He had been an officer for like a week before being promoted to detective. Now, he was a captain, seeming to skip over the rank of lieutenant. He was never popular with the average beat cop, but didn't have time for the lower police classes. He was in his spotless navy dress blues. He entered the room with Dent and two fully armored officers.

"Have a seat, Cruz," he said. He was already seated before I finally did. Dent and the officers stood behind him. I gave Dent another dirty look.

Monitor had a mustache now. Maybe he thought it made him look more senior. Not to me. Dark brown hair. Fake tan. Perfect, fake teeth. It was scary that he could actually be chief of police one day.

"I thought they got rid of you," I said to Monitor.

"No, Cruz, I run my own special unit here at Central."

"Do you now."

"I do. Who do you think has gotten himself caught in our web?"

"I'm not good at guessing. Who?"

"Cruz, you need to understand a few things. As my detective has already told you, none of your usual friends here at Central will be helping you out today. That's number one. Two: you will be formally arrested. Three: you will be going to jail, likely for quite some time. No one cares what high profile cases you've solved. No one cares about the cases you helped Metro PD close. That's past. All that matters is today and the seriousness of this crime you'll be arrested for, charged, and convicted of."

"What crime?"

"Is that how you want to play this? Pretend?"

"I've already asked your pet behind you twice to tell me why I'm being threatened with arrest. Who do you think you're talking to? I'm not some street punk. I know what proper police procedures are. What am I being—?"

"Murder," Monitor said. He placed a photo on top of the table and turned it around so I could see the face clearly. They watched for my reaction.

"Who's he?" I asked.

Monitor smiled. "He's the man who's going to send you to jail for a long time, Cruz. Do you want to confess or are we going to play games?"

"Confess?" I asked. "Are you being serious?"

"Very serious."

"Confess to what?"

"Confess to killing your business partner."

"Business partner? I don't have a business partner."

"If you confess, Cruz, we can work with you. Speak on your behalf to the district attorney and judge. Knock some years off your sentence."

For the first time, I felt a bit light-headed. Monitor was deadly serious. Dent was right. Unfolding before my eyes was a nightmare like I had never faced before in my life. These men were going to send me to jail and I was maybe hours, or minutes, away from that reality.

"I want to make a phone call," I said.

The officers had taken my mobile before we had even entered the building. I knew what his response would be.

"You can make your call after you're booked."

Once I was booked, I'd be in the system. Thrown on the hellish roller coaster of the Metro justice system, and there would be no way to escape until they allowed me to get off. All control of your life was ripped away from you.

I rubbed my forehead. "Can I have some time to think? I need to think."

"Sure, Cruz. You can think about it. We'll leave you here. Think. When I get back, you'll give me that full confession or my men here will jam you into the system, where you'll remain for years to come."

Monitor got up from his chair and led his men out of the interrogation room. I knew the games interrogators played. I used them myself in my detective business. They'd leave me in the room for even longer, maybe closer to two hours, maybe turn up the heat so I'd literally be sweating. I was in one of the nice interrogation rooms, but I was getting the grungy interrogation room treatment.

Ten minutes later the door opened. Monitor stood there.

"Mr. Cruz," he said.

"Captain." I stared at him with a sinister grin. He watched me with his own smirk.

"When did you manage it?" he asked.

"Why ask me? You're smarter than me, Monitor. I shouldn't have to tell you."

"Liquid Cool? Liquid Slippery. Criminals always think they can outsmart the law. All they do is slip right into our handcuffs for a fun, free trip to Metro Prison."

"Nice speech. I've given it myself to clients whose cases I've turned down."

"You haven't stopped a thing, only delayed the inevitable."

"We shall see."

"Yes, we shall. Your attorney is here."

"I know."

"We'll show her in for you. Only real criminals manage these sorts of things."

"Or private detectives a lot smarter than you. You and that dummy of yours are so dismissive of me, but I've taken down some serious bad guys here on Earth and Up-Top. Can you say the same? I hired the doorman for my residential building. He's also ex-police, and a professional. He called me the second your pets showed up at my place. If you've had my attorney waiting outside in the lobby, while you or your dummies were interrogating me, the judge will be quite put off with you, not me. Are you so sure I won't get bail now?"

"We'll show your criminal attorney in."

"How you've been treating me is criminal, Monitor. You'd better make sure I'm guilty of whatever you think I did, because if I'm not, every single police officer in Metro, including the chief, will hound you out of the city. I have friends Up-Top too, so you wouldn't find a job there either."

Monitor left the room. He was unmoved and realized what I was doing. Stalling for more time. Our little chatting was all considered an official and illegal interrogation by the court, if my counsel was waiting. He left the door open in the rush. However, Dent stood in the doorway.

I didn't say it aloud, but I'd get even with both of them one day.

CHAPTER 4

Wize Gal

The fact of the matter was that I did murder someone—technically, and the police knew about it. Specifically, Chief Hub knew it. It was the aftermath of my first two major high-profile cases, which began my "fame." The entire Animal Farm Syndicate was wiped out by the Metro PD after they unwisely tried to do the same to me. Every feral gang and its members were killed or put in jail for life except for one person—their crime boss, Monkey Baker. I knew he wouldn't rest until he got revenge against me. Well, I killed him before he could kill me. I was allowed to get away with it because Monkey Baker planned to blow up the entire Concrete Mama to get me. But even if Monkey Baker hadn't done that, I wouldn't have been charged.

Metro PD and the courts took criminal threats against citizens and police *very* seriously. The penalty was severe, and if the police had any notion that a threat made by any criminal against them was credible, said criminal would likely have an accident in the near future. Chief Hub allowed me to get away with the demise of the crime boss, Monkey Baker, not so much because the plot was a real, planned terrorist act; it was because he knew that Monkey Baker would have killed me if not stopped, just as he had killed his fellow police officers. Metro PD and City Hall wanted him bad and didn't care how or who. If I hadn't killed Monkey Baker, the Metro PD would have done it. Monkey Baker's gangs had killed police. You did that and you were dead. They'd get you.

Other than that one "justified" instance, no one would really believe I was capable of killing someone, outside of self-defense. There were crimes in the realm of possibility that I was capable of—this was, after all, Metropolis dripping with crime everywhere—but not cold-blooded murder. Yet that's what Monitor had accused me of and the fact he and his team were running my case meant that others felt it was a possibility too. How quickly things had changed. My last major case, Biopunk Blues, the police and I were working together. Now we were on opposite sides.

What evidence did they have?

Finally, some good news for me. My defense attorney had arrived! Wize Gal. My posthumous mentor, Wilford G., had introduced us. Back then I thought she was just a waitress, but later learned she was a ruthless paralegal attorney. Registered as a paralegal but could, if she wanted, practice as a trial attorney. She was that good.

She was a petite brunette who liked her sharp business suits. She entered with a black briefcase in her right hand and closed the door.

"Don't say one word," she said and opened her briefcase as she placed it on the table.

The contraption was a high-grade jammer. She gestured for me to sit and lean forward.

"Cruz, what have you done?"

"Wize, I'm innocent."

"Cover your mouth with your hands when you talk. They do have lip-readers."

I did as she said.

"They said murder."

"Yeah, Cruz. Murder."

"Who?"

"When you go bad, Cruz, you go for the top. Royalty. A Moon Monarch."

My eyes opened wide. "Get him back in here."

"What?" she asked, putting her hand in front of my mouth.

I stood from my chair and waved at the corner camera in the room for them to come back in.

"What are you doing, Cruz?"

"I've been framed, Wize. I bet I've been framed so hard that even you couldn't get me off. But I'm still innocent."

"What are you talking about?" she asked me.

"I didn't murder anyone, but I was there when he was."

Monitor re-entered the room with Dent and the same two other officers.

Wize stood from her chair. "Cruz, as your defense counsel, I have to insist you stop talking."

I looked at Monitor. "You have solid evidence against me? Let me guess. Video recordings?"

"Entering and leaving the scene," Monitor said. "And audio."

"And plenty of eyewitnesses," Dent interjected with a snarl.

"He framed me good," I said.

"Cruz, stop talking!" Wize said.

"There is no 'he,'" Dent said. "It's all you, and we have you."

"Who?" Monitor asked. "Who are you claiming killed him?"

"Monitor, do you really believe I'm that stupid to kill someone and not just leave one piece of evidence, but a hovertruckload of it?"

"Why not? Criminals do so all the time."

"Monitor, not even you believe I'd be that stupid."

"Then if not you, who?"

"I never thought he existed. But he's real."

"Who?" Monitor asked again.

"Cruz, stop talking!" Wize Gal yelled.

"The Three-Armed Man," I said.

"What?" Wize looked at me as if she thought I was certifiably crazy.

"You never quit, Cruz," Monitor said. "How do you know about him? Listening to the urban legends from your criminal friends on the street. He doesn't exist."

"Like Mr. Candy didn't exist. We never knew about the Orochi Corporation or the Super Cyborgs. There's a lot out there,

Monitor, that you, me, and the rest of Metro PD isn't aware of. Doesn't mean they don't exist."

"Didn't you have a case with biopunks, Cruz?" Monitor asked. "I heard one of them had three breasts. We're fashioning lies from your past cases."

"He's not a biopunk, Monitor. Far from it. I'm sure of it. I'd say he's from Up-Top. They don't have biopunks Up-Top. Up there it's bio-modification. Genetic engineering."

"Your imaginary killer is a gen-e spaceman? If that's how you want to play it. Cruz, do know you're going to be arrested?"

"Probably, but I'll get bail."

"Why is that important?"

"You know how I feel about being shot. I don't like it. I feel the same about getting framed. I know who and I'm going to get him. Have no doubt about it."

"A person who doesn't exist."

"Person? You mean hit man. Monitor, I know he exists, and not because of any rumors. I fought with him, physically."

"What?" Wize asked me.

"I fought him and chased him."

"Fought him, Cruz?" Monitor asked.

"Yes, Monitor. I was there when he killed that man. I had no idea the man he killed was a Moon Monarch. I fought this Three-Armed Man, chased after him, but he got away."

"Too bad you don't have any proof," Monitor said.

"Do you want me to tell you what happened, or listen to my attorney and stop talking?"

Wize yelled at me, "You will stop talking."

"I don't care, Cruz."

"Monitor, I know you don't, but you might want to check with your bosses first."

"Cruz, I'm the boss here."

"No, you aren't." I looked the camera. "Talk or go mute? Tell your puppy dog what to do."

"Shut up, Cruz," Dent said as he stepped forward. Monitor held him back.

"Cruz, I think it's that time. Arrest time," Monitor said.

There was a knock at the room door. Monitor left Dent and the officers there as he disappeared out the door. We waited, and Monitor returned. He sighed heavily.

"Cruz, sit down and tell your story."

"Cruz—" Wize Gal began.

"Save it, Wize. You need to hear the story too."

"Why am I here if you won't listen to me?" she asked.

"I told you. You get me out on bail to find him." I sat down again in my chair. "The Three-Armed Man."

CHAPTER 5

The Three-Armed Man

My Liquid Cool office was like a fortress. Visibly, it appeared as a normal office, but had plenty of surveillance and security measures. I could comfortably fend off any attackers, whether gang members, corporate samurai soldiers, killer robots, killer cyborgs, or the lone gunman in an illegal changeling suit. But as a sole proprietor detective agency shop, a client couldn't always come to the office. Besides, I'd lose all my street skills if all I did was stay in the sanctuary of my comfy private office.

I met clients at their office or residence for initial consultations to determine if I'd take their case, drop by to give updates, get additional information, or pick up bonus payments. I'd meet with potential clients only after we'd done a full background check and we got a retainer—only part of which was refundable if I didn't take the case. I always did my own recon before walking into any new office or residence. It was basic business common sense. Getting shot was never good for business.

When I was in the field, I preferred to stay in the field and not have to come back and forth from the office. Usually, I'd schedule all my client visits for half a day. The hovertraffic wasn't too bad as I made my third stop for the day. The previous ones were consultations with potential clients, but this one was an update for an existing one, a Mr. Prince.

I touched down in a public parking lot about a block away from his megatower home office. To walk a block in Metropolis meant you'd be walking a while, but I never minded. It gave me a chance to see the neighborhood, get a feel for the people, and, more importantly, take whatever steps I had to to keep my classic red Ford Pony safe and secure.

Mr. Prince was the CFO of a major megacorp with offices on Earth and the Lunar Colonies. Most of my corporate cases these days fell into two categories—finance or security. Mr. Prince's case was the former, and I had started a week ago. He'd hired me to do legwork for his internal confidential investigation of possible financial improprieties within the company, or as normal people would say: someone was stealing company funds. His was a multi-billionaire megacorp, and they had me chasing millions in missing funds. I suppose I wouldn't let it go either. If you allow one employee to steal and get away with it, then in no time, you'd have many more doing the same thing.

My activities had become quite extensive. Following people, watching black market mail drop centers, planting tracking and surveillance devices. Mr. Prince had me doing the work that in-house security would normally be doing. He didn't want in-house security to know what he was doing. That meant he was trying to take down someone within the company to increase his own power. People said we hadn't had any wars on the planet for such a very long time. Actually, we had wars every day in the shadowy megacorp world on Earth, complete with lots of dead bodies. You just didn't hear about it on the news broadcasts.

I'd thought it was especially true of Japanese-owned megacorps, but quickly learned that everyone else was every bit as ruthless. The Japanese were just at it longer than everyone else, that's all. Street gangsters came in all ethnicities, cultures, countries, and both genders. So did the corporate ones.

Mech City was a district I'd been in before. The area was dark but flashy, a mix of Average Joes and Janes but also a criminal class. The megatowers were mixed-use commercial and residential. Mr. Prince lived in one of a trio of triangular two-hundred-story buildings. The tower had its own visitor parking, but I never used it.

The first time I met Mr. Prince, I had parked on the roof of the visitor parking bay which had quite a bit of security, with a combination valet and security guards, though I didn't let them park my Pony by any means. Owners of classic hovervehicles don't let strangers drive their prized possessions. But from what I observed they all seemed like a very professional, efficient, and diligent operation. I left my meeting, retrieved my Pony, and was on my way. Until I happened to land on the side of the street before getting into hovertraffic.

What was disturbing wasn't that I found one tracker on my Pony's exterior; I found six of them. Based on the type of trackers and how they were placed, I was certain that it wasn't one person planting six devices, but six different people each planting their device. I didn't like it. So, I decided never to park in Mr. Prince's building ever again. There was no way to know if the attention I attracted was aimed at me, for some unknown reason, or was because of me working for Mr. Prince. He did tell me it wasn't out of the realm of possibility that others might know I was working for him. If you were a working detective in Metropolis, you had to be cautious (or paranoid) at all times—if you wanted to stay working, or alive.

The building's lobby had several doorkeeps—male and female. I checked in at the counter, gave my name, and they directed me to the resident elevators. They knew who I was from my previous visits, so they didn't need to check my ID. The elevator capsule arrived and I got on when I was sure I could get on alone. I didn't want to travel up to the one hundred thirtieth floor with anyone else, especially when unknown people might be taking note of all Mr. Prince's visitors.

The megatower was a bit different than others because there was also a security guard on each floor. I came out of the elevator capsule and the security station was opposite the elevator bank. A single guard noticed me from behind a counter and returned his attention to a monitor screen. A lot of security in the building, but I wondered about their true effectiveness since six different people had planted tracking devices on my Pony in their parking lot the first day I had visited.

28

Mr. Prince's apartment was at the very end of a very long winding hallway. I knocked once and opened the unlocked door.

"Hello, Mr. Cruz." I heard his voice from within the luxurious apartment.

There wasn't much furniture in the open living room and dining area, but what did exist was impressive. Expensive couches, chairs, tables, and statues. Hanging from the ceiling were birdhouses with birds, chirping away and watching me with their beady little eyes.

I walked into the home office, which was where Mr. Prince really lived. It was large, open, and packed. Home office, bedroom, reading room, and exercise room all in one. A clutter of things. Mr. Prince sat on a hover-lounge chair behind a desk with multiple screens.

"Mr. Prince."

"Have a seat."

I did so, or did so after I could find a stool tucked away behind boxes and suitcases of stuff. Mr. Prince clearly had the hoarder gene.

"What do you have for me, Mr. Cruz?"

I reached into my jacket for my written notes. Mr. Prince preferred written updates delivered. No email. No digital files. Handwritten on real paper. I walked over to him and handed the report to him, then returned to my stool. He read them carefully.

"Very good," he said to himself, as he flipped to the next page. "Very good. I have what I need to bring in security."

"Bring in the police, you mean."

He stopped reading to look at me. "Not yet. We don't have enough yet. All that would happen is all the low-level operators would be rounded up, but their higher-ups would still be free. But I'll soon have enough to bring them in as well."

"And you'll have exposed an embezzlement ring within the company."

"Yes, the board of directors will be quite appreciative." He began reading my notes again.

"Will you need me to do anything else?"

"I will have you continue on. As long as there are rocks to turn over, you should continue to turn them over. Many worms to uncover."

"Or snakes."

"That too."

"What's the next assignment?"

"I am almost at the end of your very thorough report, Mr. Cruz."

I waited quietly as I looked around the room again, or what I could see despite all the clutter. I noticed something glistening on his desk.

"What's that?" I asked, pointing.

He barely took his eye off my report, reached over and handed it to me. I smiled as I took the wedding ring from him.

I'd heard of them before. It looked like a diamond, but as you stared at it the stone changed colors and the intensity of those colors also changed. It was an empathy stone said to read the wearer's emotional state and moods. Such jewelry only came from Up-Top.

"You're taking the plunge," I said.

"I've never understood the many metaphors likening marriage with death."

"You'll see," I said, still smiling. "Congrats, Mr. Prince. You're going to make a great couple."

"Thank you, Mr. Cruz."

I handed him back the ring and he returned it to his desk.

"When do you ask her?"

"Maybe tomorrow," he answered.

A new life would soon be beginning for my client and his girlfriend. I heard an eruption of chirping from Mr. Prince's birds outside, and began to turn around. I glimpsed a look of shock come over Mr. Prince's face at his desk, looking past me. I dove but—

Those silly birds probably saved my life.

I not only heard a pulse blast behind my head, but felt the heat. There was a crashing sound ahead of me. I didn't need to look, but when I did my eyes confirmed my assumption. Mr. Prince had been blasted across the room, through furniture, junk, and exercise equipment into the wall. But I had already turned to fire my own weapon. I was on my back as the attacker was upon me.

Pop!

My pop-gun didn't really make such a sound, but was how I described it. I blasted his pulse gun from his hand. He made the mistake—his third—in thinking I was going to shoot him with my omega-gun that I pulled from my jacket. My pop-gun on my left forearm was always ready. The man was lean but extremely muscled, and big, much taller than average. He grabbed my right arm. No one had ever grabbed my gun arm before I could shoot. He was that fast. Then he grabbed my left arm, so I couldn't use that arm either.

What the—!

A third arm came out from the man's chest and grabbed my neck. He stood and lifted me up, off my feet, choking me in midair. I could see his sneering face clearly. His squinting blue eyes, his smiling super-white perfect teeth, pale skin, bald head. I kicked at his body with all my might, but he laughed it off. In moments, I'd be unconscious or dead.

I pointed my right foot hard to the ground and kicked again. A blast. The three-armed man yelled out and dropped me to the ground. I fought to collect myself and aimed, but the man was gone. I heard the chirping birds outside the room. I shook my head, jumped to my feet, and ran after him.

The front door was wide open, which was why I spun around to fire my weapon the opposite way. I'd never experienced anything like it before in my life. He knocked my omega-gun out of my hand with one arm, punched me in the face with the second, and pushed me out of his way with the third. He bolted out of the room through the open front door. I grabbed my weapon from the ground to give chase.

I expected him to be waiting outside to fire at me, which was why I threw myself out the door with my omega-gun set for machine-gun fire. All I saw was a figure disappearing down the hall, running at a speed I didn't think was possible. I heard the elevator.

The floor's security desk near the elevator was empty when I reached it. I looked at the elevator indicator on the wall and a capsule was going down. At that very moment, another capsule arrived. I was about to jump in when I stopped myself. I let the door close, but I wasn't in it.

I looked around, then walked over to the security desk. No one was there. Nobody behind the counter. All around the hallway were cameras. I looked at the elevator indicators and all four capsules were on their way up. Something was not right about the situation. I ran back to Mr. Prince's room as fast as I could.

"Why did you run?" Monitor asked me.

"Something wasn't right," I answered. "The floor security wasn't there."

"Yes, they were, Cruz," Dent snapped. "They identified you as you ran from the man's place and—"

Monitor raised his arm to gesture for him to stop talking.

"I tell you he wasn't there. But that's not important. What's important is why was my client killed and why am I being framed for it? This is far too involved to have been an accident. This was planned. This three-armed man must have waited until I arrived, then killed Mr. Prince. He wanted Mr. Prince dead and me framed for it. But why? Why go through all this to frame me?"

Wize Gal, Monitor, Dent and the officers looked on. No one talked for awhile. We just stood there in the room. There was a knock on the door, and another officer peeked in. Monitor followed him out of the room.

Wize walked to me and gestured for me to sit back in my chair.

"Cruz, you're going have to listen to me, or you can get yourself another defender. You're not a cop. Your job isn't to help them solve their cases," she said.

"I'm the one being jammed up here."

"You're not helping yourself, Cruz. You're only putting yourself in greater legal jeopardy."

Monitor returned to the room.

"Okay, Cruz," he said. "We'll start again. We'll start at the very beginning, but before we do that, Cruz, I'm placing you under arrest for the murder of Mr. Apollo Michelangelo."

PART TWO

Flashback

CHAPTER 6

Animals

The first time I met Mr. Prince was one of my busier work days. I was scheduled to be out of the office most of the day on client calls and potential client meetings. I left it to my secretary/office manager PJ's judgment to determine who was too lazy to come into the office, and those who might be legitimate paying clients who might take their business elsewhere if I wasn't more flexible. Just because I was "famous" didn't mean I could get too full of myself.

Living in the supercity of Metropolis could be deadly if you went someplace you weren't supposed to. People were creatures of habit and usually only went to places they lived, worked, or were familiar with—whether they were normal residents or the criminal class. As a generalist street detective, however, I went everywhere.

I left Rabbit City for my first client call and had I known what was coming, I would have skipped it altogether and stayed in my bed.

For some reason, I was a kid whisperer. I don't know what it was about me that attracted crazy maniac children. Though I seemed to also attract crazy situations, that was different and I was sure that all Metropolitans encountered the same thing.

I parked my Pony in the megatower's secure parking bay and made my way to the elevators. Lucky me, they lived only a few levels up. Unlucky me, adolescent kids were everywhere in the halls hanging around.

"Why aren't you all in school?" I asked a group of them clustered together, all on their devices.

They ignored me and I looked at their devices. They were having a group chat.

"Is there some reason you can't talk to each other like normal people? Maybe if you were in school, you'd learn how to do that."

"We're not your kid, old man," one said.

"I am not old."

"Today's a holiday," another said, but I didn't believe him.

"See. That's all you had to tell me. I was concerned about your well-being. It's what we adults do when it comes to the youth of our city. Now all you have to do is talk to each other instead of texting."

"Hey, old man, when you mouth-talk you can't send cool images or change the fonts."

"Mouth-talk?"

I was going to have a long conversation with the wife tonight. We had to keep Cruz Jr. and Kat far, far away from the youth of today.

The door of my potential client was close to the elevators. I rang the bell and stood to the side—a habit I picked up from the police. You don't want to be standing in front of the door in case someone decides to shoot you through it.

Cruz, do people shoot you through the door often?

Shut up, Dent. I'm telling my story.

The door opened and instead of preteens, an army of children stood there, all dressed in animal suits, which was very appropriate. Hyperactive didn't even begin to describe these kids. They literally couldn't keep still, and their eyes and mouths opened wide with glee at the sight of a new adult to torment.

"Who are you?" a couple of them asked in unison.

"Cruz."

"The detective!" one of them yelled and almost fell over.

"Do you want to see a magic trick?" one of the kids asked me.

I attempted a method of communication that I often used with little children, including Cruz Jr., and was equally as unsuccessful.

"No," I replied forcibly.

"I'll show you."

"No."

"Pull my finger." The kids started laughing like hyenas. I think one of them was in a hyena costume.

"No."

"I will!" another kid said.

38

He pulled the other kid's finger. The "pull-ee" vomited out fake green slime. Then the puller vomited out fake yellow slime. How cute.

The kids were on the ground, laughing hysterically. A puddle of green and yellow slime around them.

I wondered how long I'd have to wait until the adults showed up. A woman appeared, wearing an apron, and she yelled at them at the top of her lungs. The laughing kids jumped up and scattered like they were street criminals running from arriving police cruisers. They were gone.

The contrast between teens and preteens was a tremendous gulf. The former didn't want to move; the latter couldn't stay still. The former were like doped-out human lampposts; the latter were like doped-up human ferrets. Was this what I had to look forward to with Cruz Jr. and Kat? Pick your poison. I think I preferred the hyperactivity. Just keep them in a padded room without any breakables and since they were so noisy, you'd always know what they were up to. With the tragically "too cool for school" teenagers who didn't like mouth-talking, you'd never know if they were even in your place or out on the street doing crimes. Maybe I'd chip them like my Pony.

The woman had raccoon-eye makeup—way too much. My wife and her fashion police colleagues would give her a ticket.

"You Cruz?" she asked.

"Yes."

"Come in and close the door before something runs out or something runs in. There are animals on this floor."

I closed the door quickly. The woman walked back around the corner. I didn't like when people disappeared, but the TV was on. When I came down the hallway, there was an open living room on one side and the woman cooking in the kitchen on the other. Someone else stood up from a chair in the living room and walked to me.

"Hello, Mr. Cruz," the man said, extending a hand.

Before I could greet him, something whipped behind me at incredible speed. I spun around, but whatever it was, was gone.

"Don't mind him," the man said, shaking my hand. "Have a seat."

"Can you tell me who 'him' is?" I asked.

"Man-eater is harmless." The woman appeared in the living room without her apron.

The two adults sat on their couch. I sat across from them. In the other rooms I heard the army of kids. I also heard something running around. My eyes scanned the room and I noticed that the walls of the entire apartment looked like rock, including handholds for climbing.

"Good exercise, rock climbing is," the man said.

"Yes, it is. My office said you have a possible case."

My mind was focused on how quickly I could get out of there. The army of kids was bad enough, but these people had some kind of wild animal running around their place. I didn't want to know what it was. The pair worked for an animal preservation park and apparently bred like animals themselves, dressed their kids like animals, and also had wild animals running about.

"How can I help?" I asked.

The man reached over and handed me a photo. It was of some monkey.

"Captain Fantastic," he said.

"A monkey."

"Captain Fantastic isn't a monkey. He's a lemur."

"Big eyes, striped tail, ears. A monkey."

"Lemurs are marsupials, not monkeys."

"I'm not a pet detective."

"He was kidnapped," the man said. "We know who did it. We know where he is. The police won't do a thing, so we want to hire you."

"All you have to do is rescue him," the woman said. "We don't care how."

Whenever clients used phrases like that, it meant the case would inevitably involve some kind of illegality.

"I appreciate—"

Whatever animal was in the apartment ran behind me faster than light-speed again. The couple saw the nervousness in my face.

"Man-eater is harmless," the woman said again.

People don't name harmless animals "man-eater."

"I lost my train of thought. Yes. I'd only be taking your money."

"Money is no object," the man said. "Captain Fantastic is very important to our family. He must be rescued. Money is no object."

"No object at all," the woman said.

All detectives liked easy money. I was no different.

"Where is he?" I asked.

"A private collector," the man answered.

There it was. The illegality. It meant I'd have to break in to someplace.

"If that's the case, the police are the ones to call."

"We have no proof to give the police."

"Then how do you know he's there?"

The husband and wife looked at each other.

"We know," he said.

"I bet you do," I said. "Give me all the details. If you can prove Captain Fantastic is yours, I can check on my own who the—"

"Kidnapper," the woman interjected.

"Who the kidnapper is. I may take the case. I need to study it."

The animal whipped past me again at light speed. I leapt up to catch a glimpse of it, but it was too fast. I missed it again. I looked at the couple again with a stern look.

"I know what you're going to say: Man-eater is harmless."

"But he is," she said to me.

"All the animals in the apartment are human friendly."

"All? Animals? There's more?" I began looking around. "Okay, well, give me all those details on the lemur."

"Captain Fantastic," she corrected.

"Yes, the captain."

"Mr. Cruz, I believe you are our man," the man said as he stood. He shook my hand again.

We walked toward the door—finally! But then I heard something rush up behind me and stop. The couple looked at what was behind me, smiling. I felt like that little kid in a horror

42

movie, full moon, pitch black, alone, with the creature or psycho standing behind me. I slowly, and nervously, turned around. Behind me was some cute hornless, spotted deer. It stared at me with big black eyes, its entire body trembling as if it were using great energy to even stand still, and running around was actually its natural state.

"Say hello to Man-eater, Mr. Cruz," she said. "As you can see, her name is a bit of a joke since deer don't have teeth and don't eat meat."

"I'm safe then."

"Harmless."

At that moment I heard the army of kids running around the corner to me. Man-eater was gone in a blink of an eye, and I wished I could've run away too.

The same kid ran to me and said, "Pull my finger this time." He was giggling.

Another kid did the honors. The kids started sniffing the air, then laughing again.

"Eww!" "What's that smell?"

The kid fell to the floor laughing.

"Stop it, children. It's a natural bodily function," the man said to them.

"Don't mind Amphi, Mr. Cruz," the woman said.

"Yes, he's harmless." I pointed at the giggling kid on the ground. "It's bad enough I have to be subjected to Cruz Jr. But I will not be skunked by you."

That only made the kid laugh louder.

Then some kind of rainbow-colored pelican-thing flew past my face, making me jump back and almost fall. Now, all the kids were on the floor laughing.

"What was that?!"

"That was Professor Seuss."

"Okay, I'm out of here!"

I ran for the door. I was literally in a zoo and had to escape immediately.

Cruz, the pet detective. Not if I could help it.

That was my first case of the day—my first stop. I'd work their case the next day, rescue their Captain Fantastic, and got a nice fee with a bonus, which they paid by video-phone with my secretary. I was not going to that apartment ever again to see their kids—each named after an animal classification—or their non-human animals. I was not interested in seeing Man-eater, Professor Seuss, or any "one" else they had crawling, flying, or galloping around their place.

Going through the day was an exercise not only at the direction of Monitor and company, but for my own benefit. I had to go through that entire day in my mind, each client visit I made, including my last one, which was the first time I'd met Mr. Prince at his home office. Recall everything and anything, no matter how seemingly insignificant.

However, something significant did happen now that I had a chance to replay the beginning of that day over in my head. When I left the parking bay of the animal people's building, I noticed that their normal security guards were nowhere to be seen. My Pony was left unguarded, which didn't sit well with me. There were surveillance cameras all around, but the human guards had disappeared as if they all went on a bathroom break at the same time, which never happened. I ignored it then, but since a similar thing happened at Prince's building, I remembered it.

CHAPTER 7

China Doll and Mrs. Fancy

I had a wife, an employee, a best friend, and lots of friends, associates, and acquaintances. That meant a ton of people always on the lookout for new cases to refer to me. It was normal to hear someone tell them a story and they'd respond with "oh, I know a private detective who can help you." The fact was that most of my solid paying clients came from referrals, either my own network or from previous clients.

That day after I left the Animal Maniac family, I was off to Funky Circle in the district of Paisley Parish to the home of the famous Eye Candy, the premiere beauty salon, image and style house in Metropolis.

It was always packed with customers from opening until its late-night closing. Women came from every corner of Metropolis to be made to look like movie stars with its "fashion police" of makeup artists, hairdressers, manicurists, pedicurists, skincare techs, tattoo artists, wardrobe stylists, and even dressers to assemble their wardrobe, if needed. The establishment was owned by Prima Donna, Matron Queen of Metropolis fashion, who still had the magic touch after so many decades and personally tended to their oldest and highest-tipping clients.

My wife, China Doll, was Prima's number one and boss in her absence. Like every other fashionista employee, she wasn't some by-the-hour laborer. This was a coveted and highly competitive career, and everyone who worked in the parlor had advanced degrees in beauty and skincare, fashion and style arts, health, and nutrition.

Despite its many levels, the nerve center of the salon remained its main ground floor. Its interior was designed like a beehive, and every section was visible, due to its transparent walls, to every other section, except the break room, full body baths, and the bathrooms. Eye Candy was carefully coordinated chaos—women sitting on chairs getting their hair and makeup done in one section, their nails and toenails in another, facials in another, tattoos in another (always temporary to change according to current fashion trends), skincare consultations in another, and style analysis wardrobing in yet another section.

I parked my Pony on the upper parking levels and took an elevator capsule down to the main level. I came out and looked out across the busy floor for a moment. In Eye Candy, my wife wasn't the only fashionista. Everyone dressed like movie stars here—employees and clients. I saw her colleagues first, then spotted her styling a female client's hair. I decided to wait and watch. I had arrived early.

My wife went by the name China Doll here at Eye Candy, but her real name was Dot. As the consummate fashionista, every piece of her clothing, every accessory, and every piece of jewelry was the trendiest and the most stylish. She was in a yellow top under a flashy, patterned short navy jacket, wearing a golden laced belt around her waist, black bell-bottom pants, and yellow heels. Her ponytail wound down her back. While I had my trademark tan fedora, she had neck scarves. She always wore a colored neck scarf—today was navy. Dot liked her rings and bracelets—every finger had a colored ring, and each wrist had multiple bracelets.

I didn't see her boss, Prima Donna, but did see her other colleagues. Busy at work were Cyan, who had a million outfits, but all were the same color of cyan; Pinkie, with her bright pink hair; Goat Girl, known for the large ring hanging from her nose septum; and Lipps, who had quite the set of augmented lips.

Before long Dot saw me, smiled, and waved. Then all her colleagues looked and waved. "Hi, Cruz!" I couldn't hear what they were saying but whatever it was, they were laughing at me.

Eye Candy had a floor with its own conference rooms for special meetings. That's where Dot led me. I was early but so was Mrs. Fancy, a longtime client of Eye Candy. Prima Donna had told me she was one of Eye Candy's original clients, which was a long time ago.

The conference room was not like any conference room I'd ever seen. The all-white walls and furniture looked like separate paint cans of red, orange, yellow, blue, and purple had exploded everywhere, but that was the artistic effect they wanted.

"Hi, Mrs. Fancy," I said, greeting the nonagenarian.

"Hello, Mr. Cruz."

"Is it dry?" I asked my wife jokingly before I sat down.

"Cruz, sit down and hear Mrs. Fancy's case."

"I thought you weren't referring cases to me anymore after the last time?"

"That was a one-off, and this one isn't from me. It's all Mrs. Fancy."

The case was my last major one—Biopunk Blues—where, among other things, I was infected with a bio-toxin and had to be quarantined for weeks. What was a private street detective doing dealing with bio-toxins? Good question. My wife had chided me for these "save the world" cases, and that's exactly what she gave me. But it wasn't her fault. Such cases found me whether I wanted them or not.

"What's it about, Mrs. Fancy?" I asked.

"Mr. Cruz, I think someone's stealing from me. Breaking into my penthouse and helping themselves to one expensive item after another."

"Over how long a period?" I asked.

"The last year."

"Called the police?"

"No need to bring them into it."

"Mrs. Fancy, which one of them is it?"

She smiled at me.

Dot looked back and forth from her and me. "You know who did it already?"

"Your husband is a famous detective for a reason, China," Mrs. Fancy answered.

"Yes, he is," Dot said.

"Find out which one of your kids is doing it, if not more than one, retrieve the items, and make sure they never do it again. Did I leave anything out, Mrs. Fancy?" I asked.

"No. That covers it."

"Mrs. Fancy, how old are your kids? They're not juvenile delinquents anymore. Don't they have jobs."

"My kids are greedy little wannabe crooks. The youngest is sixty."

"How many kids do you have again?"

"Eight greedy little wretches. Do you and China want them? You can adopt them if you like."

"You know I love ya, Mrs. Fancy," Dot said, "but Cruz and I will have to decline."

"They probably pawned all the items already."

"Jewelry?" I asked.

"And some paintings. All gifts from my useless ex-husbands, but mine is mine."

"I'll take care of it, Mrs. Fancy. I know how to talk to wannabe crooks. They dislike prison even more than real crooks."

"Whatever you have to do is fine by me."

"You want the items back or the cash?"

"I have plenty of cash. I want the items back."

"Consider it taken care of," I said.

50

"Excellent." She reached into her purse and handed me an electronic check. "I'm old-school when it comes to payments."

I looked at the very large check as I took it off her hands. "Your money is always good at Liquid Cool."

It took me all of one day to close the case. It actually was the youngest of her kids illegally letting himself into his mother's penthouse apartment to steal things, but all eight of the kids were in on it. I had my secretary organize a meeting with all of them at the Liquid Cool office, making sure they knew their choices were to come to me or the police would be coming for them. One meeting and five minutes of me telling them what they'd do immediately, without raising my voice. All the items were returned the next day via courier to my office, I sent over the master of office security, Buggs, to Mrs. Fancy's penthouse, and I dropped off photos of the children to the penthouse security guards so they'd be added to the permanent entrance ban list. How did I get the kids to act so quickly and promise never to do so again? I simply told them that their mother was "updating" the will. They knew what that meant. Mrs. Fancy was filthy rich.

It was the kind of case I enjoyed the most—quickly solved, quickly paid. Nothing about Mrs. Fancy, her crooked kids, or her case that I solved in a nano-second had any links to Mr. Prince whatsoever. I had my secretary do full background checks, criminal and business, on all eight "kids," which I did routinely. I would have remembered if there was any link to Mr. Prince whatsoever, and now that I knew he was actually a Moon man, I saw nothing that connected any of them to any individuals or businesses off-world.

Nothing else out of the ordinary happened at that stop to Eye Candy, so I was off to my third one for that day.

CHAPTER 8

Phishy and Bonnie Rockets

I took the exit lane from the hovertraffic after about twenty minutes on the way to see my crazy associate, Phishy. He also had a client for me that day. But if Phishy was referring them, it meant they would be a character of some kind too. I was right, of course.

Phishy always wore a dark-colored vest and pants, with some off-white, long-sleeved shirt extravaganza with colored fish all over it. He was a street hustler, a slider, moving from one scheme or job to another. He did whatever scam he could get into to bring in some extra cash. Never anything illegal enough to get him a solid prison stint. Only at the level where if he were ever caught, he'd pay a fine and be on his way, not even a blot on the record. Cops and courts couldn't be bothered with nonviolent street hustlers. In a vile world, you had to set your priorities properly.

He was a man of the streets and friend to every sidewalk johnny and sally out there, which was why I had him run my Sidewalk Johnny Brigade—my own street intel network, which was as good as the police's confidential informant network. The Brigade had proven its value over and over, getting important information to me to solve a lot of cases. On the streets, knowledge wasn't just power, it was the insurance to keep from getting dead.

I was still in the air, descending, but Phishy and the group of sidewalk johnnies he was hanging with on the corner had already spotted me. He jumped up and down, waving his arms, and smiling as I landed the Pony nearby. I exited and there was Phishy spinning around on the sidewalk, doing his chicken dance to greet me. I stood there, waiting until he finished his dance jig for me, with laughing sidewalk johnnies gathered around.

"Are you done, Phishy?" I asked. I had long since given up getting him to stop greeting me with his dance. Phishy was Phishy.

Phishy was also, of all things, a licensed gun dealer, which really made you question the sanity of Metropolis bureaucrats. However, I had seen for myself that he was actually quite professional in that side of his business. He was solely responsible for getting me my Up-Top weapons. To this day, I didn't know how he got them. Even the best legitimate gun dealers or the shadow market couldn't have done so, but Phishy did. I was lucky to have him.

All the sidewalk johnnies and sallies greeted me with handshakes, nods, and waves. I used to have a much lower opinion of them in the past. Homelessness had been eradicated long ago, like polio and cancer; housing was mandatory for all, even for those without a legacy. But sidewalk johnnies were like the weeds you heard about that ruined a home's plush green lawn in the old days. Hanging around, watching trouble, causing trouble, hustling, looking for a hustle, but doing little of anything meaningful. But they were harmless, and my Sidewalk Johnny Brigade was of a higher class.

Sidewalk johnnies and sallies all had a "turf." For most, it was a street, a corner, or alleyway. Many never ventured beyond it. But in a supercity with massive streets, that was fine. You connected with them and could stay abreast of everything that happened worth knowing in that area.

The "hellos" went on for a bit. Some of the sidewalk johnnies that hung out with Phishy wore Liquid Cool T-shirts and fedoras too, which annoyed me to no end, but there was no point in protesting. They were going to do what they were going to do.

"Phishy, what do you have for me?"

"Oh, Cruz, I got a case for you."

"Who?"

"My friend Bonny."

"Bonny? Have I ever met her?"

"Oh, no. Bonnie Rockets."

"Bonnie Rockets? Phishy, what is a Bonnie Rockets? Do I need to run now?"

Phishy flashed his contagious smile. "No, Cruz. Bonnie is cool. Not Liquid Cool, but cool."

"Is she? Where is she? What's it about?"

I followed Phishy to an alley not too far from where more johnnies were clustered together. They looked like a much rougher group that didn't have much use for smiling and niceties of any kind. Phishy stopped me and I saw him gesture. A woman came out of the crowd. She wore a long flowing black slicker with the hood pulled snug around her head.

"Phishy," she said. "This is him?"

"This is Cruz," he told her.

"That's me," I said.

"Let's walk where we can have some privacy," she said.

The alleyway had a back entrance to a retail establishment. We walked in and down a dark hallway into the main area. It was a large but quiet diner. She had us sit in one of the booths. The place appeared empty, but I did hear a few conversations in hushed tones around us.

She reached out and shook my hand. Actually, she squeezed it.

"Not soft. You've done manual labor."

"I have. Hovercar restoring."

She gave me back my hand. "As long as you're not one of those baby-soft detectives who never leave an office and never set foot on the street. Phishy spoke highly of you."

I glanced at a smiling Phishy.

"What's your case? But before that, tell me what a Bonnie Rockets does in Metropolis."

"Same as Phishy. I'm a gun dealer."

"Probably deal with customers he won't," I said.

"That's for sure," she said. "Though I'm starting to think Phishy's smarter than me. I'm getting too old for this racket. Money is good, but you can't spend money if you're dead. It's getting harder and harder to remain a legitimate gun dealer in the city. Legitimate clients are acting like gangsters themselves more and more. I'm having to spend all my money on bodyguards and weapons to protect myself."

"The burden of the trade."

"Yes, you understand. You have to deal with the same madness being a private eye. You're wondering what I could possibly want with one myself."

"Yeah. You don't seem like someone who needs help from anyone."

"That used to be true. Like I said, I'm getting too old for this racket. Mr. Cruz, I got robbed. We used to call them highwaymen. Crews who'd walk right up to you and steal everything you had. That's what happened to me. I was doing some business, bringing in the supply, four cases of high-quality weapons. We were hit right outside the establishment."

"The client you were making the delivery to?"

"Unless I have proof of it, I can't even think that. I don't think the client had anything to do with it. I've done business with them many times. Longtime clients. They have the money and they do honest business."

"How many guards did you have?"

"I had four. All well-armed, well-trained, and vicious. But the robbers had a dozen. Better-armed, better-trained, and got the drop on us. Came out of the shadows. Must have been waiting for hours before we arrived. I always have a scout in a hovercar near the site to recon the area, and a stationary lookout before we approach wherever we're doing business."

"They knew you were coming?"

"Yes."

"What do you want to hire me for?"

"I want to know who did it."

"The weapons?"

"That's just it. They haven't shown up anywhere. I would have heard."

"Bonnie, was this the first time this happened?"

She looked at Phishy. "You brought me the right guy, Phishy."

"I told you, Bonnie. Cruz will find them."

"You're right, Mr. Cruz. It wasn't the first time. More like the sixth time. That's why I had vicious bodyguards instead of bodyguards."

"I'll take the case."

"I thought you might."

"Call up my office and speak to PJ."

"PJ. That Punch Judy cyborg secretary of yours?"

"Yes. Pay her and I'll get started."

"I'll call her as soon as I have you on your way."

Another case I solved quickly. Bonnie knew the same thing I suspected. It was an inside job. She was just too close to the situation to investigate it herself. I got her employee list and simply spent an afternoon checking into all of them. I used my Sidewalk Johnny Brigade. Stationed them at all their residences. The beauty of using sidewalk johnnies was that there was nothing unusual about them hanging around. I called each bodyguard and said, "I know you're the one who's been stealing Bonnie's weapons. The police are on their way to your place, and they'll rip apart your entire apartment to find the weapons. Stay where you are, I'm on my way."

Twenty calls. Two of the guards dashed out of their apartments like rabbits in a panic. They led us to their own private storage units, and we took plenty of pictures. We called the police on them to take it from there. The two guards were secretly starting their own legal gun sales company but thought the quickest way to do so was destroy the business of their employer and take all her clients. It didn't quite work out for them.

Again, there were no connections between the client or the perpetrators and Mr. Prince. I always kept an eye out for any suspicious hovercars out of habit. In a supercity as huge as Metropolis, if you were being followed, even a novice could reasonably do so without being spotted.

After Bonnie walked us out of the diner and we returned to where my Pony was parked, I said my goodbyes to Phishy and company, then headed out to my next client stop.

CHAPTER 9

Run-Time and Mr. Gist

I had thought that there might be a connection between the client to my best friend, Run-Time. He was a megacorp CEO himself, moved in those circles, both on Earth and Up-Top. If Mr. Prince was really from Up-Top, and his murderer too, I wanted to find a connection. I didn't need to see the evidence from Monitor and company. If they were going to arrest me, then it was rock solid, which meant that the entire frame-up had to have been done *before* I first met Prince that day. That was the theory I was working from. But why would an assassin from Up-Top frame me, especially with my reputation of causing all kinds of chaos for bad guys? A very risky proposition.

My posthumous mentor, Wilford G., said in his book, *How to Be a Great Detective with 100 Rules*, "Do it by the numbers." In other words, you may have suspicions, theories, and feelings about people and things, but cover your bases. Verify all the facts, double-check even what trusted people told you, and never assume anything. Many a case has gone unsolved because of people blindly making assumptions. Don't be that fool. I was going through everything that happened that day I met Mr. Prince—before, during, and after.

I was off to Peacock Hills, one of the "new" money business districts in the supercity where there wasn't a president or CEO over the age of forty-five. As I flew into the Let It Ride Enterprises megatower, I always thought to myself how the monolith buildings looked like gargantuan fingers extending into space through the city's rain cloud cover. Each glowed in the colors of white, yellow, and blue. As with most of the city's buildings, the roof lighting of each structure reflected off the sky giving them the appearance of having angelic halos.

Let It Ride was one of the few places that I allowed valets to park my classic hovervehicle. I knew it was in good hands, and I often used Let It Ride mobile hovercar security services whenever I had to go to a part of Metropolis where parking my Pony unguarded was unwise.

I exited the elevator on the penthouse floor and greeted the three women sitting at the reception desk. "Good morning, Mr. Cruz," the receptionists responded in unison. It was only after having my own secretary at my Liquid Cool office that I realized there was no such thing as a real secretary or receptionist in Metropolis. They were the gatekeepers of your business. They vetted whoever showed up and if they didn't like them, they weren't getting through, so it paid to be nice to them. My cyborg secretary had an electric rifle behind her desk. I wondered what weapons these women had.

"Good morning, ladies," I greeted.

They always seemed to coordinate their colored outfits the day before. The Caucasian woman with the British accent was dressed in white, the Asian woman with the Southern accent was dressed in red, and the Black woman with the West Indian accent was in blue.

They announced me on the vid-phone and I could hear Run-Time's voice saying, "Send him up."

I took the stairs up to the private second floor of the penthouse level, and to his office at the very end of a long hallway. The door was open and in I went.

My best friend, best man at my wedding, Mr. Run-Time himself, founder, President, CEO, and COO of Let It Ride Enterprises. Monday through Thursday, he wore his slim-fit business suits and slim ties, and on casual Fridays and the weekends, if he came in, he left the tie at home. The only casual thing he wore was his trademark flat hat. He told me that he only became a hat connoisseur because of me back in high school. That's when I began wearing fedoras. You'd never see his head without it, and you'd never see him wearing it backwards.

Run-Time was a big deal in Metropolis, a "Who's Who" among the wealthy business elite. But, like me, there was nothing "elite" about him. He owned all the top car washes, hovercar body shops, hovercar rental shops, hovercycle rental shops, hovertaxicabs, and hoverlimousine services in the city. Anything that had to do with private transportation, Run-Time had his hands in it. The hovercar remained the top luxury item in the city, despite ubiquitous public transportation and commercial hovertaxicab services.

He stood behind his desk, and sitting in the chair in front was an older man. Run-Time came out from behind his desk and we exchanged hugs; I hadn't seen him in a while. Then I shook the hand of his guest.

"Nice to meet you, Mr. Cruz," he said.

"This is Mr. Gist," Run-Time said.

We all took our seats. I sat in the other chair in front of Run-Time's desk and turned it at an angle so I could better look at the man. He was slim, well dressed, dark eyes, black hair slicked back and down to his shoulders.

"Thank you for seeing me so quickly," he said.

"Run-Time said it was important, so I'm here," I said.

"I appreciate that. You must be a busy man like us all. I'll get right to the matter at hand."

"I'll see if I can help."

"Mr. Run-Time is in luxury human transport. I'm in international and interspace cargo transportation—retail mostly, some government."

"Big business," I said.

"Bigger than mine," Run-Time added.

"I do all right," he said. "I don't have to tell you how dangerous the business is though. Hijacking is not as rare as the media would have you believe. Depending on the cargo, if I have one transport of cargo, I'll need two or more of security to escort it to the destination. That's how I met Mr. Run-Time. To shuttle my personnel back and forth from jobs. Personnel can be gone for weeks or months at a time for a single flight."

I wondered if I would have yet another case that had to do with someone stealing something from someone else. It seemed to be the theme of the day.

"I run a very tight operation, Mr. Cruz. Hijacking from competitors and rogue gangs is my number-one threat, but skimming is a close number two. Things disappear all the time in the business despite your best efforts. There are so many things in flight all over the planet, from the planet to off-world. It's hard to protect it all, all the time. You automate as much as you can. Use surveillance cameras everywhere. All our security and cargo personnel are body-cammed like the police.

"Years ago, we tried robots despite union protests, like they do off-world, but that was a disaster. Robots were sabotaged and hacked. A worse security risk. Mr. Cruz, I believe that I may have a serious skimming operation within my company. I don't know how they're doing it, but Run-Time tells me you've done quite a few corporate espionage and corruption cases before with very favorable results. My people can't get to the bottom of it. Maybe it's time to bring in an outsider with a fresh set of eyes."

"Do you have any suspicions as to who it might be?" I asked.

"Who? That question is easy. Anyone. That's the problem. It could even be my own security chiefs. I hate to be paranoid, but sometimes you have to be in this business."

"Is there a favorite type of product they like to take?"

"Anything that can easily and quickly be sold on the black market." He reached into his jacket and handed me a data disk.

"Every missing product, dates, shipping details, employees involved for the last three years."

"Three years?"

"It's been steadily getting worse."

"They don't think you can find them or stop them."

"Yes. I'm hoping that attitude is what will help you catch them."

I put the data disk in my jacket. "I'll take the case, Mr. Gist. I'll kick around for a bit and see what I come up with."

"Thanks, Mr. Cruz. I feel better already."

I solved the case in three days. I remembered because the day I solved it and collected the last half of my fees from Mr. Gist was the second time I met with Mr. Prince about his case.

Mr. Gist's case wasn't exactly hard to solve. His security team was turning everything upside down within the company to find the thieves. I simply bypassed all that and went straight to the streets. Mr. Gist's security men weren't criminals and didn't know the criminal world. I did. There were a finite number of fences on the black market, and I had committed most of them to memory (more on my memory later). With Phishy's help, I found the right people who led me to the exact fences that the thieves were using. All I had to do was wait for the thieves' courier to show to sell more stolen products. It was just my luck that he showed up the very next day. The courier was good—he wore a solid disguise, changed hovertaxis often in case he was being followed, changed out of his disguise in a secure location. Perfect. Except for the fact that I got the fence to plant my tracker on him, and the courier didn't scan his own body. How did I get the fence to help me burn his own customer? I told him he'd get to stay in business and I wouldn't call Metro PD on him. He thought that was fair, since he knew the entire Metro PD and I were "friends."

We found the thieves in Mr. Gist's megacorp, and I felt sorry for the man. Once we identified one thief and they were carted off by the police, each one started identifying other co-conspirators to get reduced sentences. When all the dominoes fell, it turned out that virtually all of Mr. Gist's security was involved, including the security chiefs, and his cargo union. They didn't think they'd get caught because everyone was involved. It was a good thing I got paid and the "check cleared" as they say, because a rival megacorp bought him out and he found himself without a job in the merger.

"Run-Time, I feel bad," I said over the vid-phone.

Run-Time laughed. "Cruz, Mr. Gist couldn't stop praising you and said anytime you have the money to visit, he'll put you up in his place to stay for as long as you want. He's happier than I've ever seen him. Early retirement, proceeds from the buyout, obscene severance payment, and he's living like a king on Lunar Colony."

"Wow," I said.

"Yes," Run-Time said. "Wow."

Even Run-Time wasn't rich enough to live on the Moon.

"Another satisfied client, Cruz," Run-Time told me.

CHAPTER 10

Mr. Prince

M r. Gist was living on the Moon. It was a connection, but it was because of a series of unexpected, though quite welcome, events no one could have predicted A coincidence and no more, I reasoned. After that meeting with Mr. Gist at Run-Time's office, I was off to my next client call.

Mr. Prince had called my Liquid Cool office first thing that morning before normal hours. PJ squeezed him in because of the size of the retainer, so I was off to see him. One could never really predict how long a client visit would last. I'd been at some that lasted all of five minutes, and others were hours long. Therefore, I never scheduled more than three or four. If I could get in another, I'd simply call the office to get another address. Run-Time said his visit with Mr. Gist wouldn't last too long, so we scheduled in Prince.

I reached the district of Mech City with its mixed-use grungy silver megatowers. My potential client told me his tower was in the center of a trio of triangular two-hundred-foot megatowers and that I could park in the building. I set the Pony down on the building's roof visitor parking bay. There was a lot of security, both valet and security guards, so I'd felt comfortable parking it where they directed and leaving it under their watchful eyes.

The setup was similar to my own Concrete Mama. Even if you parked in the visitor parking, you still had to go down to the main lobby to check in. The only exception for my building was for those who lived in the upper half. This building had no such exceptions.

The building's lobby had several male and female doorkeeps in purple uniforms, including caps. I gave my name at the check-in counter and they asked for my ID. Once they scanned it into a computer terminal, one returned it and another directed me to the resident elevators. Floor one hundred thirty was my destination.

When I exited the elevator capsule, I saw a security counter across from the elevators manned by a floor security guard. He looked up from his monitor to study me. I said a quick hello and turned right based on the numerical signs and arrows of the floor's apartment numbers. The residents of the building really took their security seriously. Mr. Prince's apartment was the last one at the very end of a very long winding hallway. I knocked once and immediately it opened.

A man stood there. "Mr. Cruz."

"Mr. Prince, I assume."

"Yes. Please come in."

Prince wore business casual but with a robe over it and slippers on his feet. He had a dark tan and perfect dark hair. He gestured me in and closed the door. A luxurious apartment with expensive furniture in the open living room and dining area. What caught my eye, this time and every other visit afterward, were the birdhouses hanging from the ceiling with live birds inside each of them, chirping away. I'd had my fill with animals from the Animal Maniac People. Hopefully, all Mr. Prince had were the birds.

"They're always happy to meet new people," Prince said. "Follow me to my office. I rarely spend any time out here."

I followed him to another room which was packed with stuff. The contrast with the outside area and his home office was startling. If he wasn't so well dressed, I'd think he was a hoarder. It was a home office, bedroom, reading room, and exercise room all in one, with stacks of boxes, papers, gadgets, and things all over. He moved to a hover-lounge chair behind a desk with multiple screens as he pulled up a wheeled stool.

"You can sit here, Mr. Cruz. Don't mind the mess. I'm simply too lazy to clean up myself and I'm in between maids." That's what he said, but in the other times I visited, I'd realize there were no maids. It was how he lived.

He recited everything he had heard about me and my previous cases and how impressed he was with my work. Then he began telling me about himself as the chief financial officer of a major megacorp with offices on Earth and the Lunar Colonies.

"I'd like to hire you, Mr. Cruz, to investigate possible, nearly certain, financial improprieties within my company."

"What kind of improprieties?"

"Missing funds."

"I'm sure a megacorp of your size would have internal security for this sort of thing."

"It does. Have you already done your due diligence of my company?"

"I have."

"Yes, we do, but my investigation has to be outside of normal channels."

"Which means you suspect the CEO or the board," I said.

"Or both."

"I see your problem."

"I report to the board, but I answer to the shareholders, Mr. Cruz. I will turn over all my files. Conduct your investigation in whatever way you deem necessary. All expenses will be covered. My only ask is that you move as quickly as possible. In fact, I would like you to make my case your priority, and I'm willing to pay to have it that way."

"I don't see a problem."

Prince wanted me to move fast for good reason. In the cutthroat megacorp world, people did disappear, and shootouts in corporate offices between hired corporate soldiers were not uncommon.

"I've heard you work discretely and intelligently, so I don't have to give you the normal proviso to 'watch your back.'"

"You don't."

"Also, I'd like you meet with me here with updates on the case."

"That'll be fine."

"Good. I'll get you those files, give you what we like to call at my company 'walking around money' to cover expenses, and get you started."

I nodded. I liked walking around money a lot. I would need it, as the case would become quite involved as I assembled the evidence of the embezzlement ring within the company. But that was only the beginning—of a lot of things.

CHAPTER 11

Monitor and Dent

I'd been taken in already, but now they were making the arrest official.

"Stay still," an officer said to me.

They had me take off my hat and jacket. A machine was scanning my head for my mug shot. It was real. I'd have an arrest mug shot. Beneath the surface there was a simmering rage within me. Detective Dent had a perpetual grin on his face. He led me over to another counter where I was made to place my palms on a screen for finger and palm prints. They'd already taken a DNA sample, so forever more I'd be in the criminal database. Even if I had my arrest expunged, I would be in that database.

"You're big-time now, Cruz," Dent said to me.

I ignored him. I was too mad and might have punched him.

"There's no need for this," Wize said to them angrily.

"Counselor, you can observe, but we don't need your commentary," Monitor said to her. "Take it up with the judge. Your client needs to know this is real."

"My client has been cooperating with you against the advice of counsel."

"Counselor, I don't care," Monitor said. "He can talk or not talk. We have plenty of evidence to hold him over for trial. Looks to me like you'll soon have a real case to try, only you've never tried a case in court before. In fact, you're not even a real lawyer."

"I am a real lawyer, and I've never needed to go to trial because I've always gotten my clients off before trial."

"Then you can do so again with Mr. Cruz."

"That's a magic trick I'd like to see you try this time," Dent said with a snicker.

"Cruz, now that we've done the proper thing, we can take you back to interrogation for you to continue your so-called story," Monitor said.

"Captain, if you feel my story is so-called, why am I wasting my time?"

"I don't know, Cruz; why are you?"

"I see why beat cops called you do-little behind your back."

"But then I'm a captain on the rise, and they're not."

"You're nothing but a jerk of the highest order, and I'm not talking to you anymore. My attorney will get me bail and I'll solve this case without you. Just remember when I do, I'll remember you."

"You do that, Cruz. But your police fan club can't help you now." He looked at Dent. "Since Mr. Cruz won't be cooperating, you can take his murdering self to jail."

"You got it, Captain," Dent said with his insufferable grin. "Turn around, Cruz, and put your hands behind your back. It's handcuff time."

"Oh, and Cruz. Your paralegal can go back home. You won't be getting bail," Monitor said, quite sure of himself.

"You can't do this!" Wize yelled.

"The chief's coming down here to tell you himself."

Wize and I went quiet.

PART THREE

Open Cases

CHAPTER 12

Chief Hub

Every fiber of my being had been transmitting that I didn't want to be formally arrested. That's why Monitor and company did it. They arrested me for murder, despite my story. By law, they'd hand my arrest record to my attorney of record. She'd ask to confer with me, which they couldn't refuse. They walked us back to the same interrogation room with me in handcuffs. They were using all the techniques to unnerve and cause the maximum psychological distress, but it did nothing of the sort to me. What I wanted now was to see the details of my arrest record. It had the name I knew him by—Xander Prince. But there was also a hyphen with another name. Apollo Michelangelo. That was an Up-Top name, and thanks to their previous slip of revealing more than they should have, we knew where Up-Top to look.

Wize Gal, being the street-smart, intuitive operator that she was, didn't need me to say a word. She was already on my same wavelength. She excused herself to call her office. She left me alone in the interrogation room. The police couldn't speak to me again unless she was present. So they hooked me up to the table and there I sat. I knew it would be a while, so I just laid my head on my arms on the table to take a nap. It wasn't my comfy bed, but when I wanted to, I could sleep anywhere.

My eyes closed and I mentally went through all the evidence they'd reveal to the courts when they brought me before the judge. They'd reveal what they had to keep me from getting bail. With no criminal record and all that I did for the city, they'd come with all their best evidence all at once. If I didn't get bail, I was through. I had to get out to find the real evidence to clear myself—and find this Three-Armed Man.

"Wake up, sleeping beauty." Dent had returned to the room, with the same two officers with him.

I sat up as Monitor came in with Chief Hub. But the body language was all wrong. Hub looked like he was a subservient to Monitor. I had seen Hub face down an entire army of the Council of Corporations. Hub would never take a backseat to Monitor, no matter how politically well-connected Monitor was or that he came from a wealthy family dynasty. Hub was the chief of police; Monitor was just a captain.

"No bail." That's all Hub said. The words were spoken with a finality that was meant to catch me off-guard.

"What do you mean no bail? I'm not a criminal and I've never been arrested before. Bail is my right."

"You have no rights," Monitor said.

"Bail is a privilege, Cruz, and you know that," Hub said. "We'll sit here for as long as it takes to get the facts—according to you."

"Or we can take you to jail right now," Monitor added.

"Chief, I've been framed!" The chief was unmoved. "For all the times I've helped the city...that I've helped you."

Hub gave me a look. "Sorry, Cruz, it's out of my hands. You won't be able to play that card today."

"I've been nothing but cooperative," I said.

"That's because you've been caught cold," Dent snapped.

I ignored Monitor and Dent again and spoke directly to Chief Hub. "I've been telling them everything from the time I arrived."

"You mean you'll tell us what you think will get you out of here."

"Well, that would be 'everything.'"

Hub looked at Monitor, nodded and left the room. Monitor stood there with the same self-satisfied smug look. How he got Hub to perform like a trained monkey, I didn't know.

"As I said. Your friends can't help you this time. There's some serious evidence on you for multiple crimes."

Another revelation. More crimes—besides murder! I'd been framed by a master.

"You're not even going to give me the presumption of innocence?" I said. "Why would I do this?"

"Maybe you were looking for a way out of the family life. Maybe a mistress or two on the side," Dent said.

I stood from my chair. I really wanted to punch him.

"Hit me," he sneered. "I dare you. I won't even move."

I sat back down. "The only smart thing you've done so far, Cruz," Monitor said. "Assaulting a detective would only add to your problems."

"I'm not going to wait all day for your attorney to return," Monitor said. "Why did your attorney have to leave Central to make a call to the office? She doesn't like us?"

"I don't like you."

"Maybe your criminal attorney is a criminal too. Those are the only attorneys who do that sort of thing."

"Wize is a personal referral from Wilford G.," I said. "Even dead, his reputation is greater than yours will ever be."

Monitor didn't like that I invoked the name of my posthumous mentor.

"I'd like a glass of water. I've been in this room for hours," I said.

"Why?" Dent asked. "No water for you. There's plenty of spit in your mouth. Drink that."

"What a thing to say. My rights are being violated all over the place."

"You're starting to talk like a perp," Dent said.

Monitor looked at one of the other officers and said, "Bring him some water."

One of the officers disappeared from the room. Outside the door, I caught a glimpse of Chief Hub in the hallway talking to a few suits. I had seen the men before—at the district attorney's office. Why would the DA be here already? It dawned on me. When did the DA's office get here? What time? How did they get here so fast? They wanted to nail me bad—and fast.

Chief Hub stepped in and said to Monitor, "His attorney is back."

"Chief, I see the DA is already here. There are lots of murders in Metropolis. I doubt any of them get this kind of personal treatment."

"Cruz, do you know how much trouble you're in?" he said.

"I've been framed."

"You keep saying that, but no one's buying it."

"This is a setup, Chief, and you know it."

"Cruz, you'd better get yourself a real good criminal defense lawyer, not a paralegal. You're likely going to spend every last penny you have in your bank account on your defense."

"It's interesting how the DA was already waiting for me when I arrived," I said.

"I know how you like to bluff people, Cruz," Hub said. "No, they weren't."

"Easy enough to find out for sure. After all, I have so many members of the Metropolis Police Division in my fan club. They'll tell me."

"Cruz, you're going to jail, not because the DA may or may not have been waiting for you when you were brought in. You're going to jail for a long time because you'll be charged and convicted of four felonies, including murder. The evidence is so solid that you might find your little police fan club will have no one in it anymore except for you."

At that point, I had to admit, I was starting to feel overwhelmed.

CHAPTER 13

Judge Dreadful

I'd been to the Metropolis Municipal Courts many times before. In fact, I worked for the courts myself in my capacity as a private detective, consulting to track down defendants, doing witness interviews, and so on. But Municipal Courts was nothing like Criminal Courts. The former was a comical zoo worthy of its own reality TV series. Criminal Courts reminded people how scary the criminal world really was and how thankful we all were to have a Metro police force even scarier to protect us.

I'd been to some very dangerous parts of Metropolis. Every city had those areas where the Average Joe didn't go if they ever wanted to be seen again. Dent and the two officers led me into the courtroom of Metropolis Criminal Courts. I was handcuffed and ankle-cuffed as if I were one of the most heinous mass-murdering criminals around. The courthouse was like an arena with high cavernous ceilings, a narrow aisle to the attorney tables and judge station, and all around you were the scariest bunch of spectators you'd ever see sitting in row after row of elevated seats facing the bench. At least when I was in the insanely dangerous Mad City I could run away. Here I was trapped.

The officers sat me down and hooked me up to the defense attorney table. There were two seats. One for me and one for my defense attorney. Adjacent to me was the prosecution table. The district's attorneys followed right after us, briefcases in hand, and sat down. There were two of them. I looked behind me and finally saw Wize arrive. She had traded in her punkish street clothes for a very professional business suit and had her own briefcase. She surely looked like a real attorney. As she sat down, the two officers stepped back to give her room but stayed close.

I glanced back at the first couple of rows on the spectator area. There was Chief Hub, other police brass that looked familiar, the head DA himself, Monitor, and Dent. I felt like the lamb being led to slaughter. I didn't recognize any other faces at first, then I saw someone waving. It was Holly Live.

"Oh, hell," I muttered.

Holly Live was an ambulance-chasing reporter, but also one of the leading reporters in the supercity. I could already hear her voice on the broadcast. "Metropolis's famous detective has been arrested for murder. Shocking details to follow." This was a total mess, but it was all necessary.

My attention returned to the front. A cyborg bailiff stood on either side of the judge's bench. I noticed they had their eyes locked on me. I hoped it wasn't personal.

The judge came through a side entrance into the courthouse.

"All rise!" a bailiff called out in a booming voice.

Everyone in the large courthouse did. When the judge sat, so did everyone else.

I had only heard of him from rumors. Judge Dreadful was what they called him, and he didn't look like any judge I'd ever seen. He looked like a combination wrestler-boxer-gang enforcer. He barely fit in his robe, almost busting out, but all muscle, no fat. He had a silver crew cut and his skin looked like leather. When his eyes gazed out to meet mine, I felt my stomach and gonads shrivel up into a ball. I was going to smile to see if that would relieve me of his death stare, but I didn't want to annoy this man in any way. I gave my ever so slight puppy-dog face. Finally, he looked down at his bench tablet.

"We'll skip the formalities," he grunted. "Prosecution, what do you want?"

Both assistant district attorneys stood. "Good day, Judge. Judge, we strongly request that Mr. Cruz be refused bail due to the seriousness of the charges."

"'Kay. Sit down."

Their butts returned to their chairs instantly.

"Defense, what do you want?"

I had to hand it to her. I would've been wetting my pants if I had to speak to Judge Dreadful. Wize was calm as could be. She stood with confidence.

"Before you answer, are you a lawyer?" he asked.

"I am, Judge."

"When did you take and pass the bar?"

"I was eighteen, Judge."

"A whiz kid. I heard about you. Passed the bar before you were eighteen but didn't join the bar association to avoid the annual fee. Are you a cheapskate?"

"No, Judge. I do primarily paralegal work, so it did not make sense for me to join the bar association if I had no intention of being a defense attorney as my primary vocation."

"But here you are."

"Yes, Judge. I take the occasional case, but I always keep the case out of the courts."

"But here you are. Didn't work this time, did it?"

"Judge, actually it would have if there wasn't a bizarre rush to judgment from the Metropolis PD and District Attorney."

"Yes, your client is innocent. Your client has never been arrested before. Your client has been an upstanding citizen and family man. Your client is every police officer's friend from that whole affair of City Hall and those spacemen versus the Metro Police thing. I'll ask again, what do you want? You need to know that 99.99 percent of the time, if the prosecution requests no bail, then it's no bail."

"Thank you, Judge, for saving the court's time with reading the obvious into the record. However, I was not going to cite any of that as the defense's reason for granting Mr. Cruz's bail."

"Then what?"

"The prosecution neglected to tell you that the victim of the primary felony count was a Lunar citizen."

"More spacemen."

"Yes, in a way, Judge. But I do know that Space Station dwellers and Lunar Colonists vehemently view themselves as separate, distinct people."

"If you don't live on Earth, you're a spaceman. Who cares if the victim was born on the Moon? He's dead and the prosecution said your client did it."

Wize held up a data disk.

"What's that?" Judge Dreadful asked.

"Mr. Prince, the victim, wasn't just born on the Moon, Judge. He was royalty. The heir to the Moon Monarch empire. They also request that Mr. Cruz get bail."

I could already hear commotion from the prosecution team and among the audience.

"Why would they do that?" the judge asked.

"To hire him to find out who killed their son, Mr. Prince," Wize answered.

She had dropped the proverbial bomb in the courthouse. I glanced back at Monitor with my own smirk. His face was as red as a beet. Dent looked like he was going to cry. The prosecution looked like they had swallowed their own tongues and were sick.

"Isn't that special," the judge said, smiling. "Prosecution. They're smarter than you. Mr. Cruz, you got your bail. Defense, who's paying it?"

"The Moon Monarch Family will be, Judge."

"Good. I can set a very high bail then. Get out of my courtroom. Mr. Cruz, you got your bail, but you will be back here in my courtroom for the commencement of trial."

I stood from my chair. "I'll have proven my innocence by then, Judge."

Wize kicked me under the table. Judge Dreadful's eyes squinted to dark slits. I knew I wasn't supposed to talk, but I wanted him to hear from me directly.

"That would be the best option for you, Mr. Cruz. I'd prove that supposed innocence before the trial if I were you. Who knows what I might do, if I were to see your face in my courtroom again. I don't like spacemen. I don't like people who wear gangster hats. I don't like smarty-pants like you. Heard you built your own hovercar in your parent's basement in high school. Yes, you're a smarty-pants. I see you and your smarty-pants paralegal, cheap skate-sometimes lawyer again, I might just make up a charge of contempt to have my bailiffs throw you in jail. They're very good at that. Smarty-pants, what am I about to say right now?"

I had ticked him off. Now he'd asked me a question directly.

"Get out of your courtroom, Judge," I replied.

"Then why do I still see your face?"

Wize gestured to the police officers to unhandcuff me. They were already doing it. Wize gathered her things. I hopped past her and ran. All I heard was laughter from the court audience, but I didn't care. I was out of there.

CHAPTER 14

La Familia

Wize later told me that we had lucked out big time. We had a name, but Up-Top databases were not easily accessible to Earth, even for the police. If Dent hadn't slipped and told us who Prince really was, we probably wouldn't have found out in time. All Wize had to do was call the Moon Monarch dome palace headquarters and say the name "Apollo." She was connected directly to the royal family. I wondered if Dent realized he helped me avoid jail.

When I ran out of the court like a madman, I came out into the pouring rain but kept going. The streets of Downtown Metro were already a madhouse but outside the government buildings pedestrian traffic was even worse, but I didn't care about that. I didn't want to run into any police officers, who might be working for Monitor, and I definitely didn't want to be chased down by the press. Using the rain as cover, I disappeared into the crowd and found a hovertaxi pickup point and waved one down. My lucky streak continued; a hovertaxi descended right away to pick me up. By this time, without my hat or jacket, I was drenched, but I didn't care. There was no way I was going anywhere near Metro PD until this was over. Wize could collect all my belongings for me. All I was thinking about was Home Sweet Home. I was going to take a super shower and bury myself under multiple layers of comfy blankets.

As the hovertaxi rose into the busy hovertraffic, I saw them. Holly Live running to me, followed by a pack of reporters. They were after me. But then I saw someone else. Dent. He looked like he had real bad intentions in mind. My hope was to get from the Concrete Mama main lobby to my bed without any confrontations.

I literally only had the clothes on my back and nothing more. The police had confiscated even my hat, and I certainly didn't have my wallet or my key device. Luckily, our doorman, Mr. Post, paid my hovertaxi fare for me. It was so nice to have solid friends in the world. I got him the job at the building; he helped me out in my time of distress.

When I came out of the elevator and finally reached room number 9732, I was home. I had to ring the bell to my own place. The door opened and it was the Hellspawn! Both my wife's parents stood there and there was an explosion of Chinese. I heard feet running and there was Cruz Jr.

"Hey Cruzie," I said as he jumped into my arms.

I heard more noise, then my parents appeared.

"Cruz!" my ma said and gave me a long hug.

Then my pops joined in. "Cruz, why are you in trouble again? The last time you were in CDC quarantine. Now all the cops are after you."

"Pops, it's all a big mistake. My lawyer is handling it."

"Lawyer? You need a lawyer?"

"Pops, was I on the news? Please tell me I wasn't on the news."

"Cruz, you were on the news."

"Good grief. That means they"—I pointed to my parents-in-law—"called Dot. Here, Ma, hold on to Cruz Jr. I want to shower and get some sleep before she gets here."

"Did you get any sleep last night?" she asked.

I shook my head. "Only a quick nap."

My pops put a hand on my shoulder and my parents led me inside while my ma took charge of Cruz Jr.

"You are a bad boy!" my wife's mother said to me.

"I am an innocent boy!"

"You are all over the news," my father-in-law said to me. "They say you are criminal."

"I am a famous detective!"

"You famous all right."

"You two aren't fooling me with your broken English routine," I said. "I know you both speak English better than me."

"Everyone speaks English better than you," my mother-in-law snapped.

I ignored them. "I'm going to take my shower and then go to bed. I don't want to be bothered. And if anyone comes to the door except for Dot or the doorman, shoot them. I know you're all armed."

"Bang!" Cruz Jr. shouted.

"Cruz, you do know he understands what you're saying," my pops said.

"But he's a baby."

"I am big boy!" Cruz Jr. said.

"Are you not aware that your son can talk?" my mother-in-law asked.

"Of course, I am. Who do you think's been teaching him all his Spanish and Chinese?"

You would have thought I'd cursed out their ancestors from their dismissive sounds and waving me off with their hands, both my parents and the Hellspawn. I was the only one in the apartment who only spoke English. Rather than delay my bliss, I ran away into my master bedroom and closed the door. I waited there for a moment with my eyes closed.

"Finally. I'm home."

CHAPTER 15

Punch Judy

When I ran out of the Metro Criminal Court building everyone was either watching me or chasing after me. But being out on bail didn't mean I was not going to be under intense focus for the next couple of months. That's how long I had to prove my innocence. I couldn't count on Metro PD or the DA's office because they were the ones convinced of my guilt. Of course, as with almost all my previous high-profile cases, something else was going on. I didn't know what it was yet, but I'd find out. I always did. I had forty-five days to clear my name. And there was no way I wanted to face Judge Dreadful in this or any other life, this reality or any other parallel universe.

The spotlight on me also meant that the media jackals would be looking for my Ford Pony everywhere. My vehicle wasn't going to leave the Concrete Mama parking spot. I hired mobile security to watch it and let our building's doormen know so they'd be on guard too for any trespassers. I was the passenger this time on the way to Buzz Town and my Liquid Cool office. My wife was flying me to work in her dark silver hover-speedster bug. A Bee was just the kind of hovercar a fashionista would drive. It was small and speedy, which was perfect for her. She traded in her former model for the family-friendly size.

I told her to take one pass around Circuit Circle so we could see if we had anyone watching the skies. Fortunately, the media didn't know my wife's hovercar. We saw them. A pack of them were camped in front of the building's main entrance, which meant a bunch of them would be on every parking level, outside any and all entrances, and the roof.

"Your fans await," my wife said to me.

"You're the one in the family who's really famous. They should pester you."

"Cruz, this woman defending you."

"Yes?"

"The news says she's not a real lawyer."

"She's a Wilford G. recommendation."

"Oh. But—"

"Dot, Wize will take care of all my legal issues just like PJ will take care of all my media jackal intruder issues at the office. I'm covered. What I have to focus on is my own defense."

"Isn't that what a lawyer's for?"

"I mean the investigation outside the courthouse. I know who really did it."

"What? You know who the real murderer is? You didn't tell me that."

"I didn't want to worry you. Besides, your nosy parents were right there."

"Cruz! What are you not telling me?"

"I know who killed my client because I was there."

"You saw him?"

"I saw him."

"You told the police?"

"Of course."

"What did the police say then? Why did they arrest you?"

"They didn't believe me. Or they were told not to believe me and to arrest me."

"How could they do that? All the help you've given them. You've solved cases for them. You've even had cops as clients and solved their cases."

"I know, I know. It's not them."

"Not them? Who?"

"Dot, everything will be fine. I know who did it and I think I know where he is. Dot! Keep your eyes on the road."

My wife drove like a hyped-up rocket and was drifting out of her sky lane because she was too wrapped up in our conversation.

"You know where the murderer is? Cruz, go get him then!"

"I can't. I have to find out why he did it and what this is all about."

"You don't have time for that, Cruz. You're back in court in forty-five days. That's not a long time."

"No, it isn't, but I'll do it," I said with a smile.

"You're going to tell me you always do, right?" she said back to me, smiling too.

"Well, it's true, isn't it?"

My Liquid Cool office was located on the one hundredth floor. Dot decided to park and walk me to the office, and when we got out of the elevator, some big-looking cyborg guys were standing right there.

"Hey, Mr. Cruz!" one of them said. "How ya doing?"

"Doing good," I said. I didn't remember his name, but I'd seen him many times before. One of PJ's friends. Phishy had his sidewalk johnny friends. PJ had her thuggish ex-felon friends. Good. She had human security on our floor.

"Oh, and hello, Mrs. Cruz," he said.

"Oh, hello," Dot said as we walked past them to the office.

"Give the door a knock and Judy will buzz you in."

"Thanks."

Another high-profile case to turn my life into a madhouse. At least PJ took the initiative to keep our corner of the universe sane. I had already made a mental note the day before that going forward, I'd have to watch out not only for the media but Dent— Monitor's attack dog. I wouldn't put it past them to try to stage some situation to get the judge to revoke my bail. I was out, but far from out of the woods and the land of freedom.

Dot knocked on the door and immediately we heard a buzz. The door unlocked. We strolled in and my cyborg secretary was standing there with her electric rifle in one hand, pointing down to the floor.

Her face seemed disappointed as she was looking at my wife.

"Where are they?" she asked. "Little man and Cruz—"

My wife's eyes widened. "What were you about to say, Judy? Were you about to call my daughter by that silly name?"

"Cruzalina is a good name."

"But it's not her name. He name is Kat! Kat as in katana."

She smiled. "That's cool. Kat as in katana. We should add that to the company bio on the Net."

"PJ, do not put anything about my family on our Net storefront. I'm the detective, not them," I said.

She turned with a huff. "Marketing, boss. Do not let cool slogans go to waste."

Punch Judy. Most called her PJ because I did. Most women called her Judy and most of the sidewalk johnnies in Rabbit City that knew her called her Punch. Her short hair was the darkest of crimson, and she had a simulated mole, a dot, above her lip. She wore one of her colored sleeveless tops, this one with an icon of the *Tour Eiffel*, leather pants, and heeled boots. She only wore sleeveless tops to show off her buff bionic arms. Back in the day, Judy was a soldier in a Neo-Paris French punk-posh gang. That was a lifetime ago now, but her pugilistic skills were no less sharp and she could punch a three hundred-pound cyborg through a wall.

"How bad has it been?" I asked as she returned to her desk.

PJ ruled the reception area. It would be like an ex-posh gang member to have an haute-couture interior designer decorating sense. With her punk rock playing in the background on an infinite loop, she had turned her space into some hipster, scenester receptionist-waiting room of the stars. Psychedelic posters on the wall, her fancy "modern" glass desk with see-through glass drawers, and a boom box on top along with her mobile computer. All of her workstation was behind a metal barrier, but it didn't look like a barrier with the decorations. The waiting area had these geometric, purple couches around a glass table on a shimmering, neon powder blue rug. The reception table had her French fashion magazines. I added the hovercar racing mags.

"No problem," she said. "I handled it all. They know not to come in here. Only paying clients allowed."

"Good," I said.

"What are you going to do?" my wife asked me.

As I walked in, my eyes focused on the neon sign on the wall outside my private office. LIQUID COOL in big, bright letters on one line and DETECTIVE AGENCY in smaller neon letters underneath.

"I'm going to have to close down for a bit."

PJ jumped up from her desk. "What?"

"Cruz, I don't know about that," Dot said.

"You said it yourself," I said. "I don't have a lot of time. I have to focus on this situation."

"You can't do that," PJ said. "You have to work your cases as normal."

"Why? I'm the one who's going to jail if I don't find the real murderer."

"Did he tell you he saw the murderer?" Dot asked PJ.

"Yes, a three-armed man."

"What?" Dot stared at me with incredulity. "Three-armed man? Didn't you already have a case with crazy biopunks?"

"Yes, but he wasn't one of them. No bio-splicing. It was natural. He moved like a real three-armed spider. Fast."

"But wasn't there a human spider in that biopunk case?"

"Dot, yes but different. That was a phony human spider. This was a real three-armed man, and he's from Up-Top."

"How you going to get him?" PJ asked.

"I need to find out why he killed my client first."

"Get him, bring him here, and I'll beat the answer out of him," PJ said.

"Yeah, PJ. That would be smart. So smart the judge would revoke my bail and have the police throw me in jail. This three-armed man didn't look like the confessing type. I have to do some solid detective work to put this all together."

"In forty-five days," my wife added.

"Forty-five days, so no other cases."

"You have to solve other cases too," PJ pleaded. "If you don't, everyone will think you're guilty. You're closing down so you can escape the law."

"Escape where, PJ?"

"I don't know, but that's what people will say. But if you work your cases like normal, everyone will say that Liquid Cool is open for business and all the charges are phony."

"I was framed," I declared.

"Exactly, and the people will say the same thing."

"Cruz, I have to agree with PJ. You can't just put all your cases on hold because of this. You'll look guilty. Perception becomes reality if you're not careful."

"You need to control the narrative," PJ said.

"Reading more business books, PJ?" I said.

"I'm VP of Client Services, I'll have you know. I have to stay abreast of the latest in best business practices."

"Cruz, she's right," Dot said. "Maybe speaking to the media might not be a bad idea. You've done it before. Quite brilliantly, I might add. You've been framed. Say so. In public."

"And work your cases," PJ interjected.

"PJ, you have client meetings scheduled today, don't you?"

She looked at her desk clock. "Your first client arrives in twenty minutes. They already paid a non-refundable retainer."

"Non-refundable?" Dot laughed. "Cruz, you're a cutthroat businessman."

"I know nothing about it." I looked at PJ. "Is my entire week filled with clients already?"

PJ said nothing, but smiled.

"How am I supposed to solve the case of Prince's murder *and* stay out of prison *and* find the three-armed man in forty-five days?"

Dot touched my chin. "But you already said you'd do it."

I sighed. "Yeah, I guess I did."

CHAPTER 16

Radio Man

Wize had given me her doomsday sit-down talk. I took her vid-call before we left for the office. She told me that no matter what happened I was going to take a big hit financially. Life was a strange thing. Before I was a detective, when I was a simple laborer, shuffling around, restoring hovercars and occasionally street racing, I didn't care about money. Because I didn't have any. Now I was making money and had a family to support, I cared about every last digit. Hearing that my bank account was about to be violently assaulted by legal fees didn't put a smile on my face.

"Cruz, it's your first time, but it won't be your last. The cost of doing business."

"I get the feeling you're nervous."

"I'm nervous because I've yet to see the evidence. They're going to spring it on us at the last minute, which means it's devastating. We'll need to have an entire legal and investigative army in place."

"Army? I thought the word was team."

"No, Cruz. We're well past teams. You need the army. You get me on the cheap, but not that army. Honestly, Cruz, they want you in jail bad. I got you bail, but you'll need that team to keep you out of prison. I say it to clients all the time: If you've gone to trial, you've already lost—even if you win. That's why I never let it get to trial. If the trial happens, it could go on for a year or more."

"A year or more?"

"After a year, you won't have any money left and your reputation will be in tatters."

"No trial then."

"Then you have to pay. I'm sorry, but that's the facts, Cruz."

I needed clients because I needed money. If it were just me, I wouldn't have cared, but a growing family and the responsibilities that go with it tend to kick natural indifference right in the nuts.

Dot had already left to go to work, but I had a couple of PJ's thug friends walk her to her Bee. She had brought an extra neck scarf to cover her head as a semi-disguise. Though I'm sure every media outlet had Eye Candy staked out, on the lookout for me, her, or what she drove.

I sat in my office at my desk with my back to the door. But it wasn't the rain droplets on the glass I was looking at. Media hovervans were illegally stopping, trying to film me through the tinted window. However, there seemed to be plenty of police cruisers around to dissuade them. I swiveled back around to look at my stack of messages. This was the system I set up which worked for me. I preferred to be untethered from my computer screen or mobile when in the field. I preferred to talk to people, either in person or by phone. There was the "hot" pile, the "hold" pile, the "hell no" pile, and a few other miscellaneous ones, which always changed.

I heard PJ buzz someone in. My first client had arrived. I assumed PJ wouldn't be greeting whoever it was with her electric rifle in hand.

"Your ten o'clock is here, Mr. Cruz."

There was PJ standing at my open doorway, speaking in her professional voice. I kept my chuckling to a minimum.

"Send him in."

PJ escorted Psi-ber Man into my office. I realized why she was acting like a kid on Christmas. Dot and I weren't famous. Psi-ber Man was famous. I had seen Mr. Radio on neon billboards for a long time, but he looked and dressed like a grunge college kid with a hoodie, neon sneakers, and slim jeans. The only indication that he was my pops' age was a slight graying at the temples.

He walked to my desk.

"I don't think I call you Psi-ber Man, do I?"

He grinned. "Radio Man is fine," he said as he shook my hand.

PJ had already closed the door on her way out. He sat in one of the two chairs in front of my desk.

"I'll always be Radio Man. The Psi-ber Man thing is the latest gimmick to increase the customer base with younger demographics."

Customer base? Radio Man had a ravenous viewer and listener base. Millions who tuned into his five-day-a-week The Psi-ber Man Frequency Show. Provocateur, commentator, reviewer, on-air counselor. His show was about "everything," which was why he was so popular. You never knew what he'd be talking about, but it was always riveting. I'd first heard his show when I was on the illegal hovercar racing circuit. His was a favorite station among racers because everyone could enjoy it. Racers could never agree on music or talk stations, but everyone liked Psi-ber Man. I hadn't known he had a personality before Psi-ber Man, but it wasn't unheard of. Personalities reinvented themselves through the ages to maintain their recognition and relevance.

We spent a little while with small talk. He was a natural professional conversationalist. Before long I knew his life's story, he knew mine, and now we could get down to business.

"Did you do it?" he asked me directly.

"No. I'm the good guy."

"I had to ask. Not because I care really, but in my business, things get around and I'll be asked. I have to be ready. There's a lot of media outside this building."

"Don't remind me."

"Mr. Cruz, if you hear my case and take it, will you be able to see it through to the end? Being accused of murder, even if innocent, tends to cause people to become distracted."

"I wouldn't have gotten bail. Besides, the trial date is forty-five days away."

"True. Okay, I believe you can wrap it up before then."

"What's it about?"

"I'm going to say some things. Don't judge me too harshly. I'm not a hypocrite or unqualified to help the many people I do on a daily basis. I take the well-being of other people quite seriously. I take my own less so."

"I didn't even ask you if you wanted any water or anything."

"Your Ms. Judy already did that. Thanks. I'll manage without any crutches. See, Mr. Cruz, I have a drug problem. That's the euphemistic phase that's used. It's off and on. I'll beat it."

"It caused you to do something you shouldn't have or be in a situation that you shouldn't have been in."

"The latter. But I'm being accused of the first part. It's what celebrities of a sort like me always fear. Blackmail. I can't go to the police because if my secrets were revealed, I feel people would judge me harshly and my reputation would be destroyed. I'm sure you can relate."

"I certainly can. But there are all kinds of celebrity drug users out there. Their use has been revealed, some have gone to jail for it, but I don't know any of them that had their careers destroyed because of it. There's more to this than drug use. Are you going to tell me?"

"I'd prefer not to."

"One question. If Ms. Judy outside were to find out, would she want to throw you out the window behind me with her bionic arms?"

Radio Man laughed. "No. She wouldn't that. She might be vexed with me, but not enough to want to do that."

"What do you want me to do?"

"Pay them."

"That's all."

"Find out if there's an end to this."

"What if they don't want it to end?"

"I'll pay you to give me some options to make it end for good. Never want to see or hear from them again. Pay them until we can get to that solution point."

I studied him for a bit. He wasn't the first client to want me to take on a case without telling me the whole story.

"I'll take the case."

"Thanks."

"I'll take it for now. If it remains simple, we're good. If it gets complex or very involved, then I'll have to re-evaluate. That's the best I can do without knowing all the details of the blackmail and who these characters are."

"That's fair."

"Did you pay Ms. Judy outside?"

"I did."

I grabbed my notebook from the corner of my desk. "Then give me the details I do need to meet your blackmailers with the first payment."

CHAPTER 17

Dent

I was almost scared because I knew what PJ was thinking. "We need earned media, not paid media. Earned is free and better." I could hear her say that with all those business books she was reading. She figured that if I solved Radio Man's case, he'd plug the detective agency on his show. Nice, but I don't think we could handle the avalanche of business.

Detective firms in Metropolis fell into two categories: the high-end, one-hundred-person firms that looked and smelled like high-end law firms, and the bottom-end, small shops that always seemed to share space with some bail bonds outfit. I wanted to stay in the middle. Not high-end but could comfortably handle high-end clients if I had to. One-man shop so I could keep my connection to the streets. The second I became a bigger firm with investigators all over the place, I'd be a prisoner in my own office. I'd be managing others, butt glued to the chair, eyes on a computer screen, and not too long after that I'd forget how to be a detective. Prima Donna who owned Eye Candy worked alongside her staff every day, and she was the best. I never wanted to get too big for my own pants. So what if I didn't have the high volume of the bigger megacorp detective firms. It also meant I didn't have all the headaches. Though, since I had been arrested for murder, the "not having all the headaches" thing wasn't quite working out at the moment.

Getting out of the building wasn't going to be easy. The media may have looked like an uncoordinated mess, but they were very good at what they did. They had to be to cover a supercity like Metropolis. They went after subjects and stories like robotic pit bulls, and nothing was going to stop them.

I had everything set and waited at the main door of the office. PJ sat at her desk laughing to herself.

"It's not going to work," she said, "but you will get a good grade for effort."

The vid-phone at her desk rang.

"Go!" she yelled.

Out the door I went. I bolted down the hall with her guarding friends clapping as I passed them. The elevator was waiting with another of our amateur guards. Up we went to the parking. I had to be fast.

The elevator opened and I ran through the pack of media like a running back through the defense of an American football game. I knocked a few of the reporters to the ground, but I didn't care. I dove into the open door of a waiting hovercar, and we were off.

The scene was either comical or scary depending on your point of view. I watched out the rear window and saw dozens of people dive into hovercars, hovervans, and hoverbikes to give chase.

"How good are you?" I asked the driver.

"I've raced hovercars before."

"I don't care about before. We need to lose these animals now. Just don't get us killed. And watch out for the police."

"Relax, Mr. Cruz. No backseat driving in my vehicle."

We shot out of the parking bay like a rocket with a line of other vehicles following. The hoverbikes were what I worried about the most. They were much faster and more maneuverable; harder to lose.

The driver was new to me, but PJ said he was a good fast driver. He was a bit on the tubby side in a nice suit, wearing driving gloves, but was calm behind the wheel. We rose into the hovertraffic quickly and he immediately began to speed up, changing a lane by rising up. We were moving ahead of the main hovercars and hovervans, but not the bikes. The one closest to us had a camera mounted on his helmet, so the maniac was probably broadcasting live.

My mobile phone began to vibrate. I looked at the number on the screen. It was Dot. *The madness was being broadcast live!* The hoverbike suddenly dropped back and I didn't need to see or hear anything to know why.

My eyes opened wide as I couldn't believe what I was seeing. "Dive!"

The driver tried to descend, but the traffic was bad. We saw flashing red and blue lights behind us.

"You really want me to run from the police?" he asked.

"If they stop us, I go to jail."

The driver made it happen. He illegally moved to the right, descended, and pulled out of the hovertraffic. All private hovercar traffic had to stay in designated virtual lanes, side by side, and one above another. The only vehicles that could fly where they pleased were the police, firemen, and garbage trucks.

He kept descending fast—twenty-five, twenty feet, fifteen—then blasted forward. The police cruiser was closing in fast. My driver dove again, hard, with the police cruiser right on top of us.

"Go!" he yelled.

I dove out of the vehicle wearing a plastic mask as he slammed the air brakes. His hovercar was totaled, breaking apart, as both vehicles crashed to the ground.

We were only ten feet or less above ground, so I landed, rolled and ran.

The plan was exit into a parking bay, jump into another vehicle, but I'd be driving, and I could lose any tails with my knowledge of the alleyways and back alleys of the supercity.

But our plan had changed. Another hovercar came out of nowhere, and this time I dove into the driver's seat. The driver had hopped into the passenger seat, and I took off before he'd strapped in and I closed the door.

We reached one hundred fifty miles per hour and I was still accelerating. The police cruiser hadn't missed a beat and took chase immediately. At least PJ's driver friend would get away. If they had gotten him, he'd be going straight to jail too.

"Man, you're running from the cops," my passenger said nervously. "They can shoot the hovercar apart and we'll be two pieces of flesh flying through the air."

I startled him by the quick angled turn I made and immediate dive. We heard a crash behind us. We couldn't see the cruiser anymore, but we saw its flashing lights and heard the ear-deafening sirens.

"Man, we're going to die!" he said.

I said nothing. I was in the driving zone of my mind. Nothing else existed except the vehicle and the road. We were traveling close to two hundred miles per hour, twelve feet above the ground, low lighting, rain, one alleyway after another.

The man screamed as I went straight down. It was an incline. I did a hard turn right and then shot up. We heard the sirens, but the lights were gone. We shot up, down, and I began to slow down as the man realized we were in a parking bay. The sirens were on the other side of its walls. I slowed to a stop and left it running as I jumped out of the hovercar.

The man followed me closely as we ran to a stairwell.

We sat in the back of one of the local diners on the street. The man was still trying to catch his breath and calm his nerves as he drank his coffee.

"I'm going to need something much stronger than this," he said and gestured to a waitress.

She came right over. "Yes."

"Do you have any alcohol?" he asked.

"Sure," she replied to him.

"The strongest drink you have. Set it right here on the table. Make it two."

"Anything for you, sir?" she asked me.

"No, my silk coffee is fine."

She nodded and left us at the table. We were at the back, but we could see outside the main front glass of the establishment, even with all the other patrons at their tables.

I counted seven police cruisers. Two were no more than ten feet away. Three were hovering above them, further away. One was circling the area and one had landed.

There was Dent. He was a ball of rage, yelling at the other officers. It didn't seem as if they liked being yelled at, so they were dishing it back at him as much as he was giving it. I thought a fight might actually break out between them—Dent versus all four officers around him.

Dent thought he had me, but he didn't.

"Cruz, you got balls of steel. You not only ran from the cops but got away from them. There you sit, sipping coffee like nothing happened. I'm not calm yet, and I've been in serious gang shootouts."

"Don't get my employee in any trouble," I said. "She's not supposed to be involved in any criminal activity."

He grinned. "I said I had been, as in a long, long time ago. I'm done with all that. Looks like you're more criminal than all of us combined. Did you do it?"

I stopped mid-sip of my silk coffee. "No, I didn't. What's wrong with you?"

"I had to ask."

"That's why I couldn't get caught. I need to find the guy who did kill my client."

"What are you going to do when you find him?"

I said nothing and simply sipped my coffee.

He laughed to himself. The waitress arrived with his two glasses of alcohol. He didn't care what it was.

"Whoever he is, I feel sorry for him with the likes of you after him. I'm starting to get a picture of you. I see how all those criminals never had a chance when they tangled with you. You look like an average guy, but you ain't. How fast did we get up to?"

"Three hundred twenty miles an hour."

He drank one glass almost all at once. "Do you know what would have happened if we'd crashed?"

"Why think about it? If we crashed, we'd be long dead before the thought could enter your brain, and there would be nothing of us or the hovercar left to put in a small baggy."

He laughed, then finished one glass and started on the other.

We waited in the diner for a couple of hours. A police hover-tow cruiser arrived so they did find the hovercar. Dent was on the scene for an hour before flying off, cursing at the top of his lungs. His fellow officers were happy to see him go. Two hours later all police had left the scene. My new buddy and I got up and walked out the back.

CHAPTER 18

Wize Gal

The Wet Cabeza was my favorite eatery. It was close to Rabbit City and was one of those places I went so often that I knew everyone who worked there, including the owners.

Inside, the layout was a large, open café, all booths and barstools at the kitchen counter, with college-kid waiters and waitresses on hover-roller skates. Upstairs, they had tiny conference rooms for rent, which was where I was.

I'd rented a room, since I couldn't go back to the office for a while, and I couldn't go anywhere near the Concrete Mama, Eye Candy, or any other place people might look.

What I needed was to find out what might be going on, so I called my lawyer/paralegal. She answered right away but told me to hold. I saw her walking to a private room. From the music I heard, until she closed the door, she was at her main casino.

"Cruz, you talk first. Then I'll talk."

"I don't like the sound of that. I'm just checking in."

"Checking in? What did you do today?"

"I was at the office seeing clients."

"How did you get from there to high-speed chases from the media and police? They're trying to get your bail revoked."

"I know you'll handle it."

"Do you?"

"Wize, I need to be out to work the case. The media I don't care about. I'll handle that. Dent is another matter. Wize, we ran from them because Dent was going to fire his weapon at us."

"What?"

"Yes."

"I don't believe you, Cruz. They wouldn't do that."

"Dent would. I was not about to have him kill me and who knows how many innocent bystanders around me. That's why we fled. But, don't tell them that. Make something up."

"Make something up. If that's what happened, then I have a duty to inform the court."

"No, Wize. That would mean I'd have to go back into court. I'm not doing that."

"You may not have a choice, Cruz. You were on TV running from the police."

"Running from the media. The police showed up. The media went away. When have the media ever gone away from a police chase? When?"

"Cruz, didn't you work a police conspiracy case already?"

"That was the Police Watch, and this isn't a conspiracy. It's Monitor, Dent, and whoever is pulling Monitor's strings. Make sure my bail isn't revoked. I'm going to take care of all of them with one call."

"You have no friends at Metro PD anymore, Cruz, at least none that can help you."

"Not them. Someone else."

"Cruz, I am quickly becoming very unpopular in this city. I own a lot of businesses in Metropolis. City Hall and the police could make my life very unpleasant if they chose to."

"Make sure my bail isn't revoked. I'll take care of it. I have to get Dent off my back. He's a loose cannon. I have forty-five days and a lot of work to do. I can't get that done with him out there."

"Forty-three days, and maybe you should stop talking to me and go do it."

"Forty-three days? What happened to the two days?"

"The court called me and apologized. They said they miscounted. Don't ask. Don't complain. Forty-three days. Do your detecting."

CHAPTER 19

Holly Live

"Cruz, you only call when you want to use me to get back at someone. Who is it this time? As long as I have my exclusive," Holly said to me. The smile never left her face as I watched her on my mobile.

"I'll send someone to get you."

"You're at an undisclosed location?"

"I am."

"But I need my camera crew too."

I didn't trust Holly Live to know about my private eatery, so I went to a place in Wharf City. Not a nice part of town at all. Criminals used it for their "business" meetings. I decided it was appropriate for mine, due to my current situation.

Holly Live arrived followed by a couple of Phishy's sidewalk johnny friends in not one, but two hovervans of her broadcasting crew. It took them like an hour to prepare the small meeting room I rented at the back of the seedy diner. We came in. All the shady patrons walked out. The owner gave us the dirtiest of looks for running off his customers, so then we had to make sure to buy food and drinks ourselves even if we didn't intend to consume any of it. I didn't want him calling anyone to cause us trouble. Wharf City was filled with that kind of people.

"Who murdered your client? You said your client was actually the member of a wealthy off-world family?" she asked.

"Yes, but I want to respect his family. In fact, I want to respect all involved, including his colleagues and co-workers at his company."

"The megacorp Bio-Matters?"

"Yes. If neither the family nor his company contacts me, then I will know I can say more. This is an ongoing investigation but—"

"But what, Mr. Cruz?"

"Metro PD is the best in the world. I've told you that privately, off-camera too. Chief Hub. Top notch. A true professional. We're lucky to have him. But even the Metro PD has bad apples."

"Bad apples? Are you suggesting bad cops?"

"I won't go that far, but I'm disturbed, and so should the people of Metropolis be, by a Captain Monitor. His 'team, especially a Detective Dent, is...They're out of control, Holly. I'll confess something to you, just between us."

Holly leaned forward.

"We did run from the police."

"Why, Mr. Cruz?"

"We were in fear for our lives. I thought this Detective Dent, Captain Monitor's lead detective, the head of his team, was going

116

to kill us. He was going to shoot us with an illegal plasma pistol from his cruiser before they'd even turned on sirens. Fortunately, I was able to snap a few pictures of it as proof. I think one of the hovercars in the lane next to us was also filming because we were being chased by media, so they'd have it recorded too."

"That's real evidence," she said.

"Do you know, Holly, what I heard?"

"What, Mr. Cruz?"

"The other officers on the scene where we abandoned our hovercar were so infuriated by Dent's behavior they almost beat him up. He was actually cursing and threatening them. I'd never seen anything like that before."

"You interned at Metro PD as a teenager, didn't you?"

"I did. In high school. Still have a lot of friends there. This Monitor and Dent. They're out of control. The city deserves better. My murdered client deserves better. His family deserves better."

"I have to ask, Mr. Cruz. Did you murder Mr. Prince? That's what you're being accused of."

"Of course not, Holly. But more importantly, you should know that Mr. Prince's family hired me to find out who did."

"Do you know who did?"

"I do. And these bad apples, Monitor and Dent, will not prevent me from bringing the real murderer to justice."

"Thank you so much, Mr. Cruz, for this exclusive." She looked straight into the camera. "Back to you, Max, at the studio."

Monitor and Dent were off my back. For how long I didn't know, but I could work my case.

CHAPTER 20

The Call

I was at home when PJ called me. She actually lived in the Concrete Mama too, on the twentieth floor. It was a coincidence. She had moved to Metropolis years ago and some genius at Housing decided it would be amusing to put her in the same building with the person who made her a cyborg—me. We were frenemies back then, but that was then.

What was unnerving was she told me she was on her way up. It was almost nine at night. I was about to go to sleep myself.

I waited by the door when I heard the elevator, and PJ came around the corner in a hooded robe.

"What are you wearing?" I asked.

She handed me her mobile. "Give it back to me first thing in the morning, *tout de suite*. No delay." She turned around and walked back to the elevator.

"Who is calling me on your mobile, PJ? What's going on?"

"He's going to call you. I don't know how he got my number. Only you'll know if he's really the guy."

PJ was gone.

I quietly returned to the apartment. I walked to my home office. Everyone—Dot, Cruz Jr. and Kat—was asleep. I closed the door and sat on a chair. I glanced at the phone. It rang ten minutes later. There was no image on the screen.

"Hello," I said.

"I saw your TV interview," a man's voice said.

"Did you?"

"I did."

"You should drop it."

"Why?"

"You're not bringing anyone to justice. You can think about that when you're sitting in jail."

"For the murder you committed," I said.

There was no response. The silence lasted for a while.

"I'm going to get you," I said.

"How?"

"I know where you are."

"No, you don't."

"You're so sure."

"I am."

"I'm going to figure out why and then I'm coming to get you. How many three-armed men can there be out there?"

I heard a low, rolling laugh on the other end.

"Any words of encouragement?" I asked.

"I was curious but now that I'm talking to you, you're not worth my spit. Not even smart enough to know you're a nobody. We're way out of your league. Have fun in prison."

The phone disconnected.

CHAPTER 21

Company Men

The damn murderer called me in person, taunted me. He was so certain that he was untouchable by me or anyone else. He knew my secretary's private mobile number. What else did he know? I had Wize meet me at the Liquid Cool office first thing the next morning to tell her in person. She had a look of worry because she was thinking the same thing I was. If he knew this much about me, what "evidence" was in the hands of the police?

"You'd better be extra careful every step of the way," she told me.

"I will. He thinks he's free and clear."

"That's not what I mean. What if he sends someone after you?"

"No. He views us as gnats. We can all buzz around as much as we like. He's moved on and already working his next job. We'll never see him again."

"Aren't you going to find him?"

"He believes he will never see me again, but he will."

"Cruz, I think we need to come up with a backup plan just in case."

"Don't lose faith, Wize. It's not the end of the movie yet. We still have a lot of plays left. You're a gambler."

"Actually, I never bet."

"You own betting parlors and casinos and you never bet."

"No."

"Well, you are an intelligent person. Don't lose faith, Wize. He made one mistake."

"What's that?"

"He confirmed he was watching from afar."

"That fact doesn't change a thing. You're the one in the court's crosshairs."

"We have our ace card."

"You say it's an ace. I say it's a card that does us no good. For all we know, these Moon Monarchs sent this three-armed man to kill Prince. I hear that stuff happens all the time up there."

I was quiet, deep in thought. Forty-two days left and lots of work to do.

"Also, there's the matter of that TV exclusive of yours."

"You didn't like it?"

"No, Cruz. I didn't like it."

All megacorps were the same. They didn't do anything unless a committee, or multiple committees, met, deliberated, argued, and game-theorized it out before a course of action was decided. Since my arrest, with all the twists and turns and my TV exclusive, their board of directors must have been meeting daily about the "Cruz situation." I gave them an opening with my TV interview. They took it.

I arrived at the office and there they waited. Our waiting area with its geometric purple couches, and glass table with French fashion (PJ) and hovercar racing (mine) magazines on its neon powder blue rug, was packed with people in black suits. Male and female, but they all looked like typical corporate human automatons.

One of them pointed to the waiting area's wall. "It will need to be updated, Mr. Cruz."

PJ had turned the wall of the waiting area into a shrine of my past cases. When she first created it, after my first major, high-profile case, my reaction wasn't positive. But I eventually saw its value, as many a future client waiting for an appointment saw those pictures, and said I had to be a legit detective. I was shaking hands with the mayor of the city, no less.

"You mean my arrest for murder?" I said. "True, but the final story is still being written. We'll add it then."

The man stepped forward and did one of those slight Japanese bows. "Mr. Current, CEO of Bio-Matters."

A woman stepped forward. "Ms. Hertz, COO and acting CFO of Bio-Matters."

A man stepped forward. "Mr. Hollo, Senior VP Corporate Security."

A woman stepped forward. "Ms. Sage, Senior VP and General Counsel of Bio-Matters."

"Thank you for accommodating us today," the CEO said.

"I knew you'd probably want to speak with me after my TV appearance," I said. "I know Ms. Sage must have counseled you to stay away."

"She did, but the full board overruled us," he said.

"Oh, you didn't want to come here either?"

"You are accused of killing Mr. Prince, our CFO. What would you have done in my place?"

"The same, and I wouldn't care if that suspect was on TV. However, I would have reviewed the court appearance recordings thoroughly, watched the TV interview thoroughly, not to mention that Mr. Prince did hire that detective for something. I'd need to inquire further. Corporate due diligence and all that."

"They have a corporate fiduciary responsibility," PJ chimed in.

"There. My employee knows the proper corporate terms better than I do. Am I speaking to all of you or just the four of you?"

"The four of us. Our staff can remain here."

I nodded and let the corporate quartet into my private office. I could hear PJ asking the staffers if they wanted any refreshments.

I took off my coat and put it on the coatrack near the door. "Let's sit over here," I said as I led them to my office's own lounge area. In the corner, I had my own arrangement of plush chairs around a glass table, the whole setup on another neon dark blue rug. I sat on the smaller couch at the head of the table and they all took their seats too. I noticed that the attorney walked back to the door and closed it before rejoining us.

We all sat and they looked at me without saying a word.

"This will go a lot better if you actually talk. I'm not a space alien who can read minds. Actually, I can read minds. No, I didn't kill Mr. Prince. Yes, I know who did because I was there. No, I don't know why the police and DA are so positive I did. They say they have evidence, but I don't know what it is. All that matters is Mr. Prince's family believes me and hired me."

"We didn't know Mr. Prince was born off-world," the CEO said. "That fact came as a surprise. Then to learn this family is the Moon Monarchs. One of the Founding Families of the Lunar Colonies."

"How did you not know Mr. Prince's background? I'd think that would be something to come up in a corporate background check. You check everything from the time of birth."

"The fact is, Mr. Cruz, Mr. Prince was using a stolen identity," Ms. Sage said. "When he assumed the identity, we don't know. Was there a real Xavier Prince or was the identity manufactured out of nothingness? We don't know. The revelation leads to more questions, not answers."

"I can't tell you why he hired me," I said.

"Why not?" she asked. "He's dead."

"I know. I was there. The courts can compel me to disclose everything, but not you. I need to do my own investigation beforehand. What I can tell you, to ease your concerns, is it wasn't for corporate espionage."

"How do you know?" Mr. Hollo asked.

"I know."

"Did you know he was using an assumed identity?" the CEO asked me.

"No. It was news to me too. But I think I know why. He was...running away."

"From his family?" the CEO asked.

"Yes. From the royal life he was born into. Honestly, I think he wanted to be an Average Joe. I can relate to that."

"We can certainly relate too, Mr. Cruz. He's not the only person in the solar system who had thoughts of running away from the responsibilities of family that one is born into. Anyone can relate to that, no matter their class."

"Yes. Well, that's my working theory."

"That explains the identity, but not why he hired you," Ms. Sage said.

"Ms. Sage, Prince wasn't killed by accident. He was murdered. The murderer was sent."

"Sent?" Mr. Hollo said with a look of shock. They all looked at each other.

"We understand now, Mr. Cruz. You think it was one of us, or someone in the company," the CEO said.

"Yes."

"Do you think it wise to tell us this so directly?"

"If you did have something to do with his death, I'll find out or the police will. There's nothing any of you can do about it. I was his detective. I know why he hired me and I had practically wrapped up the case."

"Meaning what?" Ms. Sage asked.

"Meaning I can't say."

"He hired you to investigate us?" she asked. "Activities at the company?"

I smiled. "We can play twenty questions, but I'm not saying any more. I told you too much already."

"Then why did you agree to meet us?" the CEO asked.

"I need you to leave me alone. My attorney says part of my problem is your megacorp putting pressure on the DA to lock me up. I need you to back off. If everyone leaves me alone, I can solve this case and we can all get back to our lives."

"You mentioned it yourself, Mr. Cruz," Ms. Hertz said. "They have evidence that contradicts everything you told us here about Mr. Prince's death."

"I don't like being framed. Even if Prince's family didn't hire me, I would have pursued the real murderer to the end of the galaxy. I take these things very personally."

"When exactly did you talk to the Moon Monarchs?" Ms. Sage asked.

"Do you doubt that too?"

"They did intervene on your behalf for you to get released on bail, and an off-world account did pay your bail. That much we verified," she said. "But speak to them?"

"The Founders of Up-Top are all, even the outwardly harmless ones, extremely dangerous. You can hear it in their voices. I did my research too. People think the Moon Monarchs are friendly space people running off-world premiere space amusement parks. All those Up-Top families are the same. Government, corporation, and crime bosses all in one. I spoke to them all right.

If they didn't believe my story, if I wasn't able to convince them, I don't think I'd be talking to any of you right now."

"Maybe they sprung you so they could deal with you themselves," Mr. Hollo said.

"That's possible, but they would have done that the second I left the courthouse. Made an example out of me."

"Maybe they're collecting more information. If Prince ran away from them, as you theorize, maybe he took some of the family treasures with him."

"We can all sit in this room and come up with a million theories. That's why I need to investigate before I'm back in court. I'm going to ask again: will you step back and allow me to investigate what this is all about?"

"We can hardly do that," Ms. Sage said.

"If you do, I promise when I give my final report to your company, the full board, the report I was delivering to Mr. Prince the day he was murdered, I'll give each one of you an advance copy—a day before."

"Report?" Ms. Hertz asked.

The four of them nervously looked at each other.

"He was investigating us," Mr. Hollo said.

Mr. CEO stood. "Your terms are acceptable, Mr. Cruz."

CHAPTER 22

Stick-Up Men

The media were still hunting me despite my exclusive with Holly Live. I had one of the sidewalk johnnies pick up a hovercar rental for me. Something fast, solid, and cheap. I still had to pay for one totaled hovercar from the police chase.

I found myself second-guessing my decision to keep working cases when there was really only one case that required all my attention. However, I had others doing the work for me. I'd work the cases. They'd get me the information I needed to solve the Prince murder. I was certain that once I knew why he was killed, I'd know who did it, and from there track down his murderer. But could I do it in time?

Wize told me that her sources at Metro PD said Dent was confined to a desk and Monitor was nowhere to be seen. That gave me some comfort, but I knew it would only be temporary. My TV interview only bought me some time.

I coasted through the rainy sky to rooftop parking. The district was called Angel's City, but it was a filthy hole of a place. All the neon lights couldn't hide the grime of the buildings or the people. The parking lot was filled with gangster-wannabe hovercars modified with all kinds of useless accessories. Many had their gang symbols painted or carved into the paint. At the far end some fat slob wearing a flat hat watched me with glowing goggles.

I waited with the hoverengine running, a few inches above the ground. The fat security guard had started walking to me when he saw another hovercar descend and inch forward to me. We were nose-to-nose. There was a single driver in the driver's seat.

If he felt I was going to get out and walk to him with the money, he was mistaken. I raised my hand with the money bag and left it to him to decide. He touched down, turned off his hovercar, and got out. He was in a black slicker with the collar raised.

I gestured him to approach from the passenger side window. The window automatically rolled down as he came up and leaned in. He had a scruffy face and longish dark hair.

"You don't look like Mr. Radio," he said.

"I'm his friend. Are we doing the payoff or not?"

"Payoff? You mean the installment payment."

"I'm here to drop it off. That's all. I don't know anything about anything."

"Is it all there?" He studied the money bag on the passenger seat.

"Yeah. You can count it."

He grabbed it, smiling.

"Count it right there on the seat," I instructed.

My hovercar rental wasn't my Pony, but that didn't mean I was going to fly into a dangerous district to do business with possibly dangerous people without doing modifications of my own to the vehicle. I had cameras all around the hovercar, and had been watching a second man crawl out from the back of his hovercar and make his way to my driver's side. I was wearing clear glasses with the displays on my right side of view.

The main man finished counting. "It's all here. You can tell your friend we're going to be doing a lot of business together."

"My friend sent me. Your friend sent the two of you."

The man stopped stuffing the money bag in his jacket.

"Two what?"

I didn't wait. I did a quick doughnut maneuver, knocking the first man off his feet, and all I heard from the second man was a scream. By the time the first man sat up, drawing his weapon, he saw I was already aiming mine at him.

"Give me the money bag back!" I yelled. "Stand slowly."

He got up from the ground.

"Slowly," I commanded.

He pulled the money bag from his jacket.

"Walk over and throw it into the back seat."

"How do I know you won't shoot me?"

I ignored him. He sighed, took a step forward, and tossed it through the open window.

"Tell your friend he's in trouble."

I ascended into the sky so fast that the man slipped and fell to the ground again. The fat parking lot security guard stood near his shack watching like he didn't have a care in the world. I was sure he'd seen far worse. I blasted toward the sky freeway. In my rear and side view mirrors I saw flashes from the roof. The first man was actually firing a laser gun at me. But I was out of range.

When the Radio Man's blackmailer called again, I'd make sure I was on the call too.

CHAPTER 23

Officers Break and Caps

The next day I was at the office early. The media jackal presence outside the building, including its parking, had all but disappeared. However, I had the eerie feeling I was being watched.

"You're here early working. That's what I like to see," PJ said when she arrived an hour later and, of course, first thing she turned on her French language music.

I'd been doing lots of research on the computer. I had access to numerous databases and had been pouring through information and jotting down what I found on a notepad.

PJ checked messages from off-hours. The phone had rung numerous times while I'd been in the office, but I didn't answer any of the calls.

"Boss!"

I looked up and she was standing in my open doorway.

"What?"

"You have to go back to the Concrete Mama."

"What happened?"

"Mr. Post called. He needs you back there."

"Why?"

"You need to go."

I stood and closed up my computer. "I'm going, but don't I get to know why?"

"You got some cop friends waiting for you."

"Wilford Junior?"

"No others. Don't look at me that way. Mr. Post would not set you up. But you have to be there. They're doing you a favor."

The hiring of our doorman, Mr. Post, had turned me from an outcast at the Concrete Mama to a hero. Everyone liked him. He was beyond professional and made us all feel like we lived in an upper-class megatower. Also, he was an ex-cop, which was why I recommended him to the tenants in the first place, and why he had more police contacts than I did. He had worked a beat.

I left Buzz Town right away and got to Rabbit City in good time. I parked my rented hovercar in visitor parking and down I went to the lobby. Mr. Post was waiting at the main entrance when I came out.

"Mr. Cruz. You got here fast. Thanks."

"PJ said it was important."

"It is," he said as he led me down the hallway to his personal office. The two "friends" waiting were "Ebony and Ivory," though I'd never call them that out loud.

Officer Break and Officer Caps were in full silver and black armored uniforms, high-powered binocular attachments over their visored half-helmets, PEACE in big bold white letters on their chests, body cameras, laser pistols and assorted weapons on their combat belts.

Officer Break was a Black policeman who had been on the force for over a dozen years. His partner, Officer Caps, was a White policeman who never spoke much, at least whenever I was around. He joined the Metropolis Police Department a year later. They were senior officers who ironically worked the Rabbit City (where I lived) and Buzz Town (where I worked) beats, which was how we had all become "buddies."

I smiled. "Officers, I haven't seen you in a while. What brings you here?"

They looked at Post and nodded. Post left as he closed the door.

"Cruz, you really shouldn't have done that TV interview," Break said.

"Why? I had no choice. Dent is a wild animal and I had to get him off my back. I can't clear my name and stay out of prison if he's after me for whatever reason."

"You'd better watch your back," Caps told me.

"What's going on?"

"Dent isn't a wild animal. He's a bad cop," Break said to me.

His comment caught me off guard. Police never said such things to civilians. The fact that they were telling me this made me nervous.

"Is there something I should know?"

"You need to know to watch your back. Monitor went ballistic at the stunt you pulled. He's before the Police Watch Commission, and you got Internal Affairs to look at Dent. It was far from his first time. Dent doesn't forget; he gets even. The only reason Dent isn't on the street now is because Monitor is still jacked up with Police Watch. Once that's done, they'll come at you hard. Monitor has a team of twelve, but I'm sure he'll get a lot more than that to target you."

"Why? Target me why? They have to know I didn't kill my client. It's ridiculous."

"It's the victim's off-world family," Caps told me.

"The Moon Monarchs."

"He's on temporary because of their pull. But that trump card will protect you only for so long. The Moon Monarchs are Up-Top, not here on Earth, not here in Metropolis."

"How much time do you think I have?"

"A day or two," Break answered.

I sighed.

"Cruz, the evidence is bad," Caps said.

"Have you seen it?"

They hesitated.

"It's bad," Caps repeated. "You might want to upgrade your defense."

"We're doing that."

"You also need to know that running from the police and admitting it on TV wasn't a smart move," Break said.

"I had to. To get Dent off my back."

"But now they can add evading the police as another felony charge," Caps said.

"I know. It was a gamble, but I had to."

"You're stacking up the felonies."

"Have either of you seen them going after an innocent person like this before?"

"You're innocent?" Caps asked.

"You know I am. Have you? Who's pulling the strings on this? It can't be Monitor. He's a bottom feeder. Who?"

"Let's just say you've been a bit of an embarrassment to a lot of the police brass. The roll call joke is if the police brass can't get a Red Ball cleared, give it to Cruz. He'll get it done."

"I'm being railroaded because of petty jealousy?"

Red Balls were high-profile cases with lots of media attention. Careers could rise or fall based on how they turned out. In my new career as a private detective, I had been in the center of quite a few, including my last case.

"Politics is a strange and petty business, Cruz. That's why Caps and I prefer the streets and not the top floors of Police One."

"Thanks for telling me this," I said. "I know you didn't have to, so I really appreciate it. I'm sure Dot and the kids will too."

"Yeah, you got a new daughter now too," Caps said.

"I do. Kat."

"We can't say much more," Break said. "Whatever you're going to do. Do it before your hearing date. Things may not go the way you want."

"I understand."

Caps put a tablet up to my face. "Who are these two?"

The pictures were of the two stick-up men from last night.

"Why?"

Caps smiled. "They were found on a rooftop parking lot in Angel's City. One was run over by a hovercar. The other one was shot in the face at close range."

"I'm not going to say anything more," I said.

"Maybe that's best," Caps said.

"I do owe you both."

"Cruz, you helped us out before. We're helping you out now. But I'd say we're even at this point."

"Yeah."

"Say hello to the wife and kids for us."

"I will."

The officers opened the door to leave. I followed them out.

CHAPTER 24

Mr. Radio

D ead? But I didn't shoot him.

The courtesy visit from my two police buddies was a wake-up call. They knew about my meeting with the two stick-up thugs. At least I wasn't arrested again. But I was still on Metro PD's radar. Officer Break said it starkly: "Whatever I needed to do, I'd better do it now."

Before I left the Concrete Mama, I made a call. Then I was off to Mech City. I drove to the other end of the district from where Prince lived, to an area closer to Nil Point—the center of the supercity's trash services.

The home of the Psi-ber Man Frequency Show was a strange building that looked like a bundle of giant antennas rising into the dark sky, taller than any other megatower around it. I'd never been to a broadcasting station of any kind before. My guess was that Radio Man's station was unlike most in the business.

The megatower was three hundred stories with two hundred ninety being transmission towers, and only the first ten were the offices. Of those ten floors, two were for security. The building's parking was underneath, which was unusual, but very spacious and I was able to find an open visitor parking. Robotic cameras in the ceiling watched my every move. I didn't think I'd ever seen so many in a parking lot, even at Metro PD.

When I came out of the elevator to the main lobby, I had to stop myself from running back in. There were real dogs everywhere—German Shepherds, Dobermans, pit bulls, giant dogs that looked like part bear, other species that I didn't recognize. The dogs surrounded me, sniffing me every which way as I walked to the guard station. They each had collars around their necks with a large green indicator light. I didn't even want to know what would happen if the lights turned red.

I looked up at the counter and there were three guards, but I couldn't tell if they were human or android. Their hair and skin didn't look real. They were in grayish uniforms, all wearing dark shades over their eyes, and they sat in chairs equally spaced apart, but I had the impression that they didn't have any legs.

"Go on up, Mr. Cruz," the center one said in a robotic voice, and he pointed to another set of elevators.

I walked with my pack of canine escorts to a waiting elevator. I got on; none of the dogs followed. When you lived in Metropolis and were in a profession that took you to different districts far and near, you had to expect the unusual at all times. I checked my body as I thought I'd have all kinds of dog fur on me. I did.

"Great!"

The elevator opened and I was blinded by psychedelic flashing lights. I had to cover my eyes and squint so they could adjust. I thought at first the hallway was filled with people, but could see that they were half-clothed mannequins. As long as they weren't androids. On one of my previous cases I had walked into such a scary scenario. On the ground were flashing yellow arrows for me to follow. Cute.

I found myself passing through walls of colored fog shooting out from the floor. Was this supposed to be a fun park? The ceiling was a giant projection screen with a panoramic view of space—stars, shooting comets, and flying saucers.

I got to the end of the hall, and there was a single open door in the darkness with Mr. Radio himself waiting.

"Mr. Cruz.

"Dead?" he asked with an uneasy look on his face.

On the other side of the wall was his studio and living quarters. The studio was state-of-the-art and all the equipment must have been worth a fortune, accumulated over decades. His bachelor-like apartment was more suited for a struggling college student. It was small but everything was in sight.

We sat in his living room. He had been eating cereal before I'd arrived. He didn't have a show today so his production crew wasn't in, but I could hear re-broadcasts on a radio in the corner.

"What does it mean?" he asked.

I pulled the money bag from my jacket and handed it back to him.

"It means you're not paying anything. I'm not sure what blackmail school they went to, but you don't kill your mark when they're paying."

"Maybe they thought you were trying to double-cross them?"

"No. Their plan was either to kill you or kidnap you."

Radio Man jumped up from his seat. He paced around, rubbing his face and hair.

"I can't believe this," he said.

"You're going to have to tell me more. You were smart to send me instead of going there yourself, but your blackmailer sent two thugs."

"You said they were dead. Did you..."

"I killed the one who was crawling on the ground to shoot me, or whatever he planned to do. I left the other one there, but the police told me that he's dead too. Shot right in the face."

Radio Man was a mess. Scared. Panicking. He jumped in place trying to calm himself down.

"Does the blackmailer call you?"

"He sends email right here to the studio, always with the subject 'PAY ME.' We ignored them. I get lots of junk and crazy stuff. My assistants read everything and they alerted me when one came in with references that no one should know about. It had a number to call. I did. He told me that after I paid up, he'd get rid of the phone. I used a temp phone myself. No way I'd let him have my private numbers."

"One of the thugs admitted they were going to blackmail you for a long time."

"Doesn't surprise me, but what now?"

"Check your email."

I saw the realization flash over his face. "You're right." He ran to a desk in the apartment studio.

His fingers were typing and he was hunched over a screen. "I got one! It's new. There's a new number."

"Call it now."

He looked around. "I still have the temp phone."

He found the phone on another desk, cluttered with stuff. As he ran back to his computer, he looked at the screen and dialed the number. He put the phone to his ear, but I joined him.

"Put it on speaker."

He did so. The phone rang and someone picked up.

"Hello. I'm on speaker."

"Yes," Radio Man said.

"If you've called the police—"

"Shut up!" I said. "I'm the one here with Mr. Radio. First, he's not paying you anything. You can do whatever you want with the blackmail stuff you have on him. We don't care, but you're not getting a penny now. You sent two guys to kill him when he was paying you. The deal is off."

"You killed one of my guys. I killed the other."

"You killed him?" I said.

"They botched the job so that's what happens. And the deal isn't over. I know who you are. We'll do a do-over."

"Do-over? I don't think so. You had your chance. It's over."

"I don't think your client will like the stuff I have on him out in the public."

"Since you're going to do it anyway, why pay you? It's over. You blew it. Don't email or call again. And I know who you are too. I'm taking a recording of this call to the police. We have your voice print and your confession of murder. That's all we need—"

He'd already hung up.

I handed the phone back to Mr. Radio. "Your case is over."

Mr. Radio dropped the phone on the table.

"I'm glad you talked to him. You'd think I'd know how to handle any situation after being on the radio for decades, but I don't think I've ever had to bluff my way out of anything dangerous."

"Bluffing? I wasn't bluffing." I showed him the recorder band around my wrist. "Call recorded. And I do know who he is. I recognize the voice. Mr. Radio, you do whatever you want in your free time, but my advice is to stay away from dope daddies who trade in illegal Up-Top synth drugs. That's the opposite of intelligent. You're not the first client I've had caught up in their scheme. Use their drugs, they get you to do all kinds of kinky crap, all recorded, you never remember what you did, the blackmail starts."

"You knew from the start?"

"I did. I'm a detective. I'm supposed to. Speaking of the words 'Pay Me.'"

He laughed. "Sure," he said. "Do you want the grand tour of the studio while you're here?"

"Yes. I'll take a few photos for the wife. I think a bunch of her colleagues watch your show. They might want an autograph too."

CHAPTER 25

Compstat Connie

That's how I preferred it. I hated loose ends. Knowing who killed the other stickup man put my mind at ease. In the detective biz, not every case was wrapped up nicely, far from it. But if the blackmailer hadn't told us he was the culprit, my mind would have wondered forever who did it. Was someone else trying to frame me for another crime? The internal guessing would've never ended.

I returned once again to the Concrete Mama to work in my own home office. I created a quick report to add to an external data file with the audio recording of the blackmailer. Then I created another email data file with Radio Man's autograph, video of his studio and him pretending to be doing a live show and mentioning Liquid Cool (PJ would love it), pictures of that, pictures of the lobby killer dogs, and an external shot of the antenna studio tower. That file was emailed straight to Dot at Eye Candy. Not even two minutes later and Dot was texting me back that the entire Eye Candy floor was going crazy and they were playing the video on the monitors for staff and customers. Gotta keep the wife happy!

I came out of the elevator on the lobby floor again to see Post.

"Can you get this to Break and Caps?" I said, handing him an envelope. "Just an FYI for them."

He nodded. "Of course, Cruz. Consider it done."

Officers Break and Caps didn't have to give me a heads-up on anything. The least I could do was show them proof that I wasn't the one who shot that thug dead in the face on that Angel's City rooftop parking. If you have friends in high places, keep them, especially in Metropolis. I had enough enemies.

I shot out of the Concrete Mama in my hovercar rental to get back to my Liquid Cool office. My days were counting down, but an important one was only a couple of days away. I wanted to be more than ready.

I'd gotten back to the office and it seemed things had quieted down. No media jackals hanging around and PJ had sent her friends home who were providing extra security. Everything looked quiet on the Liquid Cool front, which was why I knew it wasn't.

I came through the door and said, "What are you typing?"

"Never you mind what I'm typing," PJ answered. "This is my domain. Yours is in your office."

I grinned and walked into my private office.

"Calls?" I yelled out, but saw she was standing at my open doorway with her electric steno pad.

"Lots of calls."

"Anything interesting?"

"Mr. Post at our building called. He said he passed over your package. What package?"

"Never you mind," I said. "What else did he say?"

"They appreciated it, and someone else wants to talk to you."

"Who?"

"He didn't say."

"Are they calling, coming by?"

"That's all he said."

"Well, that's no kind of message."

"Cruz, I can't force people to leave a proper message."

"Well, if he calls again, I'll talk to him. I wonder who he could mean."

I sat at my desk and PJ was gone.

That was fast, I thought. For Officers Break and Caps to get the information and already respond. Mr. Post was the best. Always went beyond the call of duty.

I noticed one message on my desk by itself, away from the stacks of messages. PJ had circled it in red. I held it up. The Moon Monarchs were sending a representative to the office to meet me. A real live Moon person would be in our office. We had spacemen, Martians, now we'd have our first live Moon person. But then I wondered what I should expect. The Moon Monarchs allowed me to get bail and then posted my bail as my fee to hire my services. But the prosecution still said I murdered their family member.

I would never be able to type as fast as PJ with her bionic fingers, but I was holding my own with my Net research. My head looked up from my notes; there was a bit of commotion outside. I stood from my desk.

My current seventy-something mentor, Compstat Connie, strolled into my office with PJ following her. She had a blue head scarf on and wore a long gray slicker; it was still pouring rain. Megacorporations had machines that knew all there was to know worth knowing. Metropolis had Connie. She was the head of Metro PD's Crime Information Center (CIC), the multi-hundreds-of-millions-of-dollars division which collected all the supercity's crime data.

But that wasn't what I was looking at. She had her own envelope in her hand. She dropped it on my desk.

"I was never here," she said. With that, she turned and left PJ and me looking at each other. PJ peeked out of my office as we heard the door close.

I picked up the envelope. It looked like the exact same one I gave Post for my police buddies. This envelope had a data disk inside too.

"What is it?" PJ asked me.

I said nothing as I sat down and connected the data disk. PJ came around to look at my screen too.

"It's password protected. Did she give you the password?"

"I know it." I did know it without her telling me. Wilford G.

We looked at the attached files, one after another, and my stomach dropped to my butt. Compstat Connie had dropped off the prosecution's evidence against me. It was bad.

"PJ, get Wize Gal in here, or better yet I'll go to her."

"But the Moon Monarch rep will be here."

"This can't wait. If I'm not back, stall him or her."

CHAPTER 26

Wize Gal

I had to drive all the way to the Old Metro district of Cascade City to the main casino-restaurant-club owned by Wize Gal. Her father owned a few in Old Metro; this one was hers, appropriately called Wize. The establishment was huge and classy, but catered to the Average Joe and Jane. The valets, male and female, were all seasoned, long-time workers. I turned my hovercar rental over to them.

Wize had a grand office in the center of the busy, bustling, and noisy place. People gambling, drinking, dancing, watching large monitors on the walls and ceilings everywhere of every sport, fight, or race worth betting on. No wonder her legal work wasn't her main career. She was pulling in wages fit for a king and queen every single hour, whether she came into the office or not.

However, inside her office neither one of us was having a good time like her patrons outside the office.

"She gave this to you?" Wize said, seated at her desk, slowly scrolling through the documents from the data disk. "You have better connections than me. You need to keep them no matter what."

I was in a chair behind her. "Is it as bad as I think it is?"

"Depends. How bad do you think it is? Frankly, I'm shocked." She looked at me. "If I were the judge, I wouldn't have allowed you bail. But he didn't see all this."

Wize continued going through the documents. "I can't believe you have insiders who gave you this. The prosecution still hasn't provided this to me. They're playing the big evidence dump game. Holding back the real evidence until the day of the hearing. I'll have to pretend we didn't get this ahead of time to be on the safe side, which means I'll have to do the initial legwork solo. I don't mind lying, and neither does my team, but I do it better than them."

"Should you be telling me that?"

"Cruz, lawyers lie. Defense and prosecutors. Grow up. That's the game. But the evidence is the final arbiter."

"From your face, if we get to hearing, and I haven't cleared myself, I'm going to jail."

"Right away and the Judge won't allow any delays whatsoever. If I didn't know you didn't do it, I'd believe you did."

"What I saw were false witnesses mostly."

"I'll need to look through it all, but, Cruz, this is a masterful frame. This couldn't have been done quickly. Both of you were targeted. You and this Mr. Prince. At least you have friends who still believe in you, despite all this."

"The behavior doesn't fit my profile. They know I didn't do it."

"You have work to do. I have work to do."

I nodded. "Yes."

"We don't have a lot of time, and one or both of us had better come through."

"Yeah."

"Cruz, I'm charging you a lot for this because I'll be working on this all day, every day, until the hearing instead of running my own business, or other things, like sleeping."

"I know. Looks like I'll be dipping into my rainy day and vacation fund for this."

"I'll get to work then."

"I'll get back to the office. I'm meeting a rep for the Moon Monarchs."

"When?"

"Now."

"Now?" She gave me a look. "Are you crazy? Those are the people who posted your bail. You need to keep them on your friendship train. Get out of here."

CHAPTER 27

Twins

There was a bit of sweat on my brow as I had run straight from the parking lot to the elevator, and now down the hall to my office. I had arrived forty minutes after my appointment with the Moon Monarch rep. I didn't expect the person to be waiting but ran anyway.

I burst through the main door and stopped with a heavy exhale. PJ was still in the office at her desk. She pointed to the waiting area.

I had expected to see one person, but there were two of them. A young man and woman with bleached white hair and clad in expensive white clothes. Up-Top space people in their all-white gear. The fashion themes of humanity were interesting to me. Metropolis, the largest supercity on Earth, wore grays and blacks for outerwear. The Space Station and Lunar Colonies loved their white and maybe silver on occasion. Mars was all about bright reds and reddish browns.

"I'm so sorry for the delay," I said. "It was beyond my control. Please tell your bosses I'm sorry too."

"Bosses?" the Moon woman said. "We are the bosses."

"You're the bosses?"

"Members of the Moon Monarch Family."

Immediately, my guard went up. Why would uber-wealthy royals wait all this time for little old me?

"Then I'm really sorry."

"Don't be, Mr. Cruz," the Moon man said. "We would have waited all night for you."

"Why is that?" I asked.

"What was his name here?" he asked.

"Prince," she answered.

Both of the Moon people had been moving closer to me from the waiting area—very slowly.

"His real name was Michelangelo," the Moon man said. "He was our godfather, a Founder. Family is very important to Founders, more important than any other concern. Someone kills a member of the Family and that person must pay. Maybe you're innocent as you claim, but we're going to take you with us to Lunar Colony, where the best torturers in the known solar system will find out for certain."

"I don't think so," I said and glanced back to PJ, who already had her electric rifle pointed at them.

The Moon people just laughed. The man waved his hand, and PJ's electric rifle flew out of her arms before she could grab it and into his hands. I shot him with my omega-gun before he could even think to turn it on us. The Moon woman watched her friend fall backwards to the floor.

The woman stood there glaring at me, and my weapon pointed at her.

"I didn't kill him...yet, but if you move, I'll shoot you too."

"How do you have a utopian weapon, Earth man?" she asked with her teeth clenched.

I shot her. I had used the technique so many times myself, and I couldn't take the chance. Who knew what other Up-Top weaponry and devices they had on them? I couldn't give them a nano-second's chance to use any of it on us.

"PJ, quick. Get them on their stomachs and restrain them."

She ran to her desk and opened one of the drawers. I kept my weapon on both of their unconscious bodies. PJ turned the woman over on her chest first and restrained her with handcuffs, then did the same for the man.

"Our scanning arch can't detect Up-Top weapons?" PJ asked me.

Around the main door was a barely visible scanning arch, painted to match the color of the walls. It could detect metal of any kind, which meant weapons, robots, androids, and cyborgs. But the Up-Top tech was superior to Earth in evading detection.

"That means after today, no more people from Up-Top in this office," I said.

"What now?"

"Handcuff their wrists together and their ankles."

"Okay." She ran to her desk again. When she stood up, her eyes stopped at the three video monitors at her workstation. "Cruz!"

I ran to her desk just in time to see one armed man in a white suit after another running down the hall. One shot at the door and it literally disintegrated to dust. I fired my weapon at the first one running through, sending him crashing into the wall.

PJ and I ducked down, but then looked at each other. If they could disintegrate our reinforced door, they'd do the same to the reception desk and possibly us. PJ ran for her rifle. With the flip of a switch, I turned my single fire to machine-gun fire and came out from behind the desk. I fired and every shot was hitting something—two more men in white were already inside the office. A third jumped in and PJ punched him with her bionic arm straight out, crashing into another one of them. PJ had her electric rifle now and started her own volley.

All I could think of was my office weapons stash. I bolted into my private office, listening to the growing gun battle outside. I came back out with my photonic stun grenades just like Metro PD used, which meant the ones I had were illegal. I let them fly out the doorway of my private office and out the hole that used to be our main door. PJ knew to turn away, and I dove to the side of the wall inside my office for cover. Four explosions. No sounds.

I came out with my weapon pointed. PJ rushed past me to her desk. We both looked at the monitors on her workstation. A hallway of unconscious bodies. Back into my private office I went and came back out with a "pig-sticker"—the most lethal stun baton on the black market, meaning extremely illegal. The Moon couple was awake, watching me, and they knew what I had in my hand.

"PJ, lockdown!" I yelled.

PJ slapped a button on her desk and a metal barrier wall rose up, covering the entire length of the wall along the hallway and closing the hole that was once the main doorway.

"Torture, you said. PJ, let's get them into some chairs, so that they'll be comfortable."

PJ picked one up in each hand as if they were bags of fluffy popcorn and threw them onto the same couch in the waiting area.

I pointed at them with my pig-sticker. "I had an acquaintance who said that's why you really posted my bail. But I didn't believe them. I said they believed me when I said I didn't kill my client, because my client was a decent guy, and I solved his case, and I was going to personally find and take care of his murderer. That's what I told the family. I was going to track down this three-armed man if I had to go Up-Top to do it."

A very strange thing happened then. Their glaring, primitive demeanor faded. The two Moon people looked at each other with surprise.

"Mutants?" the man said to the woman.

"You told the family you saw the murder?" she asked me.

"Yes. I was right there when it happened! I saw the murderer. A three-armed man."

"You mean one of those biopunk freaks you have on this rock of yours."

"This rock is called a planet! And this guy was no biopunk. He had three arms and moved and used them as if he came out of the womb with them. Genetic manipulation is an Up-Top thing," I said.

"You told our father this?" the man asked.

"Your father? Is that who he was? Yes, I told him the entire story."

"Can you prove it?" she asked me.

"Liquid Cool secretly records all initial client calls as standard practice," PJ replied directly.

"Yes," I said. "Are you claiming you were told differently?"

"Show us the recording!" he demanded.

"Okay, we'll play along. PJ, bring them into my office."

PJ dragged them both into my office, and I was already seated at my desk and found the recording on my computer.

"Here."

I turned my screen around so they could watch the entire call between me and the Moon Monarch man with silver hair and beard. The two looked at each other again, but their rage wasn't directed at me anymore.

"Release us!" he demanded.

"We're leaving. Let us out," she said. "More will come if you don't."

I looked at PJ. She picked them up and took them back out of the office. There was nothing on the monitors and the hallway was empty. Their Moon servants were undoubtedly retrieving more weapons to play with us with. I hit the all-clear button and the metal wall lowered. We unlocked the shackles on their feet only and pushed them out through the hole into the hallway. I tossed sets of keys on the ground. PJ had already hit the lockdown button on her desk again, and the wall rose shut.

"Boss, look at this."

I joined PJ at her desk. On the monitors were a lot more white suits, and they were all carrying much bigger guns.

"I wonder what those guns do," I said.

"We need to get Phishy to get some for us."

The white suits got their bosses out of their restraints, tossing handcuffs and keys to the ground. They followed the male and female duo back down the hall, not to the elevators but to the stairwell.

"They probably have their spaceship on the roof," PJ said. "Maybe I can see it when it flies away and get a picture." She grabbed something from another drawer and ran to the main bay window in my private office. I waited and watched the monitors.

My Moon Monarch saviors actually planned to be my executioners.

The vid-phone rang.

"I got it!" PJ's voice called out. "Boss!"

I walked back into my office and came around my desk. On the monitor were the young male and female Moon maniacs. They were seated in what looked like a hoverlimo.

"Mr. Cruz, my name is Apex and this is my twin brother, Nadir," she said. "We apologize for our actions. We were given incorrect information. We loved our godfather very much and were very distressed when he disappeared."

"Your father didn't tell you the truth?" I asked. "Why would he do that?"

"The answer is obvious," Nadir said.

"We will deal with Father. This three-armed man. We've heard of him."

"Have you? How?"

"We never thought he was real though," Apex said. "The underworld has many stories of mutant contract killers. We always thought they were to frighten people like bedtime stories of boogiemen hiding under beds and gremlins in space engines are meant to scare children. It would seem these mutant stories may be real after all, some of them at least. Can you find this killer?"

"I know what he looks like. If people would leave me alone to do my detective work, I think I can."

"You won't have any other interference from us or anyone else in the Moon Monarch Family," Nadir said. "We can guarantee that."

"Call us when you've located this three-armed man," Apex said. "If he's Up-Top, we'll take care of him."

"What's going to happen to your father?" I asked.

"Don't worry about him, Mr. Cruz. The only place you might see him in the near future is in the Utopia obituaries." Apex spoke with the coldness of open space.

"I'm not sure what to say."

"The Family will transfer additional monies to your account to cover your fee in finding our godfather's killer, any damage to your office, and any additional expenses. We look forward to your call."

She hung up.

PJ stood next to me with her mouth hanging open. "*Incroyable*. Did they just tell you they're going to kill their father? He tried to get them to kill you? What kind of ruthless people are these space people? We need to keep these crazy people off our planet."

"PJ, these crazy maniacs just told us that there's an internal coup within the Moon Monarch Family, and maybe a lot of people will end up in their obituaries. Mr. Prince was the heir to the head of the Family."

"How do you know that?"

"That's what this is all about. He escaped from them, and who can blame him? They somehow found him after all these years, one of them had him killed, and now it'll be a private war in the shadows to see who will be the new head of the Family. These are Up-Top Founders. They got humanity into space, the Moon, and Mars to create new societies. They didn't accomplish any of that by being sweet and nice."

"Corporate gangsters," PJ said.

"That's the Up-Top government. But I suppose they became what they had to become to beat out the criminals, megacorps, and Earth for control of space." I shook my head. "How do I get into these kinds of cases?"

PJ smiled and ran out of the room.

"Let's see how much she paid us!" I heard her yell from her desk.

There was a scream of exhilaration. She appeared at the doorway.

"We're rich!"

I looked up at her. "Did you forget the trial?"

She frowned. "We're poor."

PART FOUR

The Investigation

CHAPTER 28

Cookie

PJ and I watched from the bay window of my personal office. We knew it was the Twins. A giant white hovercraft encircled by a ring of smaller, shiny silver hovercraft left from the roof of our building. Dark colored hovervehicles were what Metropolitans drove, with the occasional contrarian like me with my Miami Vice Red Ford Pony. Space people liked their white and shiny silver colors. The Twins' hovercraft and hover-entourage merged into the busy sky traffic in the distance. We had escaped their wrath for now, but I expected future problems from these Moon Monarchs. Assuming I wouldn't be sitting in Metro Prison in just over a month.

When I returned home, I shared the encounter with Wize Gal. On my vid-phone screen she looked like she hadn't slept in a day, and my news didn't help matters. I made sure she knew I was simply telling her to keep her abreast of things. I didn't expect or want her to do a thing.

I told her to go and sleep but knew she wouldn't. After I looked in on a sleeping Cruz Jr. and Kat, I did my best to get some sleep myself, careful not to wake up Dot. At least there was normalcy for our kids.

Despite the violence, I was glad I'd met the Moon Monarch Twins. I knew where I stood. I solved the old Prince case, but the new Prince case was what I'd be consumed with until the hearing with Judge "Dreadful."

I met Cookie at Prince's apartment first thing in the morning. The building landlord had locked the residence down for the initial police investigation. The scene was processed and all potential evidence was collected. Today was the first day the scene could be entered and the megatower landlord with the floor's security let us both in.

"Stay as long as you need and call me directly if you have any requests," the landlord said to her. He gave me a short, cold look, turned, and walked away with the same guard.

When we entered the residence, most of the furniture and things were still there. The bird cages from the ceiling remained, but Animal Control came for the birds to put them in a sanctuary.

Cookie was Prince's girlfriend. I hadn't met her in person before but knew she existed from the photos of her in the apartment. They made a happy couple from the pictures. It was a simple matter to track her down and find her contact info after the murder. I made arrangements to be there when she took charge of all his things. Prince had a will and left everything to her.

She stood in the middle of the living room for a moment with a sad, pained expression. Her long brown hair came down to her waist under her slicker. She had long nails. Long thick eyelashes. When I did call her, I expected her to hang up on me, but she didn't. She told me that she knew I didn't do it. Her boyfriend spoke too highly of me.

I waited on her. She moved to Prince's office-bedroom where he really lived. I followed.

"They took everything," she said angrily.

The room was completely empty. I had expected as much.

"You'll get everything back when the police are done. It may be a while, but you will."

She sat down on the floor, trying not to cry.

"Guess we can't go through his things if there are no things to go through."

I sat on the floor too. "It's okay. We can talk, finally."

"What do you want to know?"

"How were things between you two?"

"We were happy. We were madly in love and happy. Sure, he was a senior member in management at a major megacorp. The company had him more than I did. But he always made time for me, and when he did...it was only about me. He never let work come in."

"Never talked work, or any troubles at work?"

"No. But I knew he was working on something. He told me about you. I knew it was important to him. He told me that it was almost over."

"Do you know what his plans were? After I finished his case."

"Go before the board. That's what he was going to do."

"How did he get along with them?"

"He hated them. All of them, but it wasn't raw hatred. It was a hate-and-shrug-your-shoulders kind of thing. Like part of the job. He was good at his job, but didn't think they were any good at theirs."

"Did he ever think about running the company himself?"

"No, he never wanted that. They tried to make him CEO many times, but he turned it down. I think that's why he hired you. He felt personally responsible. If he were running things, whatever was happening wouldn't have. But he'd never take the CEO job. He told me he didn't want the spotlight. He wanted to be in the background. He enjoyed it that way. I guess I know why now."

"Do you think his colleagues knew what he was doing?"

"That he hired you? No. He was too careful and much smarter than any of them. Not the kind of man you'd want to play poker against. He had that kind of demeanor. You know what he hired you for. What would have happened if he'd presented what you found to the board?"

"There would be a new board."

"But you don't think they had anything to do with his murder?"

"No, but I'm looking into it anyway."

"I don't understand why. Someone from Up-Top sent a killer after him. That's what happened?"

"Your boyfriend was a member of one of the Up-Top royal families. He ran away from them, and they found him, or I believe someone told them where and who he was."

"And they had him killed?"

"To make sure he never returned."

"You saw the man?"

"I did."

"Do you know where he is?"

"I'll find him."

"Then what will you do?"

"Morgue or prison. It'll be his choice."

"Morgue is better."

"Cookie, now that all this has happened, is there anything that comes to mind? Something strange, unusual, unexpected, out of the ordinary. Something that happened. Something you heard or saw."

"No, nothing. Life was normal. Life was good. Now he's gone."

"I'm so sorry. He was a good guy. The police didn't leave anything in here. Maybe we should still look around the rest of the apartment."

"Yeah."

I stood and helped her up. Walking around the place, without the chirping of the birds that even I had grown accustomed to from my visits, gave it all an eerie feel.

"Did you get everything he left in the will?" I asked as we made our way to the sitting area at the rear bay window.

"Yes, but nothing that could help you. Lots of money. All this will go to me, but nothing from his previous life, before he came to Earth."

"I'm actually not surprised. I imagine all those years ago, he simply gave it all away to start life anew. He was never going back."

"Why did they kill him?"

Cookie broke down crying. I put an arm around her to console her. She knew the place better than I did. There were no secret compartments or safes anywhere. Prince, at least on Earth, was not a complicated or secretive man. He was what you saw. Anything that could have possibly been helpful was in the hands of the police.

Prince had given no clues at all of his previous life, had never once slipped. He said he was an only child and that his parents had died. Both facts we now knew were false, but he was leaving Up-Top all behind him.

"What did he like to do in his spare time?"

"He spent all his time with me," Cookie said.

"Any hobbies?"

"He always liked to do what I wanted. Shared my interests. The only thing I can think of...a hobby he showed interest in, that wasn't mine, was music. I could tell he enjoyed it."

"Listening to music? Concerts?"

"I think he may have played instruments in his past. I never knew why he didn't take it up again. I had thought he was bored of it or grew out of it. But thinking back, I always had the impression he could pick up any instrument and play it. We were at a museum once, and they had instruments from around the world and Up-Top. The way he looked at them..."

"A familiarity."

"Yeah. That he could pick up and play any of them. We never went back to that museum."

I nodded.

"Does that help you?" she asked.

"It might. We'll see."

CHAPTER 29

Pike the Fed

I told Cookie to never return to the apartment again. Call a moving team to pack everything up and ship it to her place. When the police released Prince's other things, have them do the same. I didn't want her running into anyone at the building alone based on my suspicions. She agreed.

As I made my way back to my hovercar rental, I couldn't help think how sad the whole thing was. Prince escaped, but only for a time. Someone ended his life and ruined Cookie's. Not only was I going to find the Three-Armed Man for what he did to them, and me, but I would find those who sent him. At least, I was going to try. I had to set my expectations. I might never find out for sure who among the Moon Monarchs sent the killer. They were Up-Top; I was on Earth. I had no resources at all up there. The most I could hope for was tracking down the contract killer.

Pike was a Fed, but not a field agent. He was a paper pusher who did his crime busting from behind the comfort of a desk. I'd known him for over a year. He had hired me for a case involving a "personal" matter, which of course he didn't want the Agency to ever know about.

A couple of times he'd steered a few items my way. A cold case or two that he looked into on his own time and needed someone in the field to poke around. I'd found evidence for one of the cases, which he was able to close. The second case had a primary suspect but no evidence. I wasn't able to find any, but I was able to uncover that the suspect was involved in other crimes. The Feds were happy to snatch him up for those.

I thought of my posthumous mentor Wilford G. That's how he became the detective legend he was. Working the streets of Metropolis for seventy years. The amount of contacts he accumulated, the number of people from all walks of life he helped and who owed him favors. Well, that's what I was doing with Pike. I was calling in a favor, which he didn't mind at all repaying.

There were millions of eating joints in the city. Pike loved to pick random places. Since he never worked the field, I always felt he was using his own "Best Places to Eat in Metropolis" list. We met at some no-name, tiny diner off the way. If you couldn't see the name of the place when you arrived, it usually meant it was some shady criminals' hangout. But as we sat at a small table and I looked around, the clientele looked more like retired cops. If you'd asked me to explain what a retired cop looked like, I couldn't tell you, but I knew one when I saw him or her.

"What is this place?" I asked him.

"Old-time ex-cop hangout," Pike told me.

When I thought of a Fed, I thought of personnel, dressed in their pressed black suits, serious, ever-observant, and ready for anything like any Metro street officer. Pike didn't look like an agent at all. Messy dark hair, mustache and the makings of a beard. He wore a vintage trench coat slicker.

A young waitress was working the establishment. One could see the kitchen in the back beyond the counter. Two elderly guys in aprons and wearing hair coverings, talking and laughing a mile a minute.

"What do you have for me, Pike?"

"Did you do it?" he asked.

"No, Pike. I didn't kill my client."

"I was a client."

"But you paid your bill."

Pike laughed. "Good thing. Lots of chatter about you."

"Chatter?"

"Someone from Metro PD tried to get us involved."

"Someone who?"

"I don't know. We underlings don't mix with the higher-ups. They keep it that way. We told them 'no.'"

"Why would they want to bring the Feds into this? It's not under your jurisdiction."

"Like I said. There's chatter about you. That interview on TV probably didn't win you any friends either."

"It was aimed at people who'll never be my friends. What about my client?"

Pike had a data disk in his hand and placed it in front of me.

"He was good. So good I can't tell if it was a stolen identity or created identity. But if he was a Moon Monarch, he'd have the cash to buy either one. You wanted to know when he came onto the grid. I'm reasonably sure it was twenty years ago."

"Anything on his real name?"

"Cruz, even we Feds can't get access to Up-Top files, unless they want to give it to us. They're not going to give it to us to investigate any Founder Family."

"Nothing at all? Apollo Michelangelo isn't a common name even for Up-Top."

"For sure. Those spacemen and Martians have the funniest names. I put what I found on there too. All open source only. There might be two of them."

"Son and father?"

"Yeah. I'm assuming the fun stuff was your client. Take a look at it. Your client was the complete opposite of what he was here on Earth."

"You said he was completely clean?" I asked.

"Clean as a priest his entire life here on Earth. The entire bio is on there. It's all legit except for a fake identity."

"Were you able to confirm family or relatives?"

"On Earth, none. Nothing I could confirm off-world."

"Anything else?"

"I gave you the entire record."

"How common is identity theft in Metropolis?"

"A never-ending battle, but we Feds manage. But fake identities like this...only government intel agencies or megacorps can create this kind of quality, not the everyday criminal riffraff we deal with."

"Thanks. I have some light reading for today."

"My advice to you, Cruz, is to watch out for what's coming. We told them 'no,' but Metro PD wouldn't have called us if they didn't feel there was a chance that we'd say 'yes.' Yes, to what kind of investigative help I don't know, but they tried. We only said no because we don't have the time to partner on a high-profile case that's already settled. Metro PD doesn't help us investigate our cases. Why should we help them with theirs, especially when it's not on our priority list?"

"I'm watching out, and my attorney is handling it."

"Attorney." Pike laughed to himself. "I thought it would be years before you got into the type of trouble to need an attorney. But you're big-time already, Cruz."

"I'm famous."

He laughed. "That you are. But not in the way you want this time."

CHAPTER 30

Phishy

I didn't wait. I sat in my hovercar in the nearby parking lot reading the entire file on the vehicle's computer screen. I skimmed over Prince's fake bio, but I didn't expect any clues. The news items on Apollo Michelangelo were what I wanted.

Everything around me looked like a typical Metropolis day. Rainy, lots of people shuffling around on the streets in their dark slickers and glowing visually-enhancing eyewear, neon signs. Lots of hovertraffic in the sky. But I felt I was under a dark, ominous cloud. I couldn't see it, but it was there. My instincts were screaming at me that somewhere unfriendly people were after me. They wouldn't stop until they had me in their grasps and probably had their evil eyes on me at all times.

I flew into the sky traffic when I saw a police cruiser in the rearview mirror at high speed. Police had their own virtual lanes above all the rest of us, and the cruiser was not alone. Three of them flew by with lights flashing and sirens blasting at incredible speed. But, thankfully, they weren't after me.

"What's going on, Cruz?"

Phishy's face was on the vid-phone. I had just called him when I heard the sirens.

"Was that the police?" he asked.

"Yes, but not after me."

"That's good."

"So, he's waiting for me now?"

"Yeah. He's there."

"How much of a criminal is he?"

"He's not too criminal, but enough to help you."

"Okay," I said. "But I called you for another job."

"Great, Cruz." He flashed his Phishy smile. "I'll come through for you."

"Did you once tell me that you knew that guy Hip-Hop?"

"Oh, yeah. The music guy. I don't know him personally, but I know people who do. You want to talk to him?"

"I want to meet him."

"He's always busy."

"Find out where he is and I'll go to him."

"Okay. What do you want me to tell him?"

"Tell him I need to consult with him on the history of the music scene here and Up-Top."

"Yes, he knows everything. When do you want to meet him?"

"Today, tomorrow, but it has to be quick, Phishy."

"But you have time before your court date."

"Phishy, I'm not taking any chances. I'm supposed to have over a month, but that doesn't mean they won't try something to move up the date."

"You're right. Okay. I'll contact him."

"Thanks, Phishy."

"Call you back."

Phishy's face disappeared as the screen went blank and I continued driving, observing all traffic laws, including the speed limit, to a place called Shanty Town in Wharf City.

CHAPTER 31

Moonbeam

The district was called Wharf City, or simply The Wharf. No "nice" people to be found there. One of the many crime hot spots of Metropolis. I'd been there before and would probably return many, many times in the future of my detective career.

Fortunately, the parking structures in the district were like armed fortresses. Recently, a new megacorp came onto the scene and bought up most of them and had already gained a solid reputation. You parked your vehicle in their parking structure and no one would touch it, not even the police. No valet here, but their facilities had some of the biggest, baddest cyborg guards I'd seen in awhile. And they didn't hide the fact that they were heavily armed. I flew in and found a spot on the fourteenth floor. Every level had an armed camp of guards. Cameras were everywhere, and I even saw flying patrol drones. The rates weren't cheap, but well worth it considering the part of the city you were in and the kind of people roaming the streets outside its walls.

When I came out of the elevators, there were about two dozen guards clustered nearby, smoking, rifles in hand, watching me closely—putting a direct eye on every single person who parked in their building. I gave them an approving nod as I walked out to the main street and into the rain.

As I approached the bar-restaurant named Shanty Town, I could see crowds of people loitering outside the place, smoking, drinking, and horse-playing. More like silhouettes with glowing colored shades. I paid them no mind as I entered the place, but had my hands in my pocket; the right one on my omega-gun.

There seemed to be an unspoken rule book that all these dives followed. No visible signs of the name of the place, and inside had the lowest light possible. The establishment was packed— male, female, shadows of people, glowing shades, lots of smoke, bottles and mugs in hands, conversations all around.

Meetings happened in the booth dining area at the far end of the place. I could have picked out Moonbeam a mile away. His special spectacles looked like two moons on top of his eyes. I saw him smile as I approached. He was alone and I sat across from him. There were three empty glasses sitting in front of him.

"Drinking anything?" he asked.

"I had breakfast already."

He found my response amusing.

"I hear you're going to jail soon."

"Have you."

"I've been there a few times. The first time is always the worst. After that, it's more like a vacation, if you can keep from getting killed, or other things."

"The jury is still out on the jail thing."

"People are saying the jury made their call a while ago. Guilty."

"Moonbeam, is it?"

"That's my street name."

"As much as I'd like to sit here and have you cheer me up, I'd like to get some information. I heard you've been to the Moon before."

"I have. Used to run my rackets up there. A bit too intense for even me. I decided to return to the slower pace of Earth. Much healthier. Are you planning on a trip before or after prison?"

"I'm not going to prison."

"Please don't say that. I've got money running on it."

His revelation reminded me of my Classic Cyborg case. "I'm the subject of the betting game again?"

"Lots of people are in on the action."

"Well, don't say I didn't warn you. I've never been to the Moon. So I have no frame of reference to compare it with the streets of Metropolis. What are the big, obvious differences besides we wear dark colors here, except for me, and they wear whites and silvers?"

"We have our modern analog tech, turning our backs on digital tech after the Crash. We want to touch it, physically plug in, physically pick up and deliver the cash. Up-Top is crypto-digital tech. Currency is digital only. Everything is digitally stored on their devices: IDs, keys, etc. What else? No cyborgs up there. We have them everywhere. Not there."

I'm not sure if he knew it, probably not. In one of my previous cases I saw a cult of cyborgs unlike any seen before. Super Cyborgs. They scared me as much as the space people who were with me. They were so dangerous we couldn't allow them to land on our space station. They were either in a deep, dark prison or dead, courtesy of the Up-Top authorities.

"Tell me about the people and the Lunar Colonies," I asked.

"There are the Space Station Colonies and Mars. On the Moon, the Lunar Colonies are actually half a dozen dome city colonies, with dozens more smaller dome colonies. Rich and poor and those in-between. I'd say the average spaceman is no different than the average guy here. People tend to be the same all over. We are all, after all, humans."

"What about the underworld?"

"Why? Are you are planning on going there?"

"Just doing research. You said the crime world was too intense for you. Why? No cyborgs. I know weapons are restricted there."

"Regulated. Everything is regulated there. You have to get permission to get pregnant there because of their density laws. They don't play around. Yes, weapons are heavily regulated for obvious reasons. Blast a hole through the dome and you literally can kill everybody. Everyone sucked into the void of space. The rich have their weapons, but they can't leave their property with them. Outside, it's licensed guards only. Also, for the relatively few who have them, personal vehicles. Even the rich use public transportation."

"No unregulated weapons, no cyborgs. What do the criminals use then?"

"Guns aren't the only weapons there are. The kind of tech used by the underworld there is freaky. Devices to blind, deafen, suck the air out of your lungs, scramble your brain to make you instantly fall asleep, forget what you're doing or your own name, make your skin crawl with holographic biting spiders. Anti-grav weapons, head-splitting migraine weapons. My favorite is the laser shank. Very popular there. For the up close and personal kills."

"Their mean streets sound meaner, despite their commercials and naming every city Paradise or something like it."

"They have crime all right. We have an entire planet. There, you're confined to a station or dome city. They have wide open spaces there too, but you know what I mean. The weapons on the street are endless. I was used to metal bullets, laser blasts, plasma blasts. That's not how it's done there. Then there are people there who don't need weapons."

"What do you mean?"

"We have enforcers who know their martial arts down here, but Up-Top, it's different. I never found out if it was training, conditioning, or genetic engineering. Maybe all of the above. I saw guys punch through someone's chest and pull their heart out. I saw guys rip apart a guy's head to yank out his brains. I have a strong stomach, always have, but I was throwing up for an entire day. I couldn't get back to Earth fast enough. I told my associates that they could keep their turf on the Moon. I wanted no part. They make far more money, but I would never have lasted. You're born into that world, you can't learn it. It's a learning curve no Earth hood can climb."

"But you still go by Moonbeam."

"It's a name. Gets me some additional cred that impresses the ignorant. Anyone who tells me they want to go there; I tell them they might as well shoot themselves in the head now and save a trip."

"What do you know about mutants?"

Moonbeam touched his shades and their glow turned off. I could now see his eyes.

"You are going to the Moon, you crazy detective. Mutants?"

"What do you know about them?"

"What do you know?"

"Nothing. That's why I'm asking."

"When I was on the Moon I met one. I never wanted to meet another ever again. You're probably thinking of something like the biopunk stoner freaks we have here on Earth. There are no cyborgs Up-Top or the silly bio-modification."

"Bio-splicing?"

"You're reading the biopunk propaganda. Bio-mod by another name. Up-Top is genetics. The word 'mutant' might mean someone with thirteen fingers or an extra arm or two here, but Up-Top is something different. Think of the word 'superhero.'"

"What? Superhero? Humans with powers like in the movies."

"Not like movies. Like for real."

"Why the word mutant then?"

"Because it's completely illegal Up-Top. I told you that you can't have children there unless the government approves it

AUSTIN DRAGON

because of their strict population density laws. Air isn't free up there. Genetic engineering is done, but all by the government. No one else can, but criminals never listen to laws."

"What kind of powers? What are we talking about?"

"The enforcer my crew ran into could boil your blood and kill you."

I gave him a look.

"Yes, you heard me. Grab your wrist, grab you around the neck, wrestle you to the ground and kill you with physical contact with his hands. I saw it with my own eyes. I heard of far more powerful ones than him."

"Moonbeam, doesn't that sound urban myth-ish to you? He must have had a device."

"I admit that he could've had some kind of device surgically implanted in his hands, but I think it was real. I heard of others."

"What about mutants with an extra arm or two, or something like that?"

"I heard of them too."

"Superhero mutants," I said again. "The solar system we live in."

"Cruz, if you really plan on setting foot on the Moon, don't worry yourself about mutants. They are a tiny part of the underworld. You need to worry about the underworld itself. Again, don't do it. Stay away."

"I may not have a choice."

"We always have a choice."

"Not for me."

"Cruz, the Moon isn't a very good place to die," he said.

"Is there a good place?"

"For us Earth-borns, not there."

"Moonbeam, ever spend any time in VL?"

"VL?"

"Virtual life."

"Virtual reality games."

"Not the games. A VL recreation of the actual streets in the Lunar Colonies. I need someone who's been there. Knows the streets and knows the mean streets. I'm not trying to become a new street thug trying to muscle in on a Lunar Colony turf. I need to be able to survive. My concern isn't just the criminals, it's everyone. Government, megacorps, everyone."

"Everyone? You have someone specific in mind."

"I might possibly have trouble from one of the Families."

"Families?"

"Yeah."

"As in Founders?"

Moonbeam just stared at me.

CHAPTER 32

The IQ Club

The earliest Hip-Hop was available was next week. There was nothing else I could do; he wasn't even in the country but overseas. I called PJ from my hovercar rental to rearrange my schedule. She told me that the group I wanted to meet with could come in sooner. I'd take good news wherever I could get it.

Two days later, I sat at my desk in my personal office staring out the bay window, watching the rain droplets drip down and the buildings and hovertraffic in the distance.

In my hand was a block of wood that my posthumous mentor, Wilford G., gave me. I was terrified of isopods. I'd beaten my severe germophobia for the most part and managed my OCD tendencies, but I never expected to beat that fear. But the keepsake seemed to be helping—but that's not why he gave it to me. It was to focus my mind on the important stuff of life whenever a defeatist mood dared show its face. Within the block of wood was a baby isopod encased in a clear, solid resin in the middle.

"YOUR DAY IS MUCH BETTER THAN HIS—OR WOULD YOU LIKE TO SWITCH PLACES?"

No, I wouldn't switch places. I had a Three-Armed Man to catch, and if I were really lucky, the people who sent him.

PJ had the repair crew in the previous two days to restore the exterior of the office to new. Yesterday our security expert, Buggs, came with his own crew to restore the scanning arch and the door security measures and add to the hallway surveillance and detection measures. Two days and a ton of money gone from the company bank account.

"Did Run-Time call yet?" I asked from my open doorway, looking at her type at her desk.

"Not yet, but he said all will be ready."

"Good."

"What will be ready?" she asked.

"If I tell you everything, PJ, how will I be able to surprise you?"

"As long as it's good surprises. Like big bonuses. Did you see I left a five-star review on Trusted Reviews about Liquid Cool?"

"What are you talking about, PJ? Trusted Reviews is for clients."

"And employees."

Trusted Reviews was the bible in customer service for Metropolis businesses. Businesses, large and small, did everything and anything for solid (good) reviews about their products and services. It was often the first Net stop for the

Average Joe and Jane when deciding what service or item to buy. Liquid Cool had plenty of those five-star reviews, and growing.

"PJ, don't mess up our reviews."

"I didn't mess them up. I added to them. Employees can leave positive reviews for the place they work."

"But only if we're hiring people."

"*Exactement.* I know you bought the office next door from Mr. Grumpy. When are you expanding so I can be a boss too? I need two assistants."

I laughed. "For what?"

"Never you mind. I'm the VP of Client Services. I need staff."

"I need to stay out of jail first before doing anything at all."

"Who are these people you have coming in?" she asked me. "Are these clients? I told you that Liquid Cool has procedures and that all client appointments are scheduled by me."

Before I started laughing again, I went back into my personal office.

Private clubs probably existed in societies the moment there were people with a few extra coins to rub together and free time to occupy. Members-only clubs, societies, secret societies, whatever term they had, they were exclusive and you couldn't join unless they wanted you in. I'd heard of these high-IQ societies before, but only in some article a long time ago. Hovercar restoration, hovercar racing, law enforcement, private investigation, criminal profiling, crime in general and fine hats were my interests, along with the latest: parenting and child psychology.

My clients had arrived. I heard them come through the door, ten minutes early. I heard PJ greet them, offer refreshments, do her small talk thing, or "client engagement" as she called it, and have them take a seat in the waiting area.

Rather than sit in my office's lounge area, I was going to stay at my desk. I had PJ get a third chair from our office storage. When I set up the appointment, the society said three of their leading members would meet with me. We rescheduled the appointment with no problem, but neither time did they tell me who I'd be meeting with.

The first man was tall. Slim, white hair, and sharp facial features. The second man was above average in height with a thick beard, slim mustache and bald head. The woman had one of those nice, shiny hairdos where the shoulder-length bangs pointed inward. All three of them wore suits, but no ties. They had hung up their slickers outside in the waiting area. PJ gestured them in. I figured either the tallest man or the woman was the leader of the trio. They sat down without even a handshake or Japanese bow. The tall man in the center, the thick-bearded man on his left and the woman on his right.

"Thanks, PJ," I said as I sat and PJ left, closing the door.

I looked at them. All three of them stared at me.

"The Pythagoras Society," I said.

"Yes, Mr. Cruz," the tall man said. "The society is a communal, ascetic one dedicated to intellectualism in all forms."

"You know my name. What are yours?"

"My name is 200," the tall man said.

"I'm 190," the woman said.

"I'm 170," the bearded man said.

I couldn't help but smile.

"Your names are numbers. I can't say I put much stock in IQ tests as an accurate measure of a person's intelligence."

"What is your measure of a person's intelligence, Mr. Cruz? Problem solving, logical reasoning, cognitive skills, mathematical ability, overall knowledge and recall, ability to simplify and communicate complex principles, or beat a robot at chess?"

"Very simple for me. Can the bad guy outwit the law—or me?"

He smiled. 200 was more emotionally expressive than the others. They remained stone-faced.

"The view of a hammer," he said.

"Everything is a nail," I said.

"Mr. Cruz, why would you accept the layman's mistrust of intelligence quotient?" 190 asked. "The assessments have been with us for centuries, the scores have always tracked. Human intelligence may be a gaseous cloud, but one can say how large or how thick that cloud is. You, for instance."

"What about me?" I asked her.

"If you put your biases aside, I'm certain you would score high enough to be eligible for acceptance to our society."

That made me laugh. "Acceptance? Me in a high IQ society. I'm a street detective."

"Who has been catching high IQ criminals," 200 said.

"False modesty aside, Mr. Cruz," she said. "You are, in fact, of genius level."

"What? Me?"

"Built a hovercraft in your parents' basement. I couldn't do that."

"Einstein couldn't do basic math. I can, but that doesn't mean I'm a genius."

"Albert Einstein could do basic math fine. That's a myth. You building an advanced hovertransport as a child is not. High IQ individuals always manifest their superior intelligence at an early age. Achieving things far ahead of their much older peers, including parents. Your solo construction of not merely a working hovervehicle, but one of the highest performance— equivalent to the work of a team of humans and machines—is indisputable proof."

"A hobby. Lots of people have hobbies."

"Is the purpose of this exercise to prove to us you're not a genius or that you're the normal layperson?" 200 asked me.

"Neither," I answered.

"Take the test," 170 said.

"Test?"

"Take the IQ test. It's given monthly. It would be decidedly less painful than getting hit by a bullet or laser in your common shootouts. Fluid and crystallized intelligence, long-term storage and recall, visual and auditory processing, decision and reaction time, and speed are the standard measures to arrive at your total IQ.

"If high enough, you would be eligible for acceptance into the society. Not as a full member since you would not be able to take advantage of our communal residences," 200 said.

"My wife and two kids."

"Yes, they would not be allowed."

I grinned. "They'll be devastated, especially the wife."

"I doubt it. But you would be eligible for a host of discounts and other benefits around the world."

"Benefits?"

"Yes," 170 said.

"I expect your long-term storage and retrieval might be exceedingly high," 190 said. "If I were bold enough to guess."

"Memory and recall?" I asked.

"Your ability to store information and readily retrieve it for the process of thinking. We've heard you've been memorizing the entire criminal database of the Metropolis Police Department. Another hobby?"

"How did you hear that? Yes, actually."

"A human computer," 190 said.

"A tool in my chosen profession."

"We know of no other detective, person or organization, doing the same."

"What's the lowest number I can get?" I asked. "170?"

170 wasn't amused by my attempt at a joke. 200 and 190 gave slight smiles.

"What can we do for you, Mr. Cruz?" 200 asked. "The news says you'll be going to jail soon."

"Why is everyone saying that? Before any of you ask. No, I did not murder my client."

"We were not going to ask," 200 said.

"I asked you to meet with me to consult, but more than that. The actual murderer of my client called me."

"Called you?" 200 said.

"To gloat. He killed my client and framed me for it. He called me on my secretary's private number."

"Ms. Judy."

"Yes. The thing of it is, she only got that private number a few months ago. She changes it frequently. So old boyfriends can't call her. The killer had her number. My conclusion is that he's been watching me and insinuated himself into my world so that he could frame me in such a way that it'll bankrupt me to get out of it and, all the while, I'll be in jail. I've figured out why he killed my client. Why he framed me is a different story. I don't know why. Maybe it's a coincidence. The killer thinking it might be fun to do so, but I don't think so.

"The main thing he said when he called me was that I wasn't smart enough to catch him. I don't think that's what he meant. I am. What I don't have is time. That's what he meant. Maybe he is smarter than me. I'm relatively sure he's not smarter than all of you."

I opened my top drawer and pulled out a folder.

"With time so short, I'm not taking any chances. I can do it, but your society can too. Find the killer. Find the Three-Armed Man."

"A three-armed man?" 190 asked.

"Yes. Not a perfect bio-splice like here on Earth. I'm positive he was born that way. Genetically altered."

"An off-worlder," 200 said.

"Off-world. Up-Top. On the Moon if I had to guess. And the Pythagoras Society has a Lunar Colony branch."

"Yes, we do," 200 said.

"I'll be distracted. Too distracted to do this. The killer doesn't think I can find him because he knows all about me. My routine. Who I know and who they know. You all will be my ace in the hole. He can't anticipate you because he doesn't know about you. You're too smart for that."

"What exactly are you asking us to do?" 170 asked.

"I want to hire your society. Temp contract for the Liquid Cool Detective Agency. You'll be honorary private eyes."

The three of them, adults, were all smiling like little kids at the sight of a hover-ice cream truck.

CHAPTER 33

Hip-Hop

O ur supercity was its own universe. I was born and lived here all my life and still there were so many areas I'd never seen. I could live to the ripe old age of one hundred and never see every district. So many ethnicities, languages, cultures, sub-cultures, groups, sub-groups were in Metropolis with its fifty million people. That also meant endless holidays.

Today was Carnival! Every year for the two days before Ash Wednesday. The Trinidad and Tobago Carnival was the long name, but no one ever said all that. Carnival was one of those special holiday occasions for those who celebrated it to temporarily toss their gray and black outwear in the closet and don their brightest colored dancing costumes. Mardi Gras was big too (a PJ favorite), but that ancient French holiday was only a day. Carnival was two full days of dancing madness, celebrations galore, including the fan-favorite limbo, and never-ending calypso music with steelpan drums. I loved those steelpan drums, and my ma said as a kid I was mesmerized by their playing. It sounded so unlike anything else I'd ever heard.

In the midst of all this was when I'd finally meet the man known as Hip-Hop. I don't know what I'd call him. Street performer, musical prodigy, amateur inventor, band promoter, street hustler. He said he was a DJ, but he was so much more. You'd see him performing on some street corner for sidewalk johnnies, but then he'd be in ritzy Silicon Dunes headlining a real concert at one of the mega-halls with super-expensive tickets sold out in ten minutes.

I'd heard of him because of his street hustling, which in his case meant the numbers racket—gambling. Phishy knew of him from his street performing and connection with the sidewalk johnny network. Then I came across his name in my research and had to meet him.

His flight arrived at Metro International and he told us to meet him there. Sometimes Hip-Hop traveled with a large entourage, sometimes he'd be solo. I was thankful that I'd have the chance to meet him at all with his never-ending hectic schedule.

Metro International was its own city, but the arrival and departure areas outside the terminal were well numbered. We waited for him at Departure Area S-44. I wanted to stay in my hovercar rental so I flew in, touched down, let Phishy out, and flew off. I circled the terminal rather than park. Parking at Metro International was the biggest racket in the supercity. What they'd charge you for fifteen minutes was what an average parking lot would charge you for a day.

My vid-phone on the passenger seat was ringing. I answered it.

"Cruz, he's here!" Phishy said, smiling.

"I'll be right there."

The other thing about Metro International hovertraffic was that it was always awful. I wasn't far, but I might as well have been. Also, here, hovertaxis were the lowest form of life. They'd cut you off, almost hit you, wouldn't stay in their virtual lane, or would illegally roof-ride you. Only divine intervention could explain why there weren't more hovercar accidents everywhere. As I descended, I saw them. Phishy was chatting it up and laughing. And there was Hip-Hop.

Hip-Hop was tall and tan, with movie star good looks. He wore a faux fur coat, topless underneath to show off his six-pack, and a big gold chain around his neck with the initials HH. He liked the big color-tinted shades, a top hat on his dark hair. But his prized possession was in his rectangular knapsack that he was never without. All the other pieces of clothing and accessories he might or might not have, but he always had his "musicalizer." He invented it, and it was what he was known for and what made his amazing performances possible.

I landed for them to pile in. Phishy got in the passenger seat and Hip-Hop got in the back.

"Mr. Cruz, where's the Pony? I wanted the Pony!" Hip-Hop yelled.

I laughed as I kept my focus on my driving. Hovertaxis whipped by us at light speed, but I found my opening and we were up, up into the sky.

"The Pony is safe in storage," I said.

"We'll be able to go for a test ride, though. Right, Cruz?" Phishy asked.

I shot Phishy a quick glance. "Whatever you say, Phishy. I thought my Pony was *my* Pony."

"Oh, course it is."

"Mr. Cruz, before we get something to eat, can you make a few stops? Carnival is a big deal for us performers."

"Wherever you need to go," I said.

"I've had a lot of requests in my time, Mr. Cruz, but you're the first to ask me about music history. I don't even put that on my bio anymore because no one cares."

"History is important."

"Yes, it is. Know what others did before you came along, so you can pick up where they left off. That's how I came up with my musicalizer. I didn't invent it. I made it a reality. That's why I wanted to ride in the Pony! We both can build things."

"Where to first?" I asked.

"Neon Blues," Hip-Hop said.

"We're on our way."

"Hip-Hop, are you DJ-ing tonight?" Phishy asked.

"All over, but after Carnival. I like to be on the streets during Carnival."

"Can your musicalizer mimic authentic steelpans?" I asked.

"Mr. Cruz, my musicalizer can mimic all music, sample any song ever made in the history of the world, my musicalizer has an AI that can give me any singing partner I want. Hip-Hop is the hippest, slickest, sexiest music performer in the world. But I, Hip-Hop, will be adding another skill to my ever-expanding hip-hoppy bio. That being the magnanimous musical head historian consultant king to Mr. Cruz of the Liquid Cool Detective Agency and his good friend, Mr. Phishy of the sidewalk johnny street nation!"

Phishy and I both laughed.

I was the one who told Phishy to contact Hip-Hop, but the DJ was just the kind of person that Phishy would have among his long list of friends he'd want me to meet. Hip-Hop was a character. As if psyching himself up for performing, he was singing to himself in the car, his head bobbing around with his eyes closed.

"Her name was Trini and her name was Toba. Trini had a Dad and Toba said to Go. Was it Babu or Bamboo? Was it Taboo or Tamboo?"

Phishy was supposed to be sitting straight in his seat but instead sat with his back to the passenger door, grinning and laughing as he watched Hip-Hop and occasionally glanced at me. No need to spoil Phishy's fun by telling him to sit back and straight.

My wife's parents had some restaurants in Neon Blues, not upscale like Elysian Heights where they lived. I saw where Hip-Hop was having us go. Carnival turned the streets into outdoor parties, along with competitions and parades. We saw quite a few hovervans at the end of one street, and that's where he told me to land. The crowds were thick and we could hear some announcer's voice booming over speakers.

"I'm hosting a musical competition for the kids, but I'll give them a performance to warm them up," Hip-Hop told us.

He jumped with a smiling Phishy following close behind. I was in the midst of an investigation, but here I was as the personal driver for a DJ. I didn't mind. Having fun was also part of the detective life. Besides, I heard my steelpan drums. I could feel my body wanting to dance.

I had my chance to see Hip-Hop use his musicalizer. The contraption reminded me of bagpipes. He removed it from his backpack and set in on the ground. The machine rose on its own to waist height as he opened it. There were legs and tubes in the center of what looked like a keyboard. He put on his boom microphone headset and his performance began. Media came out of the crowds with camera attachments and hovercam drones circling. I didn't have to worry about the media spotting me because they weren't the news reporters. They were with the entertainment desk.

First, he gestured for dozens of kids to draw near and line up behind him. His machine started flashing, spinning, and blasting calypso music. The dance parade began with him as lead. The kids followed, then the crowds watching, and then it seemed like the entire street itself. Of course, Phishy was right next to him. Phishy loved any kind of crazy dancing. Even some of the reporters danced as they filmed the group.

I could listen to steelpan music all day, but my eyes locked on someone in the distance.

"Is that—?"

I stared for a while in the distance. I lost sight of her, but it was Ms. Hertz, the CFO from Prince's company. Why was she here?

I had returned to my hovercar rental to use my hand scanner for trackers. Not an advanced model, but something was better than nothing. I didn't think for a moment that seeing Ms. CFO was a coincidence. But just as I reached the vehicle and was opening the doors I heard running behind me and turned.

Hip-Hop was running to me holding his musicalizer contraption in one hand and a gun in the other. The next second, I heard a strange noise behind me, and my hand went for my own weapon under my slicker.

"Cruz, let's get out of here!" Hip-Hop yelled. He threw his backpack into the vehicle and dove in.

Four figures in costumes were coming at us fast. Normally, I would have thought it was part of the Carnival. It wasn't just about fancy colorful clothes, but also elaborate costumes. Hip-Hop had a gun and these characters had something in their hands too. I followed Hip-Hop's lead, ducked into our hovercar, and in moments we were in the air.

The people chasing Hip-Hop were in clear view in my side and rearview mirrors. One was wearing a robber mask around his eyes and a small black cowboy hat on his head, pants that looked like chaps, and boots. Another was dressed in red and looked like a devil, complete with fake horns on his head. The third man was dressed as a fat Marie Antoinette character with stuffed bust area and super padded hips. The final man had a costume that looked like he was sitting on a donkey. We were being chased by guys who belonged in a circus, but it was Carnival. Two of them looked like they were about to fire at us but stopped themselves and ran in another direction.

"Hip-Hop! Where's Phishy?"

"He got away."

"Got away where?"

"Into the crowd."

"Why are you being chased?"

"They're not chasing just me."

The moment he said that, there was a crash and the vehicle's rear jumped up until I corrected. It was an illegal street car trick to stall a hovercar in midair. Not something a legitimate illegal racer would do because you'd seriously damage your own vehicle, but a trick known by all.

I could get away with totaling one hovercar because of my stellar driving record and advanced defensive driving classes, but insurance wouldn't let me get away with a second.

"I don't know what you've gotten me into, Hip-Hop, but you will tell me after I lose your friends."

"They're not my friends!"

I zipped around one corner and saw the chasing hovercar clearly. It was the junkiest vehicle I'd ever seen, which was why they didn't mind crashing it into people. It was a flying tank—old but effective. How nice, I thought. The one who looked like a robber was at the wheel and the devil was shotgun. They'd gotten to their monstrosity of a hovercar pretty fast.

"Hold on!" I yelled and slammed the air brakes.

Of course, I caught the pursuers off guard. They drove so wildly that the vehicle quickly jerked out of its virtual lane to avoid me and crashed into another hovercar. I dove our vehicle immediately as we heard another hovercar crash into them above.

Rather than descend to the ground to exchange info and wait for the police, which was the law, they did the opposite. They pulled out and dove after us.

"Who are they, Hip-Hop?" I asked. "I'm not going to ask again."

"They're collectors."

"Collectors? Collecting what?"

"A collection agency."

"Hip-Hop!"

"I owe some money."

"You're a gambler."

"It's not like I'm addicted. I'm behind on a few payments. I don't know why they're so impatient."

I dropped the vehicle to the ground and landed. Their hovercar junker began descending, as I got out of my hovercar.

"What are you doing, Cruz?"

The junker landed on the ground with a thud. I pointed my weapon and began firing. The windshield was gone. I shot off the side view mirrors. The rearview mirror. Blew about the engine block. Shot the seats inside to bits. I kept firing; their hovercar kept falling to the ground in pieces. I didn't see them but knew they were curled up inside the floor of the vehicle.

I reached the junker and leaned over the side, pointing my omega-gun at them.

"Is there something I can help you four gentlemen with?" I asked.

The four of them looked up slowly, all of them covered with debris.

"We don't think so. Tell your friend he can pay us tomorrow," the driver in the robber costume said.

"Oh, thank you," I said. "I'll give him the message. Anything else I can do for you four gentlemen?"

"No, thank you. We'll call a hovercab."

"You have a nice trip."

I left them there, got back into my hovercar rental, and we were gone.

Phishy was fine. He called me and from the chatter in the background, he'd already moved on to his next thing for the day. But he told Hip-Hop he'd show up at his next performance. I, of course, would not.

Hip-Hop and I were at my favorite eatery, the Wet Cabeza. Overly extroverted people like Hip-Hop always had to be the center of attention and any stranger would soon be their best friend after not too long. We hadn't even walked into the establishment when he stared talking to a group exiting and before I knew it, he was doing an impromptu performance in front of the diner. I couldn't believe it. Soon everyone inside Wet

Cabeza was outside, including the wait staff, dancing and doing the limbo to his bring-the-Carnival-to-you performance. Finally, I had to get him inside, but it took another thirty minutes or so of him signing autographs. Most of the people didn't even know who he was, but they were asking for autographs in case he was famous.

Our food arrived at where we were seated. The place was still buzzing about him. The man could eat. He had two plates of food just for himself.

"I have a high metabolism," he told me.

"If you say so." I had a diner specialty—humble pie. I'd gotten them to add it to their menu, and they thanked me for it. It was popular with their clientele. It was made from some kind of natural cross-bred apple. Humble pie was apple pie, was always damn good, and went well with my silk coffee.

"Tell me about Apollo Michelangelo."

"The son, you mean?"

"Is there something to know about the father?"

"Not really. At least, for me. In the Up-Top world, Apollo was...a god, until he disappeared. Child prodigy. Could play anything at all. He was known for a kind of classical music fusion he created. Made classical music popular with pop culture."

"When did he disappear?"

"Decades ago. All kinds of rumors as to why."

"Is that all there was?"

"He was a member of one of the Founder Families. Imagine being born in this universe and never having to work a day in your life. Be able to buy anything, and I do mean anything, you want. Have babes throwing themselves at your feet. Can't buy it? Have someone make it. Power and wealth like that can twist apart anyone."

"Power corrupts."

"He leaves all that behind to live as a nobody here on Earth and gets killed."

"Murdered," I corrected.

"His family?"

"Maybe. A professional hit."

Hip-Hop nodded. "Makes sense. They couldn't take the chance he'd return and want his throne back."

"He was the heir to the Moon Monarch Family? No one else?"

"No one else. Firstborn gets it all."

"Who's next in line?"

"The siblings. I think there are four or more of them."

"It's not the next one in age."

Hip-Hop shook his head. "No. It's whoever can get the most votes from the entire Family."

"Votes?"

"That's how they do it there."

"Then it could literally be anyone."

Hip-Hop nodded. "You'll never find out who killed him. Too many people involved. Whoever the next ruler of the Family is will be able to reward their allies in ways you and I couldn't imagine."

"You know a lot about this for a DJ."

"Who do you think first invented a musicalizer? Apollo did. I saw a show that he did when he was only six years old. He was a musical genius at six! He didn't use it when he got older, but I always remember that. Inspired my own version. That was a long time ago, but I became obsessed with him and his family."

"You say there's no way I could find out who sent the murderer."

"What would you do about it if you could find out? Nothing. The Up-Top authorities wouldn't touch them, and they have a lot more power. You and I are nobodies. You really shouldn't go after the killer either."

"The killer made that a bit difficult."

"Yeah, the framing thing. You're in a tough spot, Cruz."

"Do you know people up there?"

"In the music scene, yeah. But that's old. Apollo is ancient history to the kids there. People have very short memories. Is this background helpful to you?"

"Yeah. I like to cover all bases."

"You were hoping for a lot more?"

"Not necessarily."

Despite Hip-Hop's party-boy demeanor, he really was a music historian. When I'd first learned of the fact from a university professor, I thought I was being toyed with. But every professor we contacted said Hip-Hop was one of the top music historians in the world. He even had a book series under a pseudonym, so I was forced to put my biases aside and treat him as the expert he was.

"What you need is someone who can tell you about the gossip world of the Monarchs," he said. "That might help you. Oh, and the conspiracy theorists. I might know a few of those."

"The problem with that is what's true and what's not."

"True, but makes for good stories."

"When he was a Monarch, lots of people liked Apollo, even if they were insincere, but who hated him?"

"Other Founder Families. His father. People said that but never said why. Also, his sister's children. Twins."

"How would I find out more?"

"Got to get to the conspiracy theorists, Cruz."

"Don't they have journalists Up-Top?"

"I wouldn't trust them."

"Why?"

"The Families control all the media up there. No one pays the salaries of the conspiracy theorists."

"You really want me to talk to these conspiracy theorists."

"I do. You'll get a blast out of their stories. They love to talk. Some of them even have their own shows. You could call into a show and get your questions answered live. Well worth the off-planet charges to call them."

"I'm sure. Give me your top referrals."

Hip-Hop looked at his mobile. "Maybe I can save you some phone charges. There's a guy by the name of Moonbeam. He's right here in Metropolis but used to live Up-Top, on the Moon. He knows the whisper-talk up there."

"Okay."

Hip-Hop was giving me the name of someone that Phishy had already put me in touch with. So I'd be meeting with Moonbeam again.

"You should hang out with Phishy and me later. Got lots more performances."

"Shouldn't you pay off your loan sharks first?"

He laughed. "Didn't you hear what they said? I have until tomorrow."

CHAPTER 34

A Bunch of Bio-Matter

Today was fine, but I was going to make sure Phishy wasn't anywhere near the "walking concert" tomorrow or for the rest of the week, in case Hip-Hop didn't settle things with his "collection agency."

That left me to wrap up another matter the next day and I was parked in the megatower of Bio-Matters—a loading lane between the visitor parking and valet section. Personally, I wouldn't have named a company Bio-Matters because it sounded too close to bio-matter, which was a word kids liked to use for excrement to make themselves sound sophisticated. But what did I know? Bio-Matters was a multi, multi-billion-dollar high-grade agricultural megacorp serving Earth. Prince (Apollo) probably picked it all those many years ago because they didn't have any Up-Top interests.

I'd been waiting for a quarter of an hour, just sitting there. A security guard had walked over to me before.

"Do you need us to call anyone, sir?" he asked.

"No," I said. "They'll be down."

Well, Ms. Hertz, Bio-Matters' acting CFO finally came down, out from the elevators, and nervously walked over to my hovercar rental. I rolled down the window a bit on the driver's side.

"Why were you following me?" I asked.

"We were not following you."

"We?"

"We need to see that report."

"I told you I would."

"Yes, but the board is aware of it—"

"How would they know? I didn't tell them. Only the four of you knew."

"How they found out isn't important now. They are and we need to review it before you turn it over to the authorities."

"I planned to just bring it with me at my hearing date. Kill two birds with one stone, as they say."

"As efficient as that may seem to you, we'd like to see it before then."

"Why? Do you know something I don't?"

"I'm sure that I know many things you don't. Will you give me a copy of that report?"

"Only you?"

"Yes."

"What about 'we'?"

"'We' will see it after I do. I'm the acting financial officer for the company."

"Tell me what you know and I'll have it delivered tomorrow. And how did you find me at the Carnival? Have you bugged my vehicle?"

"No, I happened to be there."

"My fault. Let's start again, but backwards. You didn't bug my hovercar?" I asked again.

"No."

"You happened to be where I happened to be in Neon Blues?"

"Yes."

"You don't look like a party gal, Ms. Hertz. No offense."

"No offense taken. I can be when the occasion calls for it. It was coincidental. Whether you wish to believe me or not is nothing I have any control over."

"What are you not telling me? You want the report now, but you know something about my hearing date?"

"No. I explained already. The board knows and I'm answerable to the board. If we need to prepare for the authorities or a scandal, then we wish to do so now, not in two weeks. We're happy to compensate you, if that's what this delay is really about."

"Yes, let's do that because I can't say I believe you all that much. Pay me what you feel the report is worth to you. After all, Mr. Prince didn't want you to know about it."

"Mr. Prince is dead."

"Yes, he is."

"We didn't kill him and you know that."

"That's the only reason I'm talking to you and considering this."

"I will have a payment approved. We've done it before."

"Paid off detectives before?"

"Yes, many times. Using private investigation is not a unique practice in the corporate world, Mr. Cruz."

"True. Then I'll await my fee and get you a copy of the report."

"How much extra would that fee have to be for you not to drive directly to the police from here?"

"You're paying me for a copy. That's all."

"I'll have the payment to you within the hour."

"Thank you, Ms. Hertz."

She abruptly walked away without a goodbye or another look. I started up my hovercar to be off on my way. I watched her pass the level's security guards to the elevator bank. There I noticed two of the other senior execs come out from a corner, talking to her, and looking back at me—Mr. Hollo, the head of security and, Ms. Sage, the general counsel. Looked like their CEO wasn't a part of the "we" club. Or maybe he was. I had more important things to worry about.

CHAPTER 35

More Moon Monarchs

"Wize," I said over my personal office vid-phone. I was back at my desk. "I have a feeling."

My paralegal/attorney looked better than the other day. At least she looked like she'd had some sleep and was wearing different clothes. She had a drink in her hand.

"A feeling? What kind of feeling?"

"The feeling of a lamb being led to the slaughterhouse."

"Why do you say that?"

"I told you. I have a feeling."

"Cruz, I didn't want to get your hopes up, but I think I'll manage to get the case dismissed."

"Dismissed?" I was surprised.

"Anything can happen in court, and you're not free and clear yet, but I think I've done enough legwork to pull that off."

"Wow. That's good news."

"Does that help you with your feeling?"

"No," I said.

"What do you mean no?"

"Wize, you're doing a great job. I know you're doing your absolute best. I couldn't ask for more."

"Then what?"

"A feeling, but I could be completely wrong."

"If you're having feelings, then I'd better be prepared for the unexpected. But I always am."

"Good. More than I can ask. I wanted to share."

"Share the feelings, Cruz. See you in over a week at court. Make sure you dress sharp, leave the attitude and weapons at home, and be guardedly optimistic."

"I will."

"But if you have any more feelings, or hard facts to share, call."

"I will."

"Don't let the day rain on you too hard," she said and hung up.

I should have known better. It was after-hours and I was in the office alone. I told PJ that there was no reason for her to stay late. That's what we had all this expensive office security for, and I was only making a couple of calls. Regardless, I had all my weaponry laid out on my desk: guns, rifles, stun grenades. Saying I was overwhelmingly paranoid didn't even begin to describe my mood.

My mobile rang. I answered it even though the number was only vaguely familiar.

"Hey, Mr. Cruz." It was the face of Angle, PJ's friend, who got me away from the police.

"Angle. How are you? Where are you?"

"Judy called us, so me and the boys are here in the parking lot. In case you have any unwelcome guests."

I grinned. "Thanks, Angle. I appreciate it. I'll come down when my client call is done."

"We'll be here. We're trying out a new box of Havanas we got. We'd offer but know you don't smoke cigars."

"I can still hang out and chat."

"Later then."

He hung up and I glanced at the time on my office clock. Knowing that there were friends nearby considerably lifted my spirits.

I'd dealt with wealthy space people before, and I couldn't say most of them were positive experiences. Always, I had handled myself well, but one could never forget the raw power these people possessed. We had one direct encounter with the Moon Monarchs, and they almost destroyed my whole office. It was my omega-gun, straight from Up-Top, that gave PJ and me the edge we needed. Moonbeam already gave me a preview of the kind of tech they had up there, off-world. That was the world these space people lived in, like its own dimension.

The call came in on time. It was late night here but early morning where the call was coming from. I knew someone in the Family was calling, but I didn't know who.

I answered it and the man staring at me looked like an exact older version of Mr. Prince. The father. The father who sent his niece and nephew to snatch me off Earth.

"Are you surprised to see me, Mr. Cruz?" he asked.

"You have a lot of nerve, but I suppose you're born with that kind of nerve in your family. Have your niece and nephew reached you yet?"

He grinned. "They did. They used to throw violent temper tantrums when they were children too. Nothing has changed. All handled by the servants. I cannot be concerned with such things anymore."

"You sent the butler to answer the door when they arrived?"

"Something like that, Mr. Cruz."

"Why are you calling me?"

"The Family has decided to allow the criminal justice system of your planet to run its course."

"That's why you're calling me? Tell me, sir, why do I seem to care more about who killed your son than you do?"

"I don't know. You didn't know him."

"I knew him better than you."

"That's true. As I was saying, you will be convicted and the Family will proceed from there."

"I didn't kill your son, Mr. Michelangelo."

"Mr. Cruz, I don't care what you say. You will go to trial, be convicted, then you will be extradited here. Unlike my niece and nephew, I have no desire to ever set foot on your dirty planet."

"So sure I'll be convicted?"

"I'm so sure that a paralegal who owns a casino will not be able to prevent it."

"Since we're good pals, Mr. Michelangelo, did you kill your son?"

He glared at me. I was thankful his eyes didn't shoot lasers and he wasn't in front of me in person.

"I'm going to find the man who killed Mr. Prince, I mean Apollo," I promised.

"Apollo Michelangelo, the Fifth," he corrected.

"You really care what I call him?"

"No, Mr. Cruz, I don't care what you say. However, when you're extradited to the lunar prison facility, my associates will interrogate you thoroughly."

"You don't care who killed your son. You obviously know I didn't do it. You lied to your relatives to get them to harm me. You Moon Monarchs are a puzzle to me. Apollo was your heir and he's dead. Now comes the power struggle within the Family for control. How do I factor into everything? Why wouldn't the Family use every resource, legal and illegal, to find out who killed him? I see why he escaped from the Family. He was a decent guy and I enjoyed working for him. Respectful, sharp, great girlfriend. He was what we call on Earth a real man's man. You wouldn't know anything about that."

"No, I wouldn't. I have never been respectful or decent. But I am a Moon Monarch and you are not. I'll—"

"Why did you set this call up, Mr. Apollo? You have no use for me. You don't care about your son. Why wouldn't you just have your butler talk to me? You're one of those people who's bored with life. You have everything in the universe, but you hate all who live in it."

"Studying psychology too, Mr. Cruz."

"I read when I can."

"I destroy people for a living, Mr. Cruz. I enjoy it. I'm going to destroy you. But I don't have to go to you. Earth will send you to me. We execute our convicted murderers by spacing up here. I'd get my affairs in order."

He reached to the side and hung up the vid-phone.

I thought for a moment. Was Mr. Apollo, beneath all the dripping contempt, actually terrified of me?

CHAPTER 36

Moonbeam's Men

I was back in Shanty Town a couple of days later. It was Moonbeam's turf so it made complete sense that he set up the meeting with his friends here. Actually, it was a place right next to his bar-restaurant hangout. I'd call it a community center, but all the citizens there were criminals of some sort. I came in and two burly guards stopped me and scanned me with devices. I showed them my pop-gun strapped to my left forearm and my omega-gun. They nodded and waived me through. As I walked, I noticed that there were closed doors along the hall—meeting rooms. I stopped at the door number Moonbeam told me, and looked down the long hallway. Next door was a much larger door, possibly an auditorium with some kind of event happening.

"That's not for you." I turned to see one of the guards walking to me with a vexed look. "Your business is in the door over there."

"You have auditoriums here? What are the rates? Maybe I'd rent one in the future."

"No, you can't rent nothing, Detective. Get to your room."

I smiled and opened the next door. Moonbeam was already standing at the table with his back to me. He turned as the guard reached me and pushed me in.

"Moonbeam, your guest is quite nosy."

Moonbeam looked at me with his glowing colored moon shades.

"I'm a curious person," I said. "It's Carnival. I thought maybe there might be steel music and dancing."

"Carnival ended yesterday and you know that," the guard said. He closed the door for us.

Moonbeam had his hands on his hips.

At the table behind him were half a dozen thugs in suits. Some were smoking, all had drinks, and all were studying me.

"This is the guy, Moonbeam?" one asked.

"He's the guy."

"This is the guy who took down the Animal Farm Crime Syndicate, and all those other outfits?" the same hood asked.

"You killed Franken-borg?" another asked.

"I did, and I didn't use a weapon."

I put on my serious face. "Where do you want me to sit?" I asked Moonbeam.

He pointed and I sat at the other end of the table.

"Gentlemen, I don't want to leave this room until I know everything there is to know about the Lunar mean streets," I said. "Moonbeam helped me along, but I need more detail, need to know the players, the rivalries, the vendettas, the rackets. All of it. As I told Moonbeam: I need to survive against the criminals, the government, and the megacorps. And it gets worse."

"Worse?" one of the thugs asked.

"I think one of the Moon Monarchs wants me dead for some reason."

"Then you're dead," another thug said. "You set foot on the Moon and you're dead."

"No," I said. "What is a Moon Monarch scared of?"

"Excuse us?" Moonbeam asked.

"Nothing," a thug replied.

I shook my head. "Gentlemen, we need to figure out what the answer to that question is. It literally is a matter of life and death. The Moon people are going to abduct me one way or another. I can feel it. They're not coming down in a flying saucer for me. Earth will be sending me in a rocket to them. I can mentally feel them finalizing their plot. I need to know why a Moon Monarch is scared of me—truly scared of me."

The thugs looked at each other. They were interested.

"Moonbeam told us all you wanted was to get the real facts of the streets. We thought we were going to be playing in v-life. That's why we're in this room. So we can run our virtual reality map programs. But it seems you're asking for more, a lot more. What's in it for us?"

"Help me figure this out and I'll make it worth your time."

"Money is what we care about."

"Then I have to get you some Moon money."

The men looked at each other again.

"Mr. Cruz, don't promise anything if you can't deliver," Moonbeam said. "My colleagues and I don't work for a digit here or a digit there. When they say money, we mean money."

I rubbed my chin.

"I have a theory. My client and I were targeted. They killed him, framed me."

"They think you know something or have something—from your client?" a thug said.

I pointed to the man. "You got it. Maybe it'll be worth something to someone, worth a lot of something. If only I had some partners I could go into a business venture with."

"Get this man a real drink!" one of the thugs yelled as he raised his own glass.

CHAPTER 37

Flash

My Ford Pony was more than a classic hovervehicle. I'd been upgrading it over the years with an array of legal and illegal modifications. I wasn't scared necessarily of having it damaged in a crash; I was scared of having Captain Monitor or Detective Dent seizing it, and discovering the modifications. Once they did, they could keep it permanently.

For the duration of this situation, my prized Pony was going to sit in its protected parking spot in the Concrete Mama building. But not alone. My best friend Run-Time's Let It Ride Enterprises also provided another highly sought-after and profitable service—mobile hovercar security. The first day I decided to keep my Pony in the Concrete Mama parking lot, I called my guy, Flash. I met him at the main entrance. He descended from the sky by rocket-pack. He was the guy I used most of the time whenever I called Let It Ride's mobile car security. He was Black, young-ish (like me), light-skinned, with a ponytail and a small goatee. Flash was always good-natured, reliable, and professional, whether driving a hovercab or, in this case, hovercar-sitting security.

"Cruz," he greeted, wearing a yellow jumpsuit over his suit clothes and blue eyewear.

I put Flash in charge of security of the Pony. He managed a crew of three guys. The extra security, even with a discount as a frequent user, was costing me a fortune, but I wanted peace of mind. Flash took the day shift and for days there was nothing to report from him or his team. That changed the day after my meeting with Moonbeam and his associates.

Returning to the Concrete Mama was easier said than done that day with the terrible hovertraffic, but I made it. Ordinarily, I would have sped and used shortcuts but, again, I didn't want to give authorities any legitimate reason to pull me over, so I drove like any senior citizen—slow and steady.

I flew into the building's parking lot and made it to my level. I saw Flash standing near the Pony in his yellow jumpsuit with Mr. Post, which concerned me. I parked my hovercar rental and got out.

"Cruz," Flash greeted.

"Mr. Cruz, how are you?" Mr. Post said.

I said my hellos as my eyes scanned the Pony. I saw nothing abnormal.

"The vehicle is fine," Flash said. "That wasn't the problem."

Flash showed me his palm tablet, and I watched a video recording of a section of the parking lot from the wee early morning hours. Dent!

"What's he doing?" I asked.

"He was heading to your vehicle when my guy on duty confronted him."

I saw the exchange on the recording. Flash's guy wasn't playing games, making sure Dent saw his long gun. Dent immediately yelled at him and showed his police ID. But then Flash's guy yelled he was calling the police himself and building security. Dent immediately changed his attitude. Told the man that wouldn't be necessary and left the way he came. Flash's man followed for a bit, but Dent got into an unmarked hovercar and flew off.

"He hasn't been back," Post told me. "We reached out to my Metro PD contacts. There were no police calls for the building."

"Why was he here then?" I asked, not expecting an answer. "Can you send me this recording?"

"Already done," Flash said.

"Thanks, Flash. Good thing the Pony was in your care. Who knows what he was up to?"

I looked at Post. "Our two friends warned me about him."

Post nodded. "'Dirty cop.'"

"Thanks, gentlemen. I have to get the recording to someone in particular."

Dent was sniffing around Pony. I didn't like it, and neither would Wize.

CHAPTER 38

Monitor Madness

I called her again, from my home office this time. Wize didn't like it at all, but was glad to have the recording.

"A perfect example of the adage: better to be safe than sorry," she said.

"That's for sure. Who knows what the crazy maniac was going to do?"

"What's your plan for today and the rest of the week?"

"I'm staying in and hanging out with the kids."

"That should be a nice change of pace. No chance of trouble doing that."

Wize obviously hadn't met my kids. Cruz Jr., who was already a teleporting ninja, was forever perfecting his craft. In a blink of an eye, he'd disappear and you'd wonder if he was in the kitchen trying to set something on fire, in the master bedroom looking for weapons, or in my home office messing up my stuff.

With my call with Wize over, it was me alone with the two kids in the apartment.

"Cruzie, keep it up! Your butt is going to be in school next year!" I had no idea where he was, but I heard a giggle in the distance.

Kat, on the other hand, was a bundle of pure sweetness. She was in that phase where all she did was wiggle around and look cute. Dot and I liked this phase. Put her in the crib with lots of colorful toys and they could make their own fun for hours. I tickled her a bit before I knew I'd have to hunt for her brother.

There was a thud in one of the other rooms.

"Cruz Jr., what are you doing?!"

I heard giggling.

"I'm going to put you on a dog leash and keep you near me at all times."

I heard feet running.

"Oh, so you understand what I'm saying."

I speed-walked from the living room where Kat was and went to the hallway. I had to secure that boy.

My mobile rang. I answered it as I peeked in our guest bedroom first to find him. It was Wize.

"Didn't we talk today already?"

"Cruz, I got a tip from a friend in Metro PD. They told me I'd better get out of my casino."

"What? What do you mean?"

"I don't know. That's all they would tell me."

I stopped walking. "Wize, listen closely. I want you to close your casino down now. Get everyone out of there immediately.

Make up an excuse. Say it's a fire alarm. Then get your staff to check every inch of the place, every room, every trash can, and the dumpsters outside."

"You think they're trying to set me up?"

"Dent sniffing around my vehicle. Now your friends tell you to vacate your business. They're on their way to you, Wize, and I don't like it. I've already been framed once. Nothing says they can't do it again and bring you in on the fun."

"You're right. Bye."

She hung up.

"Cruz Control, come on out. We're going on a trip and you'll be watching your sister."

I suddenly heard his voice behind me. "Where's Daddy?" I looked down and Cruz Jr. was standing there. How did he do that?

"Get your cool hat and let's get ready."

Cruz Jr. ran off to his room, cheering.

It was good to be driving the Pony again. I sat in the driver's seat watching. The police weren't visiting Wize's place in Cascade City; it was a full-out raid.

"Police cruiser!" Cruz Jr. yelled out. He was laughing, having the time of his life.

Both he and his sister were securely strapped into their child seats in the backseat. Kat was looking around at all the lights and sirens, not knowing quite what to make of it all.

The casino was cordoned off by police. On the ground and in the air, it was a real red-and-blue siren party with over a dozen

231

police cruisers in total. Behind the police tape, patrons and spectators looked on. Behind all of them, in the parking lot, was me. There were other people in hovercars watching, but I had the best view.

Since I had my real vehicle back, my mobile also rang on the vehicle dashboard. I answered it.

"Hi!" Cruz Jr. said when Wize's face appeared on the screen.

"Hi, young man," she said to him.

"Where are you, Wize?" I asked her.

"I'm at home. Where are you?"

"Outside your casino."

"Cruz, you shouldn't be there."

"Why not? I don't see Monitor anywhere, or Dent. I don't see any of Monitor's men, but this is his doing."

"They raided me, Cruz. They said they were acting on tips from their monthlong investigation of my business into illegal activities associated with organized crime. What BS."

"BS," Cruz Jr. repeated.

"Cruzie, stop listening to the adults talk. Count how many police cruisers you see now and I'll quiz you and your sister."

"She can't talk, Daddy."

"Then you should win the game easy."

He laughed at me, but I succeeded in diverting his attention away from our conversation for the moment. He started counting.

"Did you find anything when you had your staff search the place?" I asked Wize.

"No, nothing, but I also called the legal firm that represents my casino. They were on site before the police arrived. The police are trying every tactic in the book to get them off the premises but it won't work. If and when they do get into the casino after our legal challenges, my attorneys will watch every move they make."

"Good."

"My father's attorney firm is also jumping in to help. We'll hit them in both civil and criminal court."

"Wize, are you ready to go to trial? When the hearing starts, will you be ready?"

Wize gave me a confused expression. "Of course I'm ready, but we have over a week."

"Be ready to go before then."

"What do you know, Cruz?"

"Wize, they tried to plant something on my vehicle."

"How do you know that's what Dent was planning?"

"He wasn't in uniform, and he wasn't body-cammed."

"A fact that I'll make sure the judge is fully aware of."

"Now they're at your place, trying to jam you up. Go after me, go after my lawyer. I'd say they figured out a way to move up the hearing date."

"Cruz, they can't do that. Besides, they have to give me notice."

"Have they given you the real evidence they have against me yet?"

"No."

"They will."

"Cruz, they have to give me notice and I get to contest it."

"How much notice do they need to give?"

"Forty-eight hours."

"Do they call you or send a process server?"

"They can do either."

"Is the casino listed as your official office for attorney of record?"

"Yes. So? Cruz, I know what I'm doing. They can't do what you're suggesting. The judge would throw out the entire case if they did."

"Wize, that's what this is about. To get you off the premises."

"Cruz, how do you know that? To go through all this? Significant police resources are involved here, not to mention the legal trouble that will come their way."

"Wize, I've done these kinds of ruses before. Distract your subject with one big thing over here, so they don't notice what you really want them to see over there. My last major case, the Biopunk Case, we took over the entire convention center in Opus Fields, hosted the international World Health Organization here in Metropolis. It was all a ruse. Wize, the police helped me with the ruse."

"But they're risking serious legal exposure—"

"Wize, you said it yourself. Someone wants to get me bad. I told you I had a feeling. In fact, I'd bet they've already served the notice and have gotten the judge to move up the hearing, or are about to."

"They can't."

"Wize, call all your employees and find out who they handed the notice to. One of them has it."

"I sent everyone home."

"And one of them has it in their pocket or jacket and doesn't even know it. But rest assured that my hearing will begin in two days, whether we're there or not. What would happen if we weren't there, Wize?"

"Your bail would be revoked and a warrant for your immediate arrest issued."

"As I thought. In other words: straight to jail."

I'd convinced her. Wize called all her people. Sometimes, I wished my inner paranoid wasn't right. The process server had "delivered" the change of hearing date to the casino. The person was a man who handed it to one of the new valets who was just getting off his shift. The server told him to give it to Wize, but of course, knew the kid wouldn't until he returned to work for his next scheduled day. The official court notice would have been in his pocket for three days! This happened before midnight, so that fifteen minutes counted as a whole day. Today, the police had turned Wize's place into a madhouse with all their officers, detectives, agents, and cruisers everywhere.

My hearing for the trial of murder before Judge "Dreadful" was tomorrow.

PART FIVE

Judge-Ment Day

CHAPTER 39

Last Supper

Wize was one of those people that was always in control of her emotions. She was unflappable—until now. Finding out that in a blink of an eye, we lost eight days in preparing for the hearing mentally knocked her off her feet. But I wasn't worried. She was a fighter and she'd get back up.

The plan was to get to the Criminal Courts two hours early—at six a.m.—and wait in the parking lot. We both expected the media to be there in force, but if we got there before they did, maybe we'd be lucky and could sneak right in.

"I have a big commercial hover-RV that I've used for the casino, but we can use it for this."

"Wize, we'll be fine. You'll be fine."

"Cruz, you're bringing me into the big-time. Can't say that my stomach is all that happy with you. I haven't barfed this much since early high school, and that was for drunken partying."

"You'll be fine. The judge won't let them get away with this."

"The judge doesn't like us either, but he won't be unfair to us. That's the card I'll play. He doesn't like unfairness at all, and what they've done against you is wrong in every which way there is. Have you told your wife?"

"Do I have to?"

"Cruz!"

I was joking. My wife was the other one who was panicking until I calmed her.

"What is this attorney of yours going to do?" Dot had asked me.

I was back at home with the kids. When I told her what was about to happen the next day, she left Eye Candy and joined us.

"She's good. I'll be fine."

"Cruz, my parents know real attorneys. I can get them to refer someone."

"No, Dot. I'm sticking with Wize. She's a fighter, like me."

"Why are they doing this to you? All the cases you solved for the police!"

"It's not them. It's one guy, and I'm sure someone's pulling his strings."

"What's his name?"

"Captain Monitor."

"I'm going to remember his name. I'm coming to court with you tomorrow."

"Dot, that wouldn't be good."

"Why? You don't want your wife there with you?"

"I don't want my wife killing Monitor in the courthouse. You've told me many times before: you've killed people with those heels."

Dot looked down at her shoes, then back up at me and started laughing.

"Maybe...you're right. I might not be able to control myself."

"Interested parties can watch the hearing remotely. So you, Cruz Jr. and Kat can sit right in front of the TV and take it all in. Just don't kick the screen with those shoes of yours."

"I should be there at the courthouse with you."

"Better here so I won't worry. I don't want them to try anything else."

"I'd bring my parents. They wouldn't try anything with them."

"Your parents? I definitely don't want them there. They'd try to smuggle in their weapons and get arrested for sure."

"I feel so helpless!"

I hugged my wife, and we looked down and Cruzie was hugging us both around the legs.

"Okay, it's family TV night," I said. "Cruzie gets to pick the movie."

"Yeah!" Cruz Jr. yelled, clapping.

That's what we did. Relax. No work. No phones. Just family, TV, and fun food for dinner. The calm before the galactic storm tomorrow.

CHAPTER 40

Wize and Company

Wize's hover-RV was huge. There was the driver's section, a lounge area behind it, then an office section, another lounge area, and a rear office. It also had three bathrooms.

The vehicle was packed with people. I quietly sat in the forward lounge area by myself. Since I'd had very little time to read, I was availing myself of it now. Not really reading, but looking at vacation getaway pictures.

Wize had brought her entire legal support team. In the first office, Wize was reviewing her case notes with a dozen other lawyers. I thought it funny. The paralegal was the boss of all the lawyers. In the other lounge area, Wize had about six interns in chairs to monitor all the media once the hearing started. In the rear office were six other researchers on computers with big headphones on. They were typing away, what, I didn't know.

We'd arrived at 5:55 a.m. The hearing would start at eight a.m. We had beaten the media there, which was the main goal. The parking lot was empty when we arrived, except for one lone hovercar at the other end. Court staff had their own secure parking level, so it wasn't any of them.

"Did the DA finally deliver the evidence?" I asked when we first arrived.

"Late last night," she told me. She had a big smile on her face. "Won't they be surprised when they see we're more than prepared?"

The police probably wouldn't arrive until seven a.m., the prosecution at seven thirty, when the doors would be opened for the courthouse. It was going to be a zoo. The media vultures would arrive anywhere from six a.m. on. We also arrived early to stake out our parking close to the stairs. We weren't going to use the elevators at all. The media would be stationed there. However, that meant fifteen flights of stairs. But we were all young and in shape. The plan was to walk into the courthouse at 7:55. Cutting it close, but Wize was going to send the interns ahead of us to scout out the path for any problems.

"Wize, do you have any binoculars in this vehicle?"

The team had taken a break and she was pacing around with a café drink in her hand.

"Binoculars? Why?"

"Do you have any?"

"Hold on."

She walked to the front driving cabin. There sat two huge guys. They'd keep watch of the vehicle when we left. Wize returned with a pair of binoculars.

I focused them on the one lone hovercar at the back of the parking lot.

"Is there a problem, Cruz?" Wize asked.

I stared at the one person in the vehicle for a while.

"No. I think I know who it is, but it's not a problem."

"Someone I know?"

"No, but I do. It's nothing. Focus on the hearing. Everything else is nothing."

She walked away and gathered her team back into the office to go over all the notes again. I put the binoculars away and returned to my vacation getaway book.

Hovercars started arriving in the parking lot just before seven a.m. A slow drip-drip of vehicles at first, then a steady flow of them. By seven thirty, it was becoming somewhat of a zoo. Where we were parked in the hover-RV, people were walking away from us to the elevators.

"Cruz, time to go," Wize announced.

"Okay," I said.

We exited the vehicle. No one could see us as the entrance to the stairway was blocked by our hovervehicle too. Wize had already sent her interns ahead. All was clear. So we started our climb to Judge Dreadful's courtroom.

CHAPTER 41

OMG

The plan only half worked. Wize's team walked ahead as we came out of the stairwell; Wize and I did our best to slink down behind them. The pack of reporters had taken positions outside the courthouse watching the other way.

Then I heard a familiar voice. "Mr. Cruz!" It was Holly Live.

We had almost made it to the courtroom without anyone noticing us. That damn Holly!

"Mr. Cruz, will you be going to jail today?" Holly asked me as her camera operator came up right behind her.

"Thanks, Holly, for the question," I said. "I've been honored to be a Metropolis detective for the last few years, on the side of its good citizens. This has been a terrible mistake, but I'll be fully vindicated when this is all over. You can quote me."

The reporters rattled off other questions, but we reached the threshold of the courthouse and Wize pulled me in.

"Good sound bite, but no talking from this point on," she said.

The cavernous courthouse was packed like the last time. The scary spectators in the gallery watched me. I'd learned a long time ago that there were lots of people who did nothing but go to court trials and watch the proceedings—their hobby or obsession. We walked down the narrow aisle. The prosecution sat at their desks in their black suits and smug looks. At the defense table, I sat next to Wize and her team sat at the table or behind us. Five of us in total were at the table. Six people were at the prosecution table. I glanced back at Monitor, Dent, and his team behind the prosecution table in the first row of the gallery. Chief Hub was sitting on the other side of Monitor. I still didn't get why Hub was around. He hated Monitor like most of the beat cops.

The same cyborg bailiffs came in and stood on either side of the judge's bench. They watched me like hawks too, like the last time.

The digital clock in the courthouse struck eight and Judge Dreadful came through the back entrance.

"All rise!" a bailiff called out in a booming voice.

Everyone in the large courthouse did. The judge sat, and so did everyone else.

The silver-haired, crew-cut, leather-faced, wrestler-boxer-gang enforcer-looking judge locked his eyes on me—then smiled. He looked down at his bench tablet then back up at me.

"I've been dreaming about this day, and here it is." He looked at his bailiff. "What do you think? Jail?"

The bailiff hadn't stopped looking at me. He nodded with confidence. "Jail."

"Yeah, I think so too."

"Judge—" Wize began.

"Save it, Counselor. We're merely engaging in some courthouse humor. I'm not going to do anything to give you a possibility of an appeal. Let's get this show on the road."

The hearing began, and that's when I felt like taking a nap. The bailiff read the case docket number. Wize talked, the lead prosecutor talked, the judge talked. All the legalese and reading of statutes went on longer than should have been allowed.

"Judge, I've reviewed the evidence that the prosecution has submitted and we move for an immediate dismissal of all charges," Wize said.

Wize lifted up a heavy folder. No data disk this time. I could see the prosecution team look at each other with dismay. One bailiff walked to our table and took the file from her to give to the judge.

The judge opened the file and reviewed it. He was speed-reading what he had. From my vantage point it looked like it was text documents and lots of photos.

"You prepared all this, Counselor? Very thorough and impressive."

"I've also submitted three complaints against the Metro Police Division, Judge," Wize said. "Attempting to plant false evidence at the scene of my client's residence, attempting to plant false evidence at the office of my client's attorney of record, me, and conspiracy."

The court erupted.

"Judge, we object!" one of the prosecutors said, jumping from his chair.

I glanced back to see the reporters were seated in the gallery too, including Holly Live, eating it all up.

"Defense Counselor, those are very explosive charges," the judge said.

Wize stood and held another folder in her hand. "A Detective Dent entered the parking lot of my client's residence, not in uniform, not on duty, in an unmarked hovercar, and approached my client's hovervehicle. We believe he was attempting to break into my client's vehicle to plant false evidence to get my client's bail revoked. It was only due to the fact that there was independent security in the parking lot, who threatened to call the police, that Detective Dent fled the scene."

The court erupted again, but this time in gasps. Detective Dent was a seething pile of flesh in his chair. The bailiff walked to the defense table again to get the second file.

"You might as well take this folder too," she said to the bailiff.

He took the folders back to the bench and gave them to the judge.

"The third folder, Judge, shows that one Captain Monitor initiated a raid on my place of employment, claiming to be part of a wider investigation into my business. We believe this to have been a ruse to plant evidence with the purpose of depriving my client of my attorney services. This raid took place the same day Detective Dent 'visited' my client's residence. Finally, Judge, you might be interested to know that the prosecution used this raid as a distraction to hide the fact that the court moved up the date of this hearing."

"Hide?" the judge asked.

"Let the prosecution state for the record as to how the notice was delivered to my office. In a surreptitious way to an employee coming off of work, who didn't even know that he was served or the importance of the notice, nor that it was supposed to be given to me immediately."

The judge placed both hands on the folders, and glared at the prosecution. Their table was a beehive of whispering. One of them finally jumped up from his chair.

"Judge, can we have a moment to confer with the police?"

"No!"

The judge's voice boomed through the courthouse. The prosecution's eyes widened, as they knew what was about to happen.

I had seen the DA when I was brought in for my arrest. I didn't know much about him. Everything I'd heard about him was mixed. He was a slick, politician lawyer, who I believe was elected the same year as the mayor. His office closed their cases and convicted lots of bad guys, a few because of me, so as a citizen I had no complaints—until now.

He strolled into the courthouse with his hand in the air like a kid in school. He moved to the prosecution table, but unlike his subordinates, wasn't panicking and ready to collapse to the floor.

"Yes, Mr. DA. What do you want?"

"My office wishes to amend and add to the charges against Mr. Cruz."

"Judge, it's too late to—"

"Defense Counselor, stop talking. Amend and add what, Mr. DA?"

"We're adding another charge of murder to the charges against Mr. Cruz."

The courthouse really erupted in astonishment.

"What! That's ridiculous!" Wize yelled.

This time I was the one to grab a hold of Wize to try to calm her down.

"Murdered who?" she asked.

"A Mr. Accent, CEO of the Bio-Matters Corporation."

Mr. Accent was dead! Mr. Prince was killed by a Moon Monarch. Mr. Accent must have been killed by one of Bio-Matters' executives—Ms. Hertz, Mr. Hollo, or Ms. Sage. Framing me seemed to be popular these days.

"My client is being setup again! He didn't murder anyone! Why didn't the DA's office charge him before?"

"We only found out this morning, Judge," the DA said. "There's no statute of limitations on filing charges of murder."

"Judge, I beat them! They knew you were going to dismiss the charges against my client on the Prince murder. They tried to plant evidence."

"That is a lie!" the DA yelled.

"Then this outrageous new charge," Wize yelled.

248

The courthouse grew quiet. Wize realized why when she calmed down and saw that I had my hand raised. Wize didn't know what to do.

"Mr. Cruz," the judge said. "I don't like defendants talking in my court. Usually it puts me in a very bad mood, but based on the circumstances, what do you want?"

"Judge, one question and one comment. When and where was Mr. Accent killed?"

Everyone looked at the DA.

"He was killed two days ago. We have witnesses to the effect."

My hand was still raised.

"And your comment, Mr. Cruz?"

"Judge, I can prove in five minutes to the court's satisfaction that I had no contact whatsoever with Mr. Accent, other than the one time he came to my office weeks ago. I had myself fitted with a police GPS tracker. So, it would appear that the DA still has a murderer on the loose, and most likely the real murderer is one of the DA's supposed witnesses, or maybe all three."

The outburst from the court was of laughter.

The red-faced DA looked up at the judge. "Judge!"

"No need to prompt me, Mr. DA. Mr. Cruz, a police GPS tracker can only be fitted by an active member of the Metro Police Division. If you have one on, then that would be a violation of your bail. You two were doing so well."

I slowly raised my hand.

"Not this time, Mr. Cruz. No more talking from you."

I quickly whispered to Wize.

"Judge, but the police GPS tracker was fitted by an active member of the Metro police."

"Who?" the judge asked.

Someone in the gallery stood and raised his hand.

Monitor looked like he was about to faint, Dent looked like he wanted to jump over the gallery wall to get at me, and Chief Hub was laughing.

"Who are you?" the judge yelled. "Identify yourself. Speak up. Get a microphone to that person."

The man in civilian clothes came down the aisle then to the prosecution table, brushing past the DA. All the prosecution looked like they were also going to faint.

"Wilford G. Jr., active duty officer, president of the Metropolis Police Union."

"Officer, as much as your title and position means in the police ranks, you have to follow the law like everyone else. You cannot do special favors for anyone, including friends. I know you know the defendant. Did you get official authorization from your superiors to fit Mr. Cruz with a police GPS device?"

"I did, Judge." Wilford G. held up a palm tablet.

"I hope the name on that authorization isn't Chief Hub, because I was told he had to recuse himself from this case."

"That's correct, Judge. Signed by Deputy Chief of Police Crest, who reports to Chief Hub."

I could see the prosecution panicking. Some of them looked at Chief Hub, but he sat there without any concern at all. I'd never met the deputy chief of police before that I could recall. But I didn't need to; I knew their boss.

The judge started laughing. He jerked around in his chair and looked at his bailiff.

"Have you ever seen something like this before?"

"Not in all my years, Judge."

"A paralegal and a detective outfoxed the entire Metro PD and District's Attorney. Looks like you lost your bet. Looks like I lost my bet. For the cameras, we're not being serious. That's more courtroom humor. Betting on cases for court personnel is illegal."

The judge pulled himself together, sat up straight, and stacked the folders nicely in front of him.

"First, charges against Mr. Cruz for the murder of Mr. Prince, alias Apollo Michelangelo, dismissed. New charges against Mr. Cruz for the murder of this Mr. Accent dismissed."

The gallery cheered. Wize, her team, and I were hugging each other.

"Judge!"

The courthouse got quiet. An angry Captain Monitor was speaking.

"I made my ruling and don't care what you have to say, Officer," the judge snapped at him.

"Judge, Mr. Prince, alias Apollo Michelangelo, was a citizen of Lunar Colony. They've been monitoring these proceedings and though Mr. Cruz has evaded Earth justice, he faces the same charge in their jurisdiction. We will be taking Mr. Cruz into custody to hand over to their authorities."

"What?" Wize yelled. "You have no jurisdiction!"

"But they do!" Monitor yelled at her. "The extradition order has already been filed with the court."

The courtroom erupted in boos.

The judge looked at his bench tablet. He tapped the screen. He sadly looked at us—the defense team and me.

"You almost did it," he said. "But they had the ultimate ace up their sleeve. Good effort, you two. You almost did it."

Wize looked crushed. Her team looked like they wanted to cry. Wilford Jr. was angry. I, however, had a smirk on my face.

The prosecution was about to celebrate themselves when they saw my face. Monitor saw my face. Wize and the others noticed my expression.

From the back of the courthouse, came a group of men. They were space people all right in their all-white outfits. Monitor looked as puzzled as the DA and prosecution. Chief Hub, however, was laughing again.

"Who are you?" Monitor asked, stepping in front of the spacemen to block them. "You're not with Lunar Colony."

"Actually, I am," the lead spaceman said. "Please step aside."

Monitor complied, and they moved to the area between the two attorney tables.

"Who are you?" Judge "Dreadful" asked.

"My name is Mr. Seraff, Judge. I'm the head of Interspace Police at Praetoria Space Station. We will be taking charge of Mr. Cruz for the Lunar authorities."

Seraff glanced back at me and smiled. "Good to be working with you again, Mr. Cruz."

Cheers again. Wize and her team were overjoyed and hugging me and each other again. We had won! Wilford G. patted me on the shoulder.

Monitor fell to his seat, looking like he'd just received the death penalty. Dent stood there, ready to explode.

"May we take custody of Mr. Cruz, Judge?" Seraff asked.

"You may," the judge said.

I shot Monitor and Dent the dirtiest look I could manage. I moved past Wize and her team, and I walked back down the aisle as everyone watched me. The entire courtroom was wild with applause. I reached the final row on the gallery and crouched down to look at a man seated in the last seat next to the aisle. He wore dark glasses and had wild dark hair covering much of his face. It was a good disguise.

"You spacemen always seem to play the same game. You tell me you'd never set foot on Earth, but then I find you on Earth. You didn't know I saw you in your little hovercar out there in the parking lot. Looks like your elaborate plan with your police and prosecution puppets fell apart. Tell me, Mr. Apollo Michelangelo, the Fourth, when did you delude yourself into thinking you were smarter than me? But you're getting your wish. I'll be going to the Moon, and I'll make you wish you never, ever met me and got on my bad side."

PART SIX

Launch!

CHAPTER 42

Metro PD

The moment I realized what Monitor was up to by raiding Wize's place, I called Phishy. I told him to get our Sidewalk Johnny Brigade into action and stake out the Metro Criminal Courts building. It was unlikely they'd anticipate that we'd guess what they were already doing, but I liked to be prepared. Maybe they'd confront us at the court building itself to keep us from getting in or delay us. I had to let my paranoid mind run wild.

None of that happened, of course. But what the sidewalk johnnies did see was one hovercar with a lone passenger fly in at five a.m. Mr. Apollo Michelangelo, the Fourth flew into the Metro Criminal Courts Building to sit in the vehicle ahead of the start of trial, three hours ahead of time. I glanced at him from time to time from Wize's hover-RV and all he did was sit there emotionless, like a dead robot. When I said what I said to his face, he had plenty of emotions. But he couldn't do anything about it with the world watching. He was exposed, and he jumped up from his seat and bolted out of the courtroom to laughs, jeers, and boos from the court spectators.

The ordeal was over. I was free and clear from the unit within Metro PD trying to railroad me, and much of the help came from units within Metro PD. Seraff told me we'd speak later, so that left me to exit the courtroom, with my legal team around me, like we won a death match of a mixed martial arts competition. We had to battle the media jackals, but we made it to the elevators. Once we got to our floor it was a mad dash to the hover-RV, as reporters spilled out of the surrounding elevators. The vehicle was already ready to go, and the big drivers shot out of the parking lot before the reporters could get to their hovercars and vans. Our vehicle was huge and slow, so they'd catch up easily.

"We can do a combat drop at Metro PD," I told a still beaming Wize sitting in the lounge chair across from me.

"Pardon me?"

"A combat drop."

"I know what a combat drop is, Cruz. You get your freedom but want to die jumping out of a moving hovervehicle."

"It's safe enough."

"Compared to what? Jumping off a megatower without a parachute?"

"I tried to do that too, once—unintentionally."

"I'm sure you did. Why Metro PD?"

"I have people to thank, and to make sure the second individuals who tried to frame me get what they deserve."

"Yeah, that wasn't very nice of them."

I told the drivers where to fly over. The hover-RV veered out of sky traffic as if it was going into the public parking structure. Wize and her team thought I was mad, as I slid open the side door.

"I'll call you later," I said to Wize and jumped.

It was good to stroll into the internal waiting room of Metro PD not under arrest. All was forgiven, and an officer led me to Chief Hub's office where both the chief and Wil Jr. were seated and talking.

"Speak of the devil," Hub said from behind his desk.

Wil Jr. smiled and shook my hand. "Remind me to never play chess with you."

"Cruz, I've never met someone as lucky as you."

I sat down in the empty chair next to Wil.

"Not luck, Chief. All planned. It's amazing what a person can do when sufficiently paranoid. Where's Monitor?"

The men grunted.

"Don't worry about him," Hub answered.

"Where's Dent?"

Wil answered this time. "Not in the building."

"As long as I don't run into them."

"You won't," Hub said.

"Are you going to tell me what this was all about with Monitor and his supposed team acting like he was running your department?" I asked.

"No," Hub replied.

"I didn't think so. I sent that report."

"We got it," Hub said.

"Prince had me investigate his belief that members of the board were stealing from the company. They were. Was the CEO really murdered?"

"Their General Counsel says it was suicide."

"Ms. Sage?"

"Yes."

"She's in interrogation now."

"Is that what's she saying?"

"Yes. He drowned. But she's here and her two colleagues have disappeared," Hub revealed. "We'll find them."

"From Prince's evidence, and what I confirmed, was it the entire board?"

"Leave it to us, Cruz," the chief said. "You don't know when to quit. Your client is dead and you're still going."

"Talk about services," Wil Jr. said with a laugh.

"Can I ask about the DA?"

"You can ask."

"May I ask about the D.A.? Was Apollo the Fourth the man behind the curtain, pulling the strings of his puppet Monitor?"

"You may ask, but you'll get no answers, Cruz. This is an internal police matter."

"Cruz, you're a civilian," Wil added. "But you can become a cop if you really want to."

"No thanks. I like being a regular private detective."

"Regular?" Hub said with a huff. "Anything else you want, Cruz?"

"I don't think so."

"I thought you were being taken into custody to the Moon by Interpol."

"I am. I leave today, or tomorrow morning. Seraff will let me know."

"Lucky you," Wil said. "I've never been to the Lunar Colonies, and here you get to go there for free. Chief, have you ever been there?"

"I like Earth fine. He can go. Cruz, enjoy vacation Up-Top."

"No vacation for me, Chief. I have a Three-Armed Man to catch."

"Oh, him. Is that all? Didn't you have a case where you were hunting extraterrestrials before?"

"Yeah, but that one was from Mars."

Wil chuckled.

"Get out of my office, Cruz."

"Yes, Chief." I stood from my chair. "And thanks, Chief. You too, Wil. A good day for the good guys."

"Cruz, be careful up there. The Moon can be a beautiful place, and a very deadly one too. You're an Earth boy. Never forget that. The people, the criminals; they're different than Earth. Also, I wouldn't go anywhere near those Moon Monarchs. If they kill you up there, Cruz. No one will ever find your body."

"They'll just space you," Wil said. "Centuries, millennia would go by, and not a living soul would ever set eyes on your corpse in the universe ever again."

Neither man was joking.

"I know," I said. "But I have to finish this. The Moon isn't far enough away from Metropolis to keep these maniacs from dropping down on our planet to visit me when I'm least expecting it."

CHAPTER 43

Party People

I didn't like it at all. I came out of Metro PD and there was Holly Live and her camera guy waiting for me.

"Cruz, I'm starting to be able to predict your moves," she said.

"I've noticed that. I'm catching a hovercab, so no time to talk."

"You always have time for me, Cruz. Any comments on the rumors that Metro's district attorney is in big trouble?"

"Big trouble with who?"

"My sources say he's on the way out after this fiasco. Can't help your reputation if you're outmaneuvered by a paralegal and a street detective. Voters tend to demand more from the supercity's top attorney."

"My attorney isn't just a paralegal."

"Oh, yes. Paralegal and casino owner."

I laughed. "You're right, Holly. He's in trouble."

She managed to get some quotes from me. My hovercab couldn't arrive fast enough, and I was finally on my way home. But I did glean some information from her through her "sources." City Council was leading the pitchfork brigade to get the DA to resign over my attempted prosecution. As flattering as that sounded, they weren't doing it because they were part of my fan club. I'd become the proxy of an internal war, far from the prying eyes of the public or nosiness of the press. The mayor, City Council, and chief of police were on one side—the winning side. The D.A., the senior police brass, and the Moon Monarchs were on the other—the losing side. People would be getting fired or "moving on to other opportunities" in the weeks and months ahead.

Soon, I'd be heading to the Moon where I already suspected another such internal war was taking place. I would be right in the middle of it, and I'd better be ready. In that case, people wouldn't be losing their jobs; they'd be losing their lives. The chief's warnings were still in my mind; the same warnings that Moonbeam had given me. But I had no intentions of dying on the Moon.

"Hello, you're listening to the Psi-ber Man Frequency, and your favorite announcer is raising his glass to Cruz—Metropolis's famous private eye and one of our own. It was a David versus Goliath death match at the Metro Criminal Courts this morning and Mr. Cruz slayed the giant. Give him a virtual fist bump in the air to show our collective solidarity. Also, Mr. Metro DA I'd be looking for a new residence as far from Metropolis as possible, because this is not only Psi-ber Man territory, but Cruz and Liquid Cool territory."

That's what I heard over my vehicle radio. I couldn't believe it. An ad spot on Psi-ber Man's show was astronomical even for thirty seconds. I just got a plug for free.

When I got to the Liquid Cool office, I had already prepared myself.

"Free media!" PJ yelled as soon as I came through the door. "That's called earned media. That's what you need as a business."

I stood there after I closed the door, looking around. It was a party. Hip-Hop wasn't only still alive, but he was performing in our waiting area with his musicalizer floating near him, and there was a crowd of people in the office watching.

He pointed; they all saw me and cheered.

"Cruz!"

"Hip hop, hop hip, please don't trip. I paid my bill, before the kill, for the thrill," he sang.

"Where's my steelpan?" I said.

He switched something on the device, and his dance pop became a carnival calypso. I heard my steel pan drums.

I didn't even see him at first but Phishy was in the office too, dancing.

The wall screen had the newsfeed and it was all about me, though the volume was off. We won. The reporters were going to say the same thing over and over again.

"PJ." I signaled her from her desk. "Phishy!"

He was so busy dancing that he hadn't heard me, so I grabbed him. I pushed open the door of my private office and they followed me in. What I saw on the desk made me do a double-take.

"What is all that?" I asked as I walked to my desk.

PJ closed the door and walked to me. "Messages. We've been busy. When are you going to hire me some staff? No. I hire them, because I get to be the boss of them. You won your case so you can keep all your money."

"Phishy, tell the johnnies that they did a great job."

"Really?" he said with his Phishy smile.

"They spotted that bastard for me."

"Spotted him? Who?"

"My client's estranged father. Mr. Apollo, the Fourth."

"You mean Prince Sr.?" PJ asked.

"Yeah."

"Yes, that man you confronted at the back of the courtroom."

"Yeah."

"I bet he's still running away—all the way to the Moon."

"That's why I want to talk to you both. He's now the second Up-Top gazillionaire to claim he hated Earth and would never set foot on the planet, and then I catch them right here. Maybe it's a common lie with them when they talk with Earth people."

"Who was the other one?"

"Mr. Omni in our Martian alien case."

"Oh, yes."

"I'm going to the Moon."

"You're going?" PJ said with a surprised look. "I thought that was a ruse. Isn't Seraff on our side?"

"He is, but I'm going."

"The Moon, Cruz," Phishy said. "Wow. All the way to the Moon. I wish I were going."

"No, you don't, Phishy. Believe me, you don't. While I'm gone, I want you both to watch out. PJ, you and I both know what they are able to do with little effort."

"I'll keep any space people, or Moonies from the office. I won't let them damage it again," PJ said emphatically.

"Don't even let them in the building," I said.

"Phishy, put the word out on the street. The police are looking for them too, but if we can find Mr. Hollo and Ms. Hertz of the Bio-Matters Corporation, and call the police on them. I don't like people trying to frame me."

"Did they kill the CEO like the news says?" PJ asked me.

"I don't know. The attorney, Ms. Sage, turned herself in, and says it was suicide to avoid scandal, but I can't say I believe her."

"I'll take care of it, Cruz," Phishy said.

"Seriously, be careful. I don't know how many of these Moon Monarchs there are, or where they all are, and they seem to have no problems coming to our planet to mess with us."

"We'll handle things here," PJ said.

"PJ, in all the messages here, is any one of them from our IQ Club people?"

"Oh yes, they called."

I looked at the mountain of messages in multiple piles on the top of my desk. She leaned over and pointed to the top of one pile.

"Haven't I trained you on Liquid Cool's message system yet? 'Hot' pile, 'hold' pile, and 'garbage' pile. Their message would be in hot pile."

I smirked and picked up the message. "Yes, PJ, whatever you say."

"Then I get to hire staff?"

"Except that," I said.

"I can be an assistant detective," Phishy chimed in. "I've been observing and I have my own fedora."

"No!" PJ and I said in unison.

CHAPTER 44

Dot and Company

That day had been awful for my parents. They were at my home, visiting with their grandchildren, and saw their son arrested in front of them. I'd never forgive Monitor for what he did, but at least my parents got to see me triumph over the system.

I returned home to get a kiss from Dot wearing her stylish cooking apron, see my Ma holding Kat, Cruz Jr. trying to scale my pops like a rock-climber, and the Hellspawn (her parents) in the kitchen cooking I don't know what. It was a full house.

"Dot, what are these people doing in our house?" I said with a grin.

Of course, I was dismissed or laughed at. But at least, I'd be able to relax with peace of mind—for now. Seraff gave me two days. I wouldn't be leaving the apartment until then. I planted myself on the main living room couch, kicked off my shoes, and put my legs up on the ottoman.

My ma appeared and put Kat in my arms. Mr. Wan appeared behind her.

"Shoes go by door!" he yelled.

"Shoes go where I want."

I felt something grabbing at my neck. I tilted my head back to see Cruz Jr. climbing up the back of the chair. My son had gone from teleporting ninja to rock climber. I looked down at Kat. She was staring at me and smiling.

Two days I had. Why couldn't it be two weeks?

Our big family enjoyed dinner, conversation, dessert, TV, dessert, laughs, TV, dessert. When the parents were gone and the kids were in bed and asleep, Dot and I could sit on the couch together and finally get to relax.

She didn't want me to go to the Moon either. What happened the first time we went to space was her reason. We had the opportunity to go to one of the Space Station Colonies. It was my Blade Gunner Case, and it reminded us how frightfully dangerous Up-Top could be. We had scary cyborgs down here, but nothing like what we had seen then. Dot told me she was never setting foot off Earth again. The Earth was plenty big enough for her. I couldn't agree more.

"Don't worry, Dot. Everything will be okay, and when I get back we can go on that vacation we've been putting off."

"Where?"

"It's a surprise. All I'll say is 'island,' 'big,' 'empty.'"

That did the trick. Thoughts of the danger ahead for me on the Moon were gone, and all she was thinking about was what island vacation I had in mind and what she'd buy.

CHAPTER 45

Seraff

When you don't want time to go by quickly, that's exactly when it flies by. My two days with the family were gone before I knew it. The day arrived and I wouldn't get out of bed. But that quickly changed when Cruz Jr. ran into the bedroom and jumped on the bed. When Cruzie started jumping, he didn't stop until you were up and chasing him away.

The day after Flash and Mr. Post called me back to the Concrete Mama because of Detective Dent's snooping around my Pony, I had the vehicle put in storage far from his reach, or anyone else's. It was one thing already taken care of as I caught my hovertaxi to the Metro FBI Building, which also had a private section of offices for visiting Interpol members.

I was led to the area by Feds in black uniform, then another officer in a white uniform led me from there. We stopped at an office and Seraff joined us. He nodded to the officer, who walked away.

"Come in, Mr. Cruz." Seraff was one of those zero-baby spacemen—born in zero-gravity. On Earth we called them all spacemen, or space people, but I'd learned in previous cases that there was rivalry Up-Top too. Space Station Colonists, Lunar Colonists, and Martians were not the big happy family as we Earthers thought.

"What do you all call Up-Top again?" I asked as he sat at his desk and I sat on the chair in front of it. Everything in the small office was white, down to the electric pens on his desk.

"Utopia."

"I need to start using the proper lingo."

"I had a lot of calls about you from City Hall," Seraff said.

"I'm sure. Anything nice?"

"Not at all."

"I wasn't clear about what you said on the vid-phone. I'm free but not free."

"You need a passport to be on the Moon. They're issued by the Lunar Dome authorities or by Interpol. Lunar Dome does it and it can take years for an Earther. We do it and it takes days, which is why we normally don't."

"Special treatment."

"Yes, but it comes with strings. You'll wear a bracelet at all times while on the Moon."

"What's going on then, Mr. Seraff? My client, Mr. Prince, was actually a Moon Monarch. Apollo Michelangelo the Fifth. I believe he escaped from his crazy family for a normal life. They somehow found him after all these many years and killed him."

"Your Three-Armed Man?"

"Yes. You're not taking me up there out of charity. Chief Hub and the top levels of Metro PD didn't help me out of charity either. What are you both working on?"

"Is my ulterior motive that obvious?"

"What are you using me for?"

"Who says anyone is using anyone?"

"My son is four years old, not me, Seraff. Neither are you. I'm using you to get to the Moon for free so I can track down this Three-Armed Man. He killed my client and tried to frame me. My client deserved much better. He was happy and deserved to live a long and full life with his girlfriend."

"A romantic."

"What are you using me for? You're Interpol. Doesn't the Moon fall under your jurisdiction?"

"It does; however, spaceports are controlled by their governments. If we're not allowed onto their world, or allowed to leave, then our jurisdiction doesn't mean much. Normally, there aren't any issues. Your client was a Utopian resident. He was murdered; therefore, we are the primary investigative authority. However, who he was complicates the matter."

"He was a Moon Monarch."

"Yes. They control Lunar spaceports."

"How do I fit in?"

"You run your investigation and do what you will."

"You say this knowing what I'm going to do. Let me, a civilian, run around on the Moon to track a killer."

"You didn't say that. You told me that you were seeking the whereabouts of a suspect in your client's murder and that upon finding him you'd notify us immediately. If he was to make an attempt at your life, and you acted in self-defense, that would all be sanctioned by Interpol."

I smirked.

"Strangely, you'll have more power than me when we touch down," he told me.

"The Moon does have its own police?"

"Dome Command. But their loyalties in this situation cannot be completely trusted."

"The Moon Monarchs control them?"

"No, I didn't say that. They have influence, which is enough. I can't fully trust them anymore than you can. To them, we're both outsiders."

"What will you do?"

"I, Mr. Cruz, will be returning the body of Apollo Michelangelo, the Fifth to the Moon Monarch Family."

"Should I attend?"

"No, Mr. Cruz. You should definitely not attend. You work your case. Interpol will work its. Besides, you wouldn't be allowed. A private and highly exclusive ceremony. Why waste your limited time with the obvious?"

"You're right."

"Of course, I am."

"You didn't tell me what's going on. They killed Prince because he was the heir apparent, and they didn't want him coming back?"

"Yes. His disappearance put everything on pause all these many years. The rivalries are back though. You'll find out who killed your client."

"What's the Family saying to you? The father aside, what are they saying?"

"Curiously, the Moon Monarchs have been silent. They know your Earth case was dismissed and Interpol has taken charge of you, at least on paper. They demanded we watch the case closely when they expected you to be held over for trial on Earth."

"They didn't know about you."

"No, they didn't. You're in Interpol's custody and on the way to the Moon. They have no influence over me. They don't know what to expect. So they're quiet."

"They're scared."

"Why do you say that?"

"Apollo Four seems scared of me. Maybe all of them are. I don't know why. Someone suggested to me that they're afraid I know something or have something from Prince, my dead client."

"Logical. What do you think it may be?"

"I have no idea. If they didn't send a contract killer and kill him in front of me, I would have wrapped up his case and he'd have lived all his days on Earth without bothering anyone. I'm going to find the contract killer and that will probably be all I can do. I couldn't even begin to guess the true reason why behind it.

If the Moon Monarchs leave me alone, I'll do that, and return to Earth."

"Do you think they'll leave you alone?"

"No, but it isn't something I can bluff to find out. They know what Prince had or knew. I don't. Do you?"

"No."

"Who is this Three-Armed Man?"

"We don't know. Never heard of him, but that doesn't mean anything. I'm on the Space Station Colonies. If you recall, we didn't know about the Super Cyborgs, until they showed up in mass from wherever they were hiding. There could be a thousand three-armed men on the Moon and we wouldn't know. We have our own problems, and lunar police have theirs. We don't share unless we need to."

"What's happening in the Moon Monarch Family now?"

"There will be a struggle to determine the new leader of the Family. It will either be quiet and uneventful, or incredibly violent. We need it to be quiet. The Moon Monarchs remain a very powerful Family on the Moon."

"Wait a minute. Aren't the Moon Monarchs *the* most powerful family on the Moon?"

Seraff hesitated in his answer. "No."

"What do you mean no?"

"There are other Families and megacorps, Cruz."

"What are you saying? The Moon isn't that big. How many other Families and megacorps can there be equal to or greater than the Moon Monarchs?"

"They exist."

"So the Three-Armed Man could have been sent to kill my client by someone else other than the Moon Monarchs."

"Possibly."

"Seraff, I'm getting a headache. I'm finding the Three-Armed Man, then I'm going home. I'm a private detective, not a lunar superhero. You and your Interpol buddies on the Moon will have to contain any internal family war without me. I already have to watch out for Apollo Four and those crazy twins, his niece and nephew."

"All part of the life of a famous detective."

"People say I'm famous because of a handful of big cases, but truthfully, in this business, the detective business, I've already had hundreds of cases. Most are simple and straightforward. No one knows about them except the client and those that account for most of my cash flow to pay the bills. My quiet cases."

"But your quiet cases are nowhere near as fun."

"Fun I can do without. You mean dangerous and filled with crazy maniacs. No, I like quiet. You're still going to put that bracelet on me?"

"Yes, for your protection. It's not a surveillance device, or even a tracker. I'm sure you'll be visiting the darker places of the Lunar Colonies."

"Wouldn't it be better to just chip me?"

"It's better not to use a subcutaneous device in this case. You want those who may want to do you harm to see it. The bracelet will let us know if your body leaves the dome."

My eyes narrowed. "Leave the dome? What does that mean?"

"You know what it means. If someone decides to space you, we can attempt to get to you."

"Space me?" My mouth dropped. "How can I get spaced if I'm under the dome on the streets? How can someone get a body outside the dome?"

"There...are ways."

"Seraff, I thought you space people were normal people, you just have an obsession with white clothes and like your flying saucer spaceships. What you're telling me is that you're a bunch of crazy people too."

He laughed. "No different than Earth, Mr. Cruz. I've told you before. We are all humans."

CHAPTER 46

Run-Time

S eraff stood and handed me my Up-Top visa.

"See you Up-Top, Mr. Cruz."

I smiled as I stood and took it from him. "See you up there, spaceman."

Seraff had offered me one of Interpol's best transports, but I wanted to leave my planet in an Earth spaceship. I wanted to travel in Let It Ride style.

A hovercab dropped me at Let It Ride Enterprises headquarters. I always liked being in Peacock Hills; its monolith towers flashing in the colors of white, light yellow, and blue, and the angelic halo glow of the roof lighting of its megatowers.

I was already on the two hundred and fiftieth floor with two big rolling suitcases with me. A Let It Ride hoverlimo waited. Standing by were two of Run-Time's three vice presidents—a tall Lebanese woman and a West Indian woman.

"Hello, Mr. Cruz," Mrs. Phoenicia, the Lebanese woman, greeted me. Mrs. Role did the same.

My luggage was loaded on the vehicle as another hoverlimo set down nearby. Run-Time got out, but he wasn't alone. His wife was with him and his kids. I had Cruz Jr. and Kat; he had three different age groups to contend with, including a preteen! I wasn't looking forward to that at all. Run-Time kissed his wife, and hugged his kids. They all waved to me.

"I'll take care of him," I said sarcastically.

Run-Time laughed as he walked to me. We got in the back of the hoverlimo and his VIP got into the front compartment. As the driver lifted off in the vehicle, Run-Time watched his family from the window. He had the window down and continued waving.

The window rose shut and he sat back.

"We're off to the Moon," I said.

"Yes, we are."

Run-Time had begun expanding his business into Earth-to-space station people transport. Cargo transport was far more lucrative but a saturated and hard market to break into. However, he was about people transport, and there were not as many competitors on the luxury side of the market.

"Where was your family?" he asked.

"Said our goodbyes beforehand. Parents and parents-in-law too. With those Moon Monarchs running around, I feel more comfortable not having them around me in public."

"I'd say you were paranoid, but I know you're not—in this case."

"Can't wait to have it all behind me."

"You've never been to the Moon yet, have you?" Run-Time said.

"How many times have you been?"

"Only once but not long. A day stop-over before I returned to Earth."

"What do I need to know?"

"I could spend our entire ride to Metro International explaining it, but it would be pointless. You have to experience it. Above all, remember, Cruz, you're a visitor. You can get away with things on Earth because you're an Earther, not on the Moon. You don't want to get on the wrong side of the law, or anyone else there."

"Tell me about their government."

"Like the rest of off-world. Megacorps are the government, and Families run the leading megacorps. Certain things they're more lax than us, other things they are much more draconian. They do live under bio-domes. Any threats to that bio-dome, or anything that can threaten life within it are taken deadly seriously."

"We'd do the same, if it were reversed."

"Yes, we would. Anything happens to that bio-dome and everyone literally dies. One other thing, to prepare you, since it's your first time. But actually it should be no big deal to you, with your history."

"What?"

"Visitors from Earth have to go through extended bio-decon."

I grinned.

"You're the only Earth person who'd smile at that."

"With my history as a former bubble boy and recovering germophobe, decon and I are old friends. No problem at all."

"I thought you'd say that. As for the politics of the Moon, Lunar Colony is actually many interconnected bio-domes, each with its own ruling council. Collectively, all the councils make up the ruling parliament of all Lunar Colonies. There's no one leader. Leadership is a ruling committee made up of the ruling Families—their Founders. Same structure as Mars and the Space Station Colonies—each station is its own government. On the Moon, it used to be that the Families could overrule the entire parliament, but that power has been waning over the decades. Founders get weaker, non-Founders get stronger."

"These Moon Monarchs are Founders."

"They are the original Founders of the Moon. The oldest Family and still powerful, but not like in the past."

"How many members?"

"Ruling members. Nearly fifty. Total members, including spouses, children, and grandchildren. Almost two hundred."

"Did you find out anything about any internal power struggles?"

"Not even I have any sources on the Moon. Cruz, you need to be very careful there. Don't do what you'd do with our politicians and megacorps. It's a whole different scene there."

"Different planet."

"No, different dimension in another universe. We're Earthers. We're nothing there. Always remember that. The average person will be respectful and nice, but even they have the same basic attitude as the ruling class."

"We're just Earthers."

"Yes."

"I heard a rumor that I need to confirm. I thought it was an urban myth."

"Yes, Cruz. Spacing does happen up there."

"How?"

"Forget about how. It happens. Don't cross the wrong people. Knowing you as I do, you shouldn't even be going there. I know you're going to cause trouble."

"Me? I'm harmless," I said, smiling.

To see the airspace around Metro International and Interspace Airport, it looked as if extraterrestrial aliens in every manner of hovercraft, aircraft, and spacecraft were arriving as part of their planetary conquest.

Departures for the space stations were one terminal. I'd been there before. The departure terminal for the Moon was new for me. It was much larger but had far less people preparing for departure. Run-Time wasn't a first-timer so he went in a different line from me. His line was short and he passed through quickly. I, on the other hand, was stuck in a long, slow-moving line. Why couldn't all these people pick another day to go to the Moon for the first time?

"Anything to declare, sir?" one security agent asked me when I finally reached the scanning arch to move to the next section of the terminal.

"Declare? Isn't that a customs question for when I return?"

The other agent was reviewing my visa and scanned it with a hand device.

"It's on both ends for those going to the Moon or Mars. Do you have any prohibited or illegal items to declare?"

I gave him a confused look. "Well...no. Prohibited or illegal items are prohibited and illegal."

He gave a fake smile. "If we find something on your person or in your luggage, then it's straight to prison."

"Oh snaps! I have my illegal thong underwear in my luggage."

I liked my joke but neither of the guards did.

"Go on through, sir," one guard said.

I stepped through the scanning arch. It gave the green "go" light.

"You didn't like my joke?" I asked with a fake frown.

"Sir, take your luggage and go."

"Illegal thong. Yeah, we never heard that one before," the other guard said.

They had already turned their attention to the couple behind me. The couple shook their heads at me in disapproval.

"Doesn't anyone have a sense of humor around here?"

The next area was Decon! One agent directed me to a large table where another agent had me lift up my luggage and place it in front of him.

"Why are you smiling?" he asked me.

"This is Decon."

"Why does that make you smile?"

"It's Decon."

"Are you some kind of weirdo?"

"I'm an honorary member of the CDC."

Oh no. As soon as I said it, I realized I shouldn't have. He was about to open one of my suitcases but froze.

"CDC?"

"I'm joking. Just a joke."

"The Centers for Disease Control."

"I'm joking."

"Are you a disease carrier?"

I sighed heavily. "A joke."

The agent spoke into his wrist communicator. "I need a supervisor to my station."

A supervisor arrived and I spent the next half hour talking to them. The supervisor disappeared and went to a nearby standing computer terminal. The agent joined him. They watched me as they searched the databases.

I kept calm, but internally, I was hoping beyond hope that they didn't find out that I had been a bio-terrorist attack victim in my last major case.

The two men walked back to me.

"That's something I've never seen before," the supervisor said. "You're pre-approved by both the Metropolis CDC and Earth CDC. What's so special about you that you'd be pre-approved?"

"I don't know, sir."

"What's his occupation?" the supervisor asked the agent.

"Private investigator," the agent answered.

"I've worked for both offices before in the past. For the head of the Metro CDC."

They stared at me.

"Sir, if you get to the Moon, and they don't like you, like I don't like you, they'll send you all the way back. Understand?"

"Yes, sir."

"Carry on," he said to the agent and walked back to wherever he came from.

I learned my lesson. I wasn't going to say another word.

The real bio-decontamination process came next. I was directed to a room that looked like a doctor's office. Another agent was waiting for me.

"Please sign these forms," she said.

I took the tablet and stylus from her.

"Read carefully and check any diseases you've had in the past."

"Yes."

I read and signed.

"When you've boarded the shuttle, you'll meet with medical personnel on board. You'll be getting two shots—vaccinations, two pills for ingestion—decontamination for the colon and GI tract, and one oral cleanser."

I closed my eyes and lowered my head.

"Sir, this isn't funny."

"I'm sorry," I said. "It sounds funny."

"Please sign that you've understood what I've said. You will not be able to decline any of the decon procedures, and you will not be able to enter Lunar Colony without them."

"I understand."

"That's all, sir. Enjoy your trip."

I was all smiles as I waited with Run-Time in the departure lounge area. Run-Time had a spaceship! Outside the bay windows of the air terminal was a Let It Ride Enterprises spacecraft! A huge double-decker passenger craft prepping for departure. The flight crew were contractors; the decon-med staff were space people. Everyone else on the craft was direct Let It Ride personnel.

"You sure you don't need accommodations?" Run-Time asked me.

"I have it covered."

"Look at you. Friends literally in high places."

"I don't want anything to come back to you."

"You are expecting trouble."

"I'm always expecting it. That's why I'm good at what I do."

"If you get in over your head, leave. Seriously, Cruz. Get to the spaceport and get out of there."

"Mr. Seraff will help, if it gets to that."

"Will he?"

"He will."

"Interpol is using you."

"I'm using them, so it's all good."

"Don't forget you can call me too."

"I know."

"A very dangerous game you're playing. Lunar Colony is a series of bio-domes, that's it. Not many places to run."

"But I have a Three-Armed Man to catch."

"Why are you so certain you'll find him?"

"I couldn't find him in a million years. That's why I had others look for him. They found him."

Run-Time leaned forward. "They found him? You know where he is?"

"They found him for me."

"Cruz, he'll have weapons. Up-Top isn't about guns like on Earth. Laser-shanks and weapons you've never seen before. You don't have any of that and your omega-gun may be an Up-Top weapon, but it's not here with you. And Seraff isn't going to lend you any of his weapons. He's a spaceman, not a Moon man. The dome authorities won't allow any Earther to carry a weapon on their turf."

"I have it covered."

"Covered? How?"

"I have other friends up there."

"But are you sure they're friends?"

"No, but I'm easy to please. A warm bed, a wicked gun, and directions to my Three-Armed Man and I'm good."

"That easy, huh?"

"Not easy at all because I have to get through my enemies first to get to him. That's going to be the hard part."

We launched for the Moon within the hour. My first trip to the Moon. I just had to make sure it wasn't an unexpected one-way trip.

PART SEVEN

Moon Landing

CHAPTER 47

IQ Man

From Earth, when you could see it, the Moon was always so beautiful. But to approach the planetoid for real, its image literally filled your entire field of vision. It was breathtaking. On the upper level of Run-Time's double-decker spacecraft, I stared out the observation lounge, large enough for all hundred plus passengers, as we began our final descent. I sat in the front row in the center of older wealthy business types and younger wealthy vacation hoppers. Tourism was big, big business for the Moon—those uber-wealthy who could afford it, but there were plenty of Earthers for once-in-a-life-time visits.

For a while there was nothing else visible on the big, beautiful white rock. Then the structures came into view. The main center dome looked to be made of a slightly glowing opaque silver material covered in lines of flashing lights. Surrounding the main structure was a network of connected smaller domes, not all the same size. We saw antenna towers, dishes, and what looked to be missile launchers. Other spacecraft landed and departed from the outermost dome spaceports. We had arrived on the Moon, and all of us were in awe.

I had always thought Metro International was a behemoth of a structure, but the Moon spaceport was far larger, and that dome was tiny compared to the main Lunar Colony mother dome, as I would soon learn the proper nomenclature.

There was, however, bad news. Run-Time's craft had been recalled to one of the Space Station Colonies. Run-Time said it was routine, but I didn't necessarily believe him. Run-Time ran his businesses professionally and efficiently. Never a wasted move or expense. He didn't want to worry me. They know I'm here, I thought to myself, as the passengers and I prepared to exit the craft.

"Are you sure about this?" he asked.

"I'll be fine. I want people to think I'm here all alone."

"But you are."

We chatted a bit more. We were each trying to convince the other that everything would be okay. Neither of us was all that successful.

"Don't let anything happen to you up here, Cruz. I don't want your wife after me. The Moon isn't a good place to die."

"You're the second person to tell me that."

"Then listen to us."

He pressed a card in my hand before I disembarked the spacecraft. All the other passengers were already gone; I was the last one. I put the card in a pocket and held my pacifier (I'll explain later) in the other. One of the flight crew had gotten me a push trolley for my suitcases. My best friend and I exchanged hugs.

"You look good in your lunar outfit," he said.

I had changed out of my trademark tan fedora and slicker for a new outfit—a white fedora and white slicker.

"I'm Up-Top now," I said. "When in Rome dress as the Romans."

I was on my way. My foot was about to touch the surface of the Moon for the first time in my life. When it did, stepping down from the Let It Ride spacecraft's floating stepladder, I smiled. An automated people mover waited.

The mover was similar to pods we had on Earth, only these didn't use hovertech, but rather some type of maglev (magnetic levitation) tech. I watched the spacecraft for a while as I raced away. Behind me a giant transparent barrier closed. I could see Run-Time's spacecraft clearly. There was no delay. It launched and flew out of the spaceport dome into space. On Metropolis, I had my own team, my connections, contacts, associates, my weapons, my Pony. Here I had two suitcases and a giant pacifier in my mouth.

The decon medical personnel on the spacecraft had given me the two shots, one in each shoulder, given me two pills to swallow, which they made sure I did, then pushed a big pacifier in my mouth.

I pulled it from my mouth. "What's this?" I asked them.

"The human body is a cauldron of germs, viruses, and bacteria. We must properly neutralize any bio-threats to the Lunar Colony. We've dealt with your blood, colon, GI, skin and hair."

"Skin and hair? When did you do that?" I asked.

She ignored me and continued. "Spit and sperm are last."

"What did you say? What are you doing to me?"

"It looks like a baby pacifier but is an advanced medical cleansing device to neutralize any bio-threats in your mouth and its saliva. Don't eat or drink anything for an hour. After that, you may experience a lack of taste for a few days."

"What are you doing to me? What about the other thing?"

"That has been taken care of." She smiled. "Your reproductive systems were done when we did the skin and hair."

I pointed the sucker part of the pacifier at her. "I'm going to tell my wife what you did to me."

The medic laughed.

The people mover arrived at the disembark section and a group of customs and security officers were waiting. I had to go through the exact same procedures as I'd gone through before on Earth at Metro International. I'd traveled internationally on Earth and didn't have to go through all this security.

The pod stopped and I got out, pulling my cart with my luggage behind me. Before me was not a scanning arch but a scanning tunnel.

"Come through," I heard a voice command, as a humanoid robot walked to me to take charge of my cart.

The scanning tunnel was only about six feet long and all silver. I didn't hear or feel anything as I stepped through to the other side.

"All clear. All genetic scans clear," a robotic voice from the machine itself said.

"Genetic scan?" I asked an agent.

"Yes, Earth man. If you had a genetic anomaly for any kind of disease, the machine would tell you. Looks like you'll live to be a hundred years old, barring any external agents."

Genetic scanning? We didn't do that on Earth.

"Anything to declare?" another agent asked.

"No, sir."

I wasn't about to take any chances here with any jokes or volunteer any information not asked.

"How long will you be on Lunar Colony?"

"Ten days, sir."

"Purpose of your visit?"

"Vacation only, sir."

He handed me back my passport.

"Have you been to Lunar Colony before?"

"No, sir."

He handed me a very thin plastic-like tablet. "Please read this carefully. Every page. Lunar Colony is safer than Earth but we do have a criminal element here too, who like to scam newbies. Do not give your information to any strangers. Do not give money to any strangers."

Another agent stepped forward. "The most important thing, sir, is don't use any illegal drugs from the streets."

"I don't even do that on Earth, so I'm not going to do that here."

"A warning, sir. Not an accusation. It's another scam. A substance harmless to a lunar child ingested by you could land you in the morgue."

"I'm here for vacation, but not that kind of vacation."

"Then I don't need to say anything about issues that might arise from the use of prostitutes."

"We can skip that part too. I'll read your pamphlet though."

"We know you will because before you can officially leave the terminal, you're required to sit in the reading area"—he pointed and I saw my former passengers all seated and reading—"read each page and initial."

"Welcome to the Moon, sir. Please enjoy your stay, and don't forget your bags."

I yelled. I admit it. The second I left the customs area, something happened. I was in the air. How could I have forgotten? I was on the Moon with its gravity being one-sixth that of Earth. On Earth I was one hundred sixty-five pounds (no, I'm not lying, that's my weight, with an upper range of ten or more pounds). So on the Moon I was less than twenty-nine pounds! I was flailing around in the air, so I stopped moving. My body landed on the ground. I calmly looked around. Some people were laughing at me, but a few others were physically challenged too. I'd heard of low gravity prep centers on Earth, but I always ignored them. I'd never expected to be on the Moon ever in my life. Other passengers obviously had been to those centers. The normal movement was to keep your legs together and simply jump. One could jump three feet at one time, or a lot more, with little effort. I grabbed my bags, not needing a cart anymore, and bunny-hopped away. I felt silly, but less silly than before when I was jerking all around in the air. I glanced back and noticed that the floor material of customs and the physical landing area was different than outside it. I was curious how they achieved Earth gravity within the customs zone, but the answer would have to wait for some time in the future when I was back on Earth and had nothing better to do with my time.

When I finally exited the spaceport terminal, I stopped again in amazement. No city was larger than Metropolis; it was a supercity. But the Lunar Colony city around me was no less impressive. There was no rain or hovercar traffic of any kind. In their place was a sunny vista along the horizon, with the images of other planets hovering above an orange sun—all a virtual projection along the inside of the dome. What was real was the intricate public transportation of winding monorails and moving pods vehicles, flashy and neon-wrapped megatowers. But that's not why I was staring in amazement. It was the people, in their white and light-colored clothing. They were flying.

There were a group of us passengers standing outside the main doors of the spaceport terminal, watching. The people of the Moon weren't hopping around like giant bunny rabbits like we were; they were far more dignified than that. The Moon people didn't walk, they floated along. It reminded us of using hoverplatforms on Earth, but it wasn't hovertech they were using. Moon people used jump-boots and micro-rockets in their clothes. The jump-boots did all the work to move them along, gliding along the air, touching down to the ground occasionally. Others had micro-rockets embedded in their jackets, tops, pants, or wrist and ankle bands to float through the air without any jumping motion at all.

Guess what we all then saw across the street? A store called a "moon-walking" convenience store with jump-boots of every conceivable color, micro-rockets of every conceivable design, and clothes with them embedded. We all laughed.

"You can't go on a vacation anywhere without them trying to rip off the tourists," one of the men said, "on or off Earth."

Of course, we all bunny-hopped across the street to the store.

The real reason I changed my clothes on Run-Time's spacecraft was that on the Moon, my tan attire would make people think I was a Martian. I needed to blend in, so I could explore the city and conduct my investigation, but first I had to ditch my luggage. Moonbeam had made some negative comments about Lunar Colony when he moved here. However, I didn't see it. I may not have liked the work I was going to have to do, but I would thoroughly enjoy their Moon cities. The nearest rail platform was where I walked to, only a few yards from the spaceport departures exits.

Under the dome, day didn't gradually turn to night like on Earth. Here, it happened every twenty-four hours within minutes, like a giant hand pulling back a curtain in the sky. Jarring at first for an Earth man, but I'd get used to it.

I think I preferred night. No projections then. A clear unobstructed view of space and the stars. Tonight, we also got to see the Earth up in the sky. I glimpsed a shooting star in the distance. From my "reading," I'd learned that space wasn't all wonderful and nice for the colonists. They faced electromagnetic storms, meteors, meteor storms, and unauthorized spacecraft from Earth or Mars. The things that looked like missile launchers on the Moon's surface weren't for that but for shooting lasers.

With my luggage tucked away safe and secure, I returned to the streets of the Lunar Colony to get a feel for the place, floating along with my white rocket boots. Everyone looked like high-class models with expensive clothes, perfect skin, hair and teeth. No sidewalk johnnies or sallies here. No cyborgs. Just perfect people. I forgot that everyone who lived on the colony was beyond wealthy compared to Earth, so what did I expect?

My destination was the Star Restaurant at the top of a commercial area called Space Mountain. I arrived and super slim model-type waitresses greeted me. The entire interior looked like it was made out of diamonds.

"I'm expected," I said. "Cruz is the name."

"Yes, sir. Follow me," one of the greeters said, and I followed her through the restaurant.

The patrons were extremely well-dressed, dripping with jewelry, and their meals had more colors than the extended rainbow. There wasn't a dish I could identify by eye. The attendant led me up a few steps to a more secluded section of the restaurant where a man sat at a table alone. He was impeccably dressed in a—wait for it—white suit. He stood as we reached him. She turned me over to him and left.

It seemed the Earth custom of handshakes didn't apply here, just lots of nodding, which was fine with me.

"Mr. Cruz, have a seat."

I sat across from him and had to shift my butt around because I was still sinking into the chair, whatever it was made of.

"It's nice to meet a member of the Lunar chapter of the Pythagoras Society. What's your name?

"I'm Mr. 300."

I stared at him for a moment. "Is that even possible? You're playing with me."

"No, Mr. Cruz, my IQ is more than 300, in fact. I rounded down to appear more accessible to you lower-intelligence mortals."

I smiled. "That was a joke."

"Yes, it was. But all I got was a smile. Mr. 200 and 170 believe you could become a member yourself if you apply yourself."

"As tempting as that sounds, I have more pressing matters and a limited window to resolve them."

"Yes, they said. Are you hungry, Mr. Cruz?"

"Yes, I am, but I'm not sure if I should eat any of your food. We walked by and I was looking at people's food, but I couldn't name a thing."

"You'll manage, Mr. Cruz. Look at the pictures and point. None of it is anything you haven't eaten before. The Moon simply likes to create its own version."

"Then I'll eat."

Mr. 300 raised his hand for the waitress.

"Is he still here?" I asked him.

He lowered his hand. "Yes."

"But do you know exactly where he is?"

"Let's eat, Mr. Cruz. At least have a good meal before you go running off, chasing after someone you should be running away from."

"I'm ready for this Three-Armed Man."

"Hardly, Mr. Cruz. But let's eat."

I was still trying to eat my purple-legged octopus dish with a fork and a pliers-like eating utensil. It was messy but good.

"Is this a genetically modified octopus?" I asked.

300 was eating his yellow soup with a spoon. "Do you really care?"

"No." I was determined to finish eating the last leg.

"How do you like our planetoid?" he asked.

I paused and looked around at the people in the restaurant. "It's...too perfect. Everyone is the same. On Earth people wear the same outerwear, but underneath they're different. There's no variety here."

"There's lots of variety. That will become clearer to you as the days go on. I noticed that you've already mastered moon-walking."

"You really call it moon-walking?"

"We do."

"It's no different than hoverboarding on Earth. I just have to get used to the fact that I weigh barely more than my infant daughter here."

"Most Earthers adjust in a day or two, then it becomes second nature. The real shock will be when you return to Earth. You'll step out of your rocket ship and, for a few moments, you'll feel as if you weigh a thousand pounds and can hardly move."

"How did you find him?"

"Mr. Cruz, I do have to caution you again. You're chasing a killer for hire. A person whose handiwork you witnessed for yourself. What do you expect to do?"

"Bring him to justice. If all that means is I call the police on him, that's fine by me. He tried to frame me and I want him in jail."

"I doubt that will happen. More likely, one or both of you will end up dead."

"Why do you say that?"

"You must have already reasoned that this man works for at least one of the colony's Founding Families, possibly many others. They're protecting him and they're not going to turn him over to you or the police. Up here, the police are less powerful than the Families. Up here, the government is the largest megacorp, more powerful than any other."

"All I want is to know where he is or how to get to him."

"I'll give you his address."

"Address? You found his address?"

"Yes," 300 said, still eating his soup.

"How did you find that?"

"That's my secret, Mr. Cruz. The Pythagoras Society believes no problem is without a solution. We had his description, his profession, his world of residence. That was all we needed to locate him, but you will soon find out why knowing where he lives doesn't really matter when he's being protected."

"I'll take care of that."

"You do know he knows you're here, and those protecting him do too."

"Of course."

"What do you plan to do when they come for you?"

"Shoot 'em."

"This isn't Earth, Mr. Cruz. Guns are not the toys of choice here."

"What do you do here on Lunar Colony, Mr. 300?"

"Why should I tell you?"

"Mr. 300, I've known that the killer was probably from the Moon. How did I know? When he killed my client in front of me, I saw a unique tattoo on one of his wrists. I'm somewhat of a student of the tattoo arts. It often ties in with the criminal world. The tattoo was from one of the Up-Top crime gangs, specifically here on the Moon. Every criminal who wishes to survive has to be affiliated with a gang or crime family. On Earth, you can be a solo player, but not Up-Top.

"Right now, I'm a solo player here, Mr. 300. The killer is either part of a crime family or affiliated with one, which means I'll have to go to them first. I need to know how you know where he is because, as a solo player, I'm not about to proceed any further without knowing how you know his whereabouts. I know he knows I'm here. He even called me on Earth from my secretary's mobile—a mobile she'd just bought. I'm not walking into any traps. Are you IQ geniuses really smart, or did his crime family feed you the information? So I'd be the dummy and walk right into their trap and never be seen again."

"No need to worry, Mr. Cruz. Though your extra caution is more than warranted. I work for Dome Security. Census, in fact. My colleagues sent me all the details of your client's murder. I reviewed the flight manifest of every passenger who arrived the day of the murder and the next day. I found him and know of him. Though I did not know he was the infamous Three-Armed Man. He has a reputation in the underbelly of the Moon. For the first time, thanks to you, we know his identity. Not that it matters."

"My lucky day. A bona fide identity. Which crime family or gang is he with?"

"The location of your Three-Armed Man is for free. Anything more will have to be at my consultative rate. Prices up here tend to be far beyond those you're accustomed to down on Earth."

"Yeah, I know I couldn't afford you. But as a colonist and me the naive Earther, if I were to ask which Family would benefit from the Moon Monarchs being in disarray...?"

"I might answer that question for anyone else in conversation, but not you. You're dangerous enough to make use of such information. Go after your Three-Armed Man, then go back home to Earth. Anything more and you definitely will not return to Earth, even with your Interpol benefactors."

CHAPTER 48

White Shadow

Seraff confirmed that Mr. 300 was part of Moon Dome Security, though he wouldn't tell me his real name.

"He's your CI, Cruz, but you don't trust him?" Seraff asked me on my secure vid-phone.

"I verify whenever I can."

"Your Mr. 300 is legit."

"I wonder what a genius like him does for Dome Security?" I asked.

"He designs better security, but that's all I can say."

"What advice do you have for me?"

"Cruz, you're going to do what you've already planned to do."

It was a good attempt at deflection. What he meant to say was that he wanted me on the Moon to do what Interpol felt I already planned to do. I was, after all, here courtesy of them.

Day two of my "vacation" on the Moon, and the awe of the place was starting to wear off. Moonbeam told me that it might happen after a week, but I was feeling it now. Despite the huge planet dome, I was feeling claustrophobic. Psychologically, I felt I was in a box, a box of tremendous size, but still a box. I also missed the rain of Earth.

I pushed the nostalgic feelings out of my mind because I was about to enter one of the "smaller" bio-domes. Now, the "fun" was about to begin, meaning danger. But I had one more important thing to do.

Moonville. That was its name. Was that its name when it was first created? I had entered, for the first time, the not-so-nice part of the Lunar Colonies, where more illegal things happened than legal. The people around me looked like clones with wigs instead of real hair, but more dark colors here. The "day" light not as bright. It reminded me of the Shadow Market on Earth. Here too, the streets were noisy and flashy; sidewalk hustlers were everywhere watching people who passed by. I had entered the Shadow Market of the Moon, the shopping center for the criminal class. I saw young people, mostly men, standing on every corner watching with their augmented-reality glasses—lookouts. I thought it strange that an entire bio-dome allowed crime, but they had a great front. Gambling. Dance clubs. Fight clubs. Just like on Earth. The legitimate entertainment business was the shield for the illegitimate business behind the scenes. I realized that I finally felt...comfortable. I was in my element. I knew criminals, even though I wasn't one. The wealthy set I didn't know, unless they were criminals too.

My contact was someone named White Shadow. Moonbeam and his associates had set up the meet. As they told me in Shanty Town on Earth, White Shadow would find me. I strolled down the neon streets and felt a presence, turned and there he was. Or was he a she? He was a Caucasian with bleached white short hair, dark shades so I couldn't see his eyes, and a one piece turtleneck outfit, all black down to the tips of his shoes. I couldn't tell what kind of fabric it was because it looked like it was painted onto his body. Then he had a white jacket on, long-sleeves but the jacket part only went down to the middle of his back. I wasn't sure if he was a he because the facial features could have been feminine or masculine.

"Follow me," he said in a raspy voice.

He ducked around a corner and I followed. At the end of an alleyway were a group of large men, dressed similarly, except they had normal, black hair or were bald. There were about a half dozen of them standing outside a door. One of the thugs had two large briefcases in each hand.

White Shadow nodded. The thug with the cases set them down on the ground, and they all opened and walked through the door into whatever establishment it was—from the noise it sounded like some gambling joint. The door closed.

I handed White Shadow a card from my pocket.

"Moonbeam sends his thanks," I said.

"Moonbeam and I are even. How are you going to pay me?"

"We handled that already."

"But you didn't pay my delivery fee yet." White Shadow gave me a smirk.

"I just get to the Moon, and already someone is trying to shake me down. We paid you. Now you're trying to change the terms after the fact. I don't like that."

"I'm not changing any terms, because we never agreed to anything before. I know Moonbeam. I don't know you."

"What do you want me to do? I need the briefcases and I'm not leaving here without them. We paid for them. Moonbeam said I could trust you."

"Moonbeam lied."

"Moonbeam didn't lie. You're lying. What do you want me to do?"

"Pay my delivery fee."

"We already paid, and I just got here to the Moon. You were supposed to rent my hotel room too."

"That's taken care of too. Nice hotel. Good view of the space mountains."

"Obviously, I'm not walking around with money in my pocket, and you didn't tell me how much this delivery fee is."

"Relax. I don't deal in money, Mr. Cruz. I deal in favors."

"Favors? I don't like the sound of that."

"The last time Moonbeam was here, he needed backup. Who do you think put that backup together for him? From what I hear you'll need the same services. The lone gunman macho-thing doesn't work up here on the Moon. Do you have someone else who'll watch your back, or do you intend to watch your front, back, sides, above, below, all at once?"

"You'll be my guardian angel?" I asked.

"Yes."

"In exchange for what?"

"I keep you alive and I'll think of something of equal value."

"Do you know who I'm going up against?"

"Yeah."

"Why would you be my bodyguard knowing that?"

"Bored."

"Really, why?"

"My motives are my own. All you need to know is that it's important to me and my associates that you stay alive and investigate."

"Who's paying for your bodyguard services for me? Moonbeam and his associates don't have that kind of money. So who's paying? I want to know so I know who to send a snazzy thank-you card and gift basket for Christmas."

White Shadow chuckled. "Why ask why? You got friends."

"Lucky me. All these friends I've never met popping out from moon craters all over the place."

I was like a celebrity. I had all these friends on the Moon who wanted to help me—Moonbeam, Seraff, Mr. 300, now White Shadow. With all these wonderful friends I was stacking up, who needed enemies?

CHAPTER 49

Gist

Moonbeam and company rented me a hotel room in the center of the main dome's tourist district, but I wouldn't be staying there. In fact, I wouldn't be going anywhere near the hotel. I took monorail public transportation to a very nice residential area in the main dome and moon-walked, with my two briefcases, to a mansion in particular. The neighborhood was street after street of dome-shaped houses, complete with synthetic lawns and white picket fences. The streets here weren't the multi-city-block-long, fifty-to-one-hundred-feet-wide streets I was accustomed to in Metropolis. These were pedestrian streets with sidewalk areas lining the edges with lots of palm trees. For a people who often made jokes about our dirty planet, they sure went to a lot of trouble to make it seem like you were on Earth. I reached my accommodations—a large, bluish dome mansion. Around the side, there was a single guesthouse that would be home for my time on the Moon. Everything was biometrics and digital Up-Top. The door recognized me before I was even ten feet away and unlocked.

Inside the guesthouse was better than a hotel room. Spacious, clean, uncluttered, all white except for blue carpeting. In the bedroom, my two suitcases rested on the side of the master bed. There was a living room area, dining area, sitting room, and kitchen. One door in the sitting room led down to a private exercise room. Another door in the kitchen led to the rooftop lounge area. There were lots of plants in the place—potted plants, bamboo-like plants, flower arrangements. Plants of any kind made Metropolitans nervous. We didn't have them because they attracted infestations of mites and, my personal panic attack maker, isopods. But the Moon supposedly had no vermin, humans excluded. Except for the plants, Dot would have loved the place, but I'd make it up to her, and this wasn't a vacation.

The room also had a large secret floor safe, which was where my two briefcases went as I lifted back part of the carpeting. I knew I'd be up the rest of the day and all night familiarizing myself with all my new toys.

Run-Time had introduced us, I solved his case, his international and interspace cargo transportation company was bought out, and now Mr. Gist was living the good life on the Moon. He agreed to put me up for my stay without hesitation. I'm sure it also had to do with wanting to hang out with another Earther. He'd have to make friends fast because I'd only be here for a short period, and most of that time I'd be working.

He was sitting in the main house in front of a bank of TVs watching all kinds of sports games simultaneously while eating pizza and drinking alcohol. I joined him for a pizza lunch. It was so good.

"You're getting around like a pro," Gist said, his eyes glued to the TVs. "It took me some time to get used to not having a hovercar. Only the police can have autonomous flying craft. Not even a hovercab. You have to walk and use public transportation for everything. Even the food delivery guy uses public transportation."

"I am getting used to it. Public transportation works fine and makes sense here Up-Top."

"More likely a way for the government to keep an eye on everyone more easily."

"Government does the same on Earth. It's the same all over. Is this real pizza toppings or some genetically engineered mystery meat?"

"It's not real meat, if that's what you're asking."

"I don't have a problem with mystery meat. I had some from Mars."

"Mars? How?"

"One of my cases. Martians came to Earth and they had food with them."

"You ate their food."

"It was good."

"That might be living too dangerously for me. You get to work with all types of interesting people. Any time you're on the Moon again, you can stay in the guest house. I have more room than I need. I lucked out with this house. The family moved to Earth, which is almost unheard of."

"And you moved up here. A nice swap."

"I've had a string of luck starting with you. Solved my case, I get a big payoff, I get my dream home on the Moon."

"You're living like a king, Mr. Gist. Doesn't the Moon have real royalty?"

"You mean the Moon Monarchs?"

Mr. Gist didn't know much. He may have been a new resident of the Moon, but he was an Earther like me. I probably know more about Lunar Colony than he ever would know. He was going to live like royalty and nothing more for the rest of his life. What he allowed me to do was stay at a place where I'd be safe and could defend myself if needed. It was my sanctuary away from Earth, and that's what I needed.

Later, when I returned to the guesthouse, there was one thing I had to do before going through my new weapons. I called the hotel where I had my rented hotel room and the front desk connected me to my voice messages. There were no voice messages, but there were forty-two missed calls. Either someone really, really wanted to speak with me, but didn't want to leave a message, or a lot of people wanted to talk to me. I'd rent a disposable phone the next day and forward the hotel line to it, but, again, I was going nowhere near that hotel.

Tomorrow I began my work. Not the hunt for my target yet. I had to lay the foundation first to get to him, especially knowing he knew I was here. Maybe one of the missed calls at my hotel room was from him.

CHAPTER 50

Moon Cops

Because I was playing around with my new Up-Top weapons, I had only gotten two hours sleep. I had an all-weapon concealed weapons license in Metropolis; I was on the Moon. If I carried and got caught by the police, I would be arrested, and unlike Metropolis I had no hovercar to stash my weapons in. Being in prison on the Moon was no more desirable than being in a cell on Earth. I agreed with Gist, I wasn't liking this public transportation-only lifestyle of the Moon. It was interfering with the way I did business.

Gist lived in District Seven, but I didn't take the nearest transport hub. I moon-walked for a hell of a long time. It's on streets you got to know a place: the kind of people, how they lived, did the neighborhood change from section to section. As I walked for the better part of an hour, there were parts of the districts I passed through where I felt that no one had walked on its pavement for years or more. People didn't do what I did. They walked to a transport hub, maybe to a neighbor's house, but never their own district. Lines of people walked to the nearest rail stop. Monorails flew by or stopped above. The districts were all very orderly—living, work, and play.

I finally got on at a rail stop in District Fifty-One. The reason I picked the stop was because of its number. The passenger cars were spotless. The one I was on had a few other people with me—a young couple and a woman. I sat and stared out the window as the transport departed at the buildings and the massive projection sky of the bio-dome.

My eyes studied everything I saw outside the monorail's window as it sped by. We had a few monorails left on Earth, but they were centuries old and servicing only a few districts. One day they'd be shut down, but the politicians had been saying that for more decades than anyone could remember.

I saw the first one after I had been on the monorail for fifteen minutes. An elongated hovercar with front wings and a dorsal rudder. The craft was flying alongside of us about twenty feet away. I ignored it, and soon it dropped back and disappeared.

Gist was lucky to have found a home so close to the center of the city. That's where I was returning to. District Two. What I learned as I sat and watched was that the lower the numbered district, the larger it was in size.

When the monorail stopped at District Two, I was already standing to get off. Nearby was the white hovercruiser. Waiting and looking straight at me were three police officers. Clad in white body-armored uniforms, with thick belts, and wearing sturdy white caps.

"Are you Mr. Cruz?" one of them asked.

"Yes."

"Passport please."

I handed one of them my document from my jacket, while another scanned my body with a hand device. He was satisfied. The one with my passport scanned it with his gloved palm, then handed it back to me.

"Thank you for your cooperation, sir," the lead officer said.

I had to bite my tongue to keep from saying something that would certainly get me in trouble. I put my passport back into my jacket and floated away. I glanced back occasionally. They were very interested in me. In moments, I was around the corner and gone.

A long time ago, I learned that the data terminals on Earth weren't connected to Up-Top. Off-worlders could access our information databases, I was told, but we couldn't get into theirs. I was on the Moon and learned it was all true. I needed to do a lot of research like any good detective, and the Moon had plenty of digital cafés. I found one called the Data Dungeon. Cyberpunks on Earth had told me about it, and I saw why. It was like a dungeon all right, but ground level, bleak, barren, brownish walls, ceilings and floors—very un-Up-Top-ish. However, each computer terminal booth was in its own crater-like alcove in the ground, well lit, all-white, multiple screens, plush work chairs, people wearing computer glasses and ear devices for their music or audiobooks. But it was a café too, so baristas were busy keeping the beverages flowing. The hourly rental rates were outrageous, but I was sure it was cheaper than if I were in the center of the touristy main city. The clientele were a cross of older adults and teenagers.

My task was simple. Find out everything I could in the public domain about the Moon Monarchs and all the other Founding Families that I didn't even know existed. I learned all the history there was to know, including the political tensions that existed, like how the Lunar Colonies were kept from expanding from a fifty-year coalition of the Space Colonies, Earth and Mars.

I'd been in the place for hours when I saw them. The two of them walked in with silver hoodies and dark shades. They didn't see me from my below-ground work area "crater." What were the odds of this happening?

I locked my terminal and climbed up the steps of my crater. When I walked out of the computer café, I looked around. There they were as I'd expected—the same lunar police hovercruiser. I approached the craft and it opened. The same officers stepped out.

"Are you three on duty or slumming on the people's time?"

"What does that mean exactly, sir?"

"Follow me. You have two arrests to make."

"Arrests of who?" a second officer asked.

"Give me a palm device and I'll pull them up."

The officers looked at each other. One reluctantly gave me his. I typed in the names. My two "friends" had plenty of media stories about them on the newsfeed.

"Ms. Hertz and Mr. Hollo. The CFO and Chief Security Officer wanted by Metropolis Police for suspicion of murder in the death of the CEO of the Bio-Matters Company. They should be on your extradition list. Let's go get 'em before they run off."

I waltzed back into the Data Dungeon with three lunar policemen behind me. Immediately, everyone in the computer café looked up at us. Hollo saw us first and almost dropped his cup. Hertz turned around from where she was sitting. We walked to them.

"Hello Ms. Hertz, Mr. Hollo," I said. "How are you two lovebirds enjoying Lunar Colony? I'm sorry your trip has to be cut short so you can be sent back to Earth to go to jail."

"How did you find us?" Hollo yelled.

"Find. I wasn't looking for you. I was working in the corner there for hours. You two walked in wearing your bad disguises, and I did my civic human duty and called the cops on you."

"You're the one who should be in jail!" Hertz yelled at me.

"Yeah, yeah. When you get back to Earth you can tell the prosecution all about it."

"We didn't kill Accent," Hollo said, standing up.

"That's not what Ms. Sage is saying."

"What?" Ms. Hertz stood up.

"The day my Earth case was dismissed and I went back to Metro PD to see my police friends. She was there saying you two were behind it all."

"What?" they both yelled.

"The embezzlement and murdering Mr. Accent."

"She was the one who said we should go on the run!" Hertz yelled.

"That lying, conniving—" Ms. Hertz began.

Hertz and Hollo couldn't stop yelling and cursing as the three lunar police took them both into custody. With the low gravity of the Moon, all the police had to do was reach down and lift them up as if they weighed less than thirty pounds, because...they did.

I'd finished my research and even managed to make a few calls from my rented workspace. Always take full advantage of a window of opportunity. I was probably being watched by others, but as the officers took their two suspects back to their hovercruiser, I shut down, packed up, and disappeared out the back door of the café before the officers' craft was in the air.

Later, I learned that the Data Dungeon was not the choice of computer cafés for the real Lunar Colonists. Only Earthers used it. We all thought we were going to a secluded, authentic data café when, in fact, only Earthers were there. I was drawn there because of cyberpunk contacts. Hertz and Hollo were drawn there because of their corporate contacts. They were researching how to live off the grid and evade Earth authorities with all their stolen cash. Unlucky for them, they happened upon me.

My all-day work sessions continued the next day. I was sure the three lunar police who kept watch over me were wondering why I was living at the Data Dungeon. What could I be researching? they were asking themselves. Seraff probably was expecting to get some kind of reports about me, but instead nothing. Gist's guesthouse to the Data Dungeon and back. For the next four days that was all I did. But that was part of my plan. I was sure everyone monitoring my every move was saying the same thing. "Do something already, Earthling!"

Tomorrow, I'd begin to cause trouble.

PART EIGHT

Utopia Syndrome

CHAPTER 51

Pinwheel

The landscape looked exactly like the natural surface of the Moon. There were dancers in white vintage American astronaut suits and red vintage cosmonaut suits. Bikini-clad models were dancing with them. Everyone laughing, dancing, and jumping to the beat of the loud pop music with the faux-space background.

Pinwheel was in the center of the dancing troupe. Long, dark hair down to her back, rainbow-colored string bikini, and a tiara on her head. They had all been dancing and jumping for seemingly hours as flying cameras filmed the action from multiple angles and levels. Their linked camera operators stood further away, the director next to them. He seemed to be doing more ogling of the models than any real directing.

"We want a break, Maestro," a model said with a pouty face.

"Yes, let's go," Pinwheel said. She held the hand of an astronaut and skipped away to the director.

She laughed when they reached the "Maestro." Letting go of her astronaut dancer, she threw herself at the director. He barely caught her. She laughed again as the three men watched her strut over to me.

"You're the guy?" she asked.

"I am."

"Normally, I don't talk to strangers, but Hip-Hop said I had to talk to you," she said.

She walked past me. I got up from my seat to follow her. The studio was filled with spectators, crew, and catering.

"How do you know Hip-Hop?" she asked.

"Friend. He did a few performance shows for me. I did a few favors for him."

"Now he's doing another favor for you. The world spins 'round and 'round."

She was like an overgrown adolescent the way she acted and spoke. We walked to a trailer, the door opened and she skipped up the steps. Inside was like a posh hotel suite. No bed but an entire lounge sitting area around a pool—the trailer was that big. She dropped down on one of the chairs.

"Maestro doesn't give us a lot of time for breaks, so you have that long. What's your name again? I forgot already."

"Call me Cruz," I said.

"Is that a commoner name?"

"Yeah, but I'm cool."

She laughed. "Hip-Hop says you are, but I don't know."

I sat in the chair next to her and handed her a photo.

She sat up and took it. "What's this?"

"Can I tell you a story?"

She stared at the photo with a confused look.

"Well, the story goes like this. There was this guy. A royal family member of one of the original Founding Families of Lunar Colony. He was brilliant. He would have been its next ruler. But then he disappeared. Never to be seen again. Decades later he was found on Earth. Living the life of a megacorp executive. He worked his way up to the top with no help from anyone. The Family found out and he was killed. Killed by a man with three arms. A contract killer. The question isn't who ordered the contract, but why? Only the Family knows that."

"Who's this woman?"

"That's his girlfriend. They had a happy life on Earth until someone on this white rock ended it."

"What does your story have to do with me?

"Why does the Artemis Family hate the Moon Monarchs so much?"

She said nothing as she watched me suspiciously.

"You don't have to answer," I said, "but I'll give you another reason to hate them. They're trying to pin the murder of their heir on the Artemis Family."

"How would they do that, Mr. Cruz?" Pinwheel wasn't the carefree adolescent of thirty-going-on-thirteen anymore. She was a cold, sneering member of the Moon Monarch's rival Family, Artemis.

"It was part of Apollo Four's plot from the beginning. They didn't think I'd get out of their frame job on Earth. I was supposed to be in prison, locked away. They tried to frame my attorney too—the plan was to move her out of the picture too, so I wouldn't have counsel. Then a story would be planted that I was supposedly working for Artemis. That I didn't witness this Three-Armed Man killing Apollo Five. The story would be I led the Three-Armed Man into Apollo Five's home to be killed. Then, probably, money tied to the Artemis Family would show up in my bank account, or a secret one in my name."

Pinwheel rose, shaking; she was so enraged but managed to softly say, "That is a lie."

"I know it is, but we need to get to the Three-Armed Man before they do. That's our proof of their plot."

"I know all about you, Mr. Cruz."

"Do you?"

"You leave this instant. I've already called my guards."

"Is that why you were tapping your index finger and thumb together like that?"

"Mr. Cruz, we know where you're staying. Who you've talked to. Where you've been."

"You've been busy."

I heard the sound of a nozzle engine. My ears had already learned to pick them out. A thug in a suit appeared, floating above the ground. My omega-gun blasted him back out of the trailer.

"How did you get that weapon into the colony?" she yelled.

"Tell them to stop." I pointed my weapon at her.

She raised her hand as six more thugs flew into the trailer. They stopped in midair.

"Why are you fighting me?" I snapped at her.

"Why approach me with this story now?" she asked. "You've been on Lunar Colony for five days. Why now?"

"I've never been on the Moon before. I had to find out who to trust."

"You trust us?"

"No. I trust that you hate the Moon Monarchs more than me. You've been at it a lot longer."

My words made her think.

"I need to think," she said then dove out of the trailer. It was a motion I'd seen other Moon people do. They'd propel themselves through the air as if swimming through it.

"Don't think too long!" I yelled. "We need to find the Three-Armed Man before they do."

The thugs followed after her and grabbed the other thug I stunned from the ground.

CHAPTER 52

Moon Mother

There was no chance I'd be let back into my place by the wife without them. I had to take photos of them. Ahead of me was the Pyramids on the Moon—the official residence of the Moon Monarchs. Cruz Jr. wanted me to get him "Moon" toys, including a pyramid replica. Stunning didn't adequately describe the massive structures etched with hieroglyphics. The monorail transportation dropped me off at its main steps, I got out, and climbed up. My head tilted back to the very tip. The building was possibly one hundred or more stories. Nothing as tall as in Metropolis but buildings on the Moon were normally no taller than fifty stories.

At the top of the steps were abnormally tall security guards, all wearing red fez hats. I didn't think I'd see another fez for a while after my last major case.

When I reached them, I said, "Mr. Cruz to see the Moon Monarchs."

"Do you have an appointment?" one of them asked.

"No, but they'll see me."

"Are the authorities waiting for you?" he asked.

I turned to see my three lunar police "friends" had landed in their hovercraft.

"No, they're my official escorts."

"Wait here, sir."

One of the guards went inside, or he disappeared through the wall. I imagined it was some kind of holo-door. About a dozen of the guards clustered in front of me.

The first guard returned.

"Sorry, sir, but they are not receiving guests. The Monarchs are busy people. You must have an appointment. Call the pyramid office at your convenience."

"Tell them I know who's behind the murder of the heir apparent to the Moon Monarch Family. Tell them I intend to bring these conspirators in the murder of Apollo Michelangelo Five to justice. They can either work with me or against me. Their decision. Tell them that."

The first guard looked at me with a red face. "The Earthling is giving orders."

"Yeah, the Earth man. My little kids are Earthlings. I'm an Earth man. Tell them, please. I'll wait, as will my escorts."

The guards glanced at the lunar police at the bottom of the steps.

"Wait here, sir."

He disappeared again through the holo-door.

The tech to make nozzle jets silent must have existed, but no one wanted them to be silent. At first, I didn't know what was coming at me from behind the holo-door, then they came through. I'd memorized the photos of all the Founding Families of the Lunar Colonies. The Moon Mother herself, the mother of Apollo Five, my client Mr. Prince. Tall, muscle-bound guards surrounded her. How many barbell presses would one have to do on a low-gravity planetoid to get a chest as big as theirs? Their physique was too perfect, so I assumed they were all implants. All of them in white suits with crimson fezes on their bald heads and beards.

She floated inches from me and stopped. Her gaudy white and crimson dress was draped in golden jewels. Her hairstyle was that of an ancient Egyptian empress, dark hair to her chest, heavy eye makeup, and some kind of golden crown.

"Who killed my son, if not you?" she asked me in a raspy voice.

Through the holo-door appeared the Twins, Apex and Nadir, with their own entourage of guards.

"I will answer your question for a question."

"Make it a good one, and answer first."

"You know the answer. A Three-Armed Man from the Lunar Colonies."

"Who sent him?"

"Who would stand to profit from chaos in the Moon Monarch Family? Artemis. It is why I've been quiet all these days. It keeps coming back to them."

The matriarch's face flushed with anger.

"I need to find that Three-Armed Man before they do," I said.

The Twins moved closer as I handed a photo to the Moon Mother.

"This was your son's girlfriend. For all you know, she would have been your daughter-in-law. What happened to Apollo Five offends me to the core. You can believe that. Will you help me get the mutant who took him away from all of you?"

The Moon Mother blinked her eyes, as if to keep from crying. "I loved my son dearly. I was devastated when he disappeared all those years ago. I know why he did. This life isn't for most. I missed him every day. I never had a chance to say goodbye. And now I will never have the chance to say anything to him ever again."

"What do you want, Cruz?" the Moon Mother asked. "My niece and nephew told me what you said about this mutant. Others have told me you lie."

"I need to know about the black-market genetic engineering market."

"That will help you find him?"

"Yes, but I must move quickly. Artemis is watching me too."

She looked at one of her guards. "Give him the information he requests."

The guard nodded as the Moon Mother rose up in the air, inches from the ground, to turn and float back through the holo-door with all her guards hovering after her. One guard remained. He handed me a thick, metal-like card. In moments, a name and address appeared, along with a phone number.

He flew back into the pyramid too.

"Where's Apollo Four?" I asked the twins. "Lost interest in finding out who killed your uncle, Apollo Five, so quickly?"

"We should talk inside," Nadir said.

"I'm not going inside your pyramid. Weren't pyramids in history really symbols of death and big, fancy crypts? I don't want to become a space mummy. But you can call me at my hotel."

"The hotel you're not staying at," Apex said. "You don't care about our uncle's murder."

"Exactly what I say about you two. But it's my actions, not yours, that tell the truth. The man I knew as Prince didn't deserve to die the way he did. All you two did was go to his funeral. I'm the one making sure his killer is brought to justice."

"What makes you think we won't do the same?" Nadir yelled at me.

"Why aren't you?" I asked him.

"A contract killer like that could hide for years on the Moon and—"

Apex restrained him.

"Ignore him," she said to her brother. "We don't need him to do what we must do."

They floated back through the holo-door too. The image disappeared and it was a solid rock wall.

CHAPTER 53

Java

In the detective biz, major clues didn't jump out in front of you with a flashing light and a megaphone yelling, "Hey Detective, this is the most important thing." Key revelations in a case were often subtle, easily missed, seemingly unimportant, but you had to be ever-vigilant to spot them. As an "Earthling," I made the same assumption that probably everyone else on Earth made. That there was only one major Founder Family of the Moon. The pioneer Family that ushered in human civilization on the Moon. It was the Moon Monarchs, wasn't it? Well, it wasn't the whole truth. That was what my casual conversation with Seraff revealed. The Moon Monarchs were only one of the Founding Families of the big white rock in orbit around Earth. The Moon Monarchs and Artemis were the leading ones, but there were a dozen such families that made the Lunar Colonies a reality centuries ago. The Moon Monarchs and Artemis weren't just rival Families. They almost went to war with each other. Their hate was as old as the very first Lunar Colony. Such facts meant that far more suspects were possible in the murder of my client, Prince.

The Moon Mother was royalty all right. Members like her were deceptively calm on the outside. Internally, you'd never know what emotions were raging, good or bad. Everything I said was already known to her. The Artemis Family could have been behind her son's murder. The media on the Moon was no different than Metropolis; they had their versions of Holly Live too. The rumor mill was wild with speculation and conspiracies, just as Moonbeam told me. Who killed Apollo Five? The Moon Monarchs? The Artemis Family? The mutant underground? Earth? Martians? The other Founding Families of the Moon? It was endless. My days of research at the Data Dungeon revealed that I wasn't even in the top ten of murder suspects of Apollo Five. But the Moon Mother, the Twins, and Apollo Four were.

In that backdrop of suspicions, I felt comfortable investigating the Moon Monarch's lead. I hopped back onto public transportation, knowing my lunar police "escorts" were never too far away.

Their motto was "Reimagine Humanity." I didn't like it. Who was doing the "reimagining," and did those who were "reimagined" have any say in the matter? The glass building that housed Re-You Inc. was also a pyramid. Their corporate information said they were privately owned, and their board of directors listing was private.

I arrived and was led by a woman in a silky white dress down to her ankles. I wasn't quite clear how she walked. She left me in a conference room bigger than my entire apartment on Earth.

The woman who came in was definitely a zero-baby. Her arms looked like they were made out of rubber. She was presentable in her silver business attire, short blonde hair, pleasant. We sat at the corner of the conference table.

"Thank you for seeing me so quickly, Ms. Java."

"We are always happy to help the Monarch Family."

"Do they own Re-You?"

"No. We are privately held."

"Did the Moon Monarchs tell you what my inquiry is about?"

"Yes, illegal genetics. Understand, Mr. Cruz, that genetic editing, as with the entire biotech industry, is strictly regulated on Lunar Colony."

"That's a new term. Same as genetic engineering or manipulation."

"Same thing."

"Regulated, but there's an illegal market?"

"I don't think so, Mr. Cruz. Lunar Colony isn't seething with human life like your planet. Such activities would be quickly found out and shut down. The risk would be too great."

"I encountered a Three-Armed Man."

"Yes, I was told. Why do you assume such a person is from Lunar Colony, or anywhere in Utopia?"

"He's here."

"Even if so, that doesn't mean he is a Lunar citizen or is the product of genetic engineering. Your planet does have a subculture known as biopunks, low-tech bio-splicing. It's not even genetic engineering or any legitimate science. Simple cut and paste."

"Yes, I know. I've met them. This Three-Armed Man wasn't a bio-punk. I'm certain of it. And his third arm wasn't a bio-splice."

"Interesting. Without seeing for myself, I couldn't even speculate."

"What does Re-You do?"

"We make humanity better. Off-world can be a harsh place. The war against human defects and diseases is a never-ending battle for science."

"You make designer people."

"No, Mr. Cruz. That's illegal. A myth. You can't pick hair or eye color, or height, or even gender. That's not what we do, or anyone else."

"We thought you did do that."

"There are many myths about life here, off-world. None of which is true. But you said a man with three arms. That's quite a bit removed from trait selection of biological offspring."

"A mutant, Ms. Java?"

Java hesitated. "Another myth."

"But is it? I've heard quite a few things."

"What have you heard exactly, Mr. Cruz?"

"Things."

"What things?"

"This Three-Armed Man is a mutant. When my informant told me that, I thought of genetic freaks, but he said something interesting. He said think of mutants as superheroes. Powers? Is that what we're talking about?"

"Mr. Cruz, no such thing exists. It's a myth."

"But there is an illegal black geneticist market?"

"Hard to do, since it doesn't exist. Mr. Cruz, your informant was leading you down the stray path. Off-world, all biogeneticists of any level are watched. They are considered members of a profession that can be a threat to national security. Designer people are strictly prohibited, despite the Earth propaganda to the contrary. Off-worlders had these ethical battles centuries ago. We had designer people back then. It became a serious problem then, a threat. We resolved it by outlawing all of it. Genetic editing is a strictly regulated practice today and the penalties for non-adherence are quite severe, Mr. Cruz, even by Earth standards."

"Are you saying that geneticists or genetic engineers or genetic editors—"

"All mean the same, Mr. Cruz."

"You're saying none of them would be left to run around unmonitored."

"When it comes to human bio-gens? No. Even if your man with three arms exists, he wasn't born here, he wasn't created here. Mr. Cruz, why is your focus on the Moon's bio-gens? Why not Earth? The Space Colonies and Mars have genetic editors and engineers too. I don't believe their monitoring regime is as robust as ours."

I smiled. "The Earthlings or the Martians did it, then?"

"Or the Spacies."

"This is interesting, Ms. Java. Trait selection was allowed in the past."

She was very slow to answer me. "It was, but that was a very long time ago, before we outlawed it."

"So all the perfect people I see roaming the Lunar Colonies are simply the descendants of the genetically perfect people of yesteryear."

"If you wish to think of it like that, yes. It was practiced and ceased ages ago. Neither one of us was born yet. What does it matter? It's illegal now."

"Sorry to make you uncomfortable, Ms. Java. I'm from Earth so I don't know the history of things up here."

"It's quite all right. I was told you are also assisting Interpol."

"Yes, they're allowing me to continue my investigation that began on Earth."

"A long way to come for an investigation."

"This Three-Armed Man killed my client and tried to frame me for it."

"I was told that."

"I'm sorry for this question, but it's important. Could one of the major megacorps on Lunar Colony conduct illegal genetic activities without anyone knowing about it?"

"Absolutely not. That is a very serious charge, Mr. Cruz. Which megacorp would you think capable of such a thing?"

"I don't know. That's why I ask."

"But why ask that?"

"To see if you believe it's possible."

"It's not."

"Well, I do know where he lives."

"Where who lives?"

"The Three-Armed Man."

"This person is real, and you know where he is?"

"Yes, I've known since I got to the Moon."

"Why haven't you told the authorities?"

"The authorities can't do anything until there's proof. Re-You is the only genetic bio-tech firm on the Moon. Is that right?"

"Precisely."

"So if there isn't an illegal market on the Moon, and you're the only legal market, then the Three-Armed Man could have been created by Re-You?"

Java slowly stood.

"As I said earlier, any number of places, including your planet, could be home to a supposed illegal geneticist market. Re-You is a legal company and has never conducted any illegal business."

"On Earth, we have a cyborg parts registry. That's how the police can identify illegal cyborgs. Every cyborg has a list of their allowable parts by law. There are investigators who specialize in reading those microscopic identifiers. They have the equivalent profession up here, off-world. Genetic investigators. They can literally determine what firms made any gene modifications to a human. We find the Three-Armed Man, alive or dead, and we'll know."

"Then good luck with your investigation, Mr. Cruz."

"You did say that Re-You is privately held."

"Yes, I did."

"Is there a chance that it's actually owned by the Moon Monarchs?"

"None."

"You know the actual owners of Re-You."

"I do."

"The Artemis Family?"

"No."

"My suspicion was correct then."

"Excuse me. What suspicion?"

"Re-You is owned by the Lunas Family, another one of the Founding Families. If that's true and this contract killer was created by Re-You, then that leads to all kinds of unpleasant questions. Founding Families assassinating heir apparents of other Families, and trying to frame their rival Families."

"No!"

Java flew out of the conference room as fast as she could. I felt the sudden desire to get out of the building as quickly as possible.

CHAPTER 54

White Shadow

White Shadow called me on my mobile. I was riding public transportation again. I could always find a car that was virtually empty.

"There are some guys at your friend's house," he told me.

"What are they doing?"

"Looking around the main house and the guesthouse."

"Make them go away."

"We're doing that. Where's your friend?"

"He's on vacation. I told him to lock up the main house and come back when we have everything wrapped up."

"Good thing you did that. I'll have to call you back." White Shadow suddenly hung up.

He called back five minutes later and didn't look happy.

"Cruz, are you crazy?"

"What happened?"

"The guys are with the Lunas Corporation."

"And?"

"And? Do you know what the Lunas Corporation is called up here?"

"How would I? I'm from Earth."

"They're called the Lunatic Corporation. They're gangsters. They have legit business but lots more criminal operations."

"Why doesn't someone do something about them then?"

"I'm sorry, Cruz, have you Earthers eliminated all crime on Earth?"

"I apologize, that was uncalled for."

"Yes, it was. I'm helping you out, remember."

"And I appreciate it. One day you'll tell me why."

"One day."

"Where are the guys?"

"Cruz, their CEO wants to meet you now."

"Meet me?"

"Now."

"I need to tell you something."

"What's that, Cruz?"

"Lunas Corp is housing the Three-Armed Man."

"The contract killer you're hunting?"

"Yes."

"How do you know that?"

"I just do."

"Then don't go. It's a trap."

"It might not be."

"Why do you say that?"

"Because I told the Moon Monarchs that the Artemis Family hired him to kill their heir, and I told the Artemis Family that the Moon Monarchs hired him to assassinate their heir and frame their Family. Then I told one of the associates of the Lunas Corporation that they're behind it all."

All while I said this to him, White Shadow was repeating, "Oh God."

"How should I play this?"

"Why are you asking me, Cruz?"

"Well, if I still have bodyguard service, I'll do one thing. If you hang up and lose my number, then I have to play it another way."

"Cruz, I have to talk this over with my guys. We may want to leave the Moon for a vacation ourselves. You should work for Lunas Corp. You're a lunatic too."

"How else would I get leverage to get the killer?"

"This is the plan? Do you do this kind of thing on Earth?"

"All the time. But I know exactly what I'm doing. Haven't you heard? I'm famous."

White Shadow hung up on me.

CHAPTER 55

Moonbeam and Comet

I had no choice but to wait and see if White Shadow would call me back. It wasn't time to call Seraff yet. Once I did that, it would be a grand mess and I was certain the Three-Armed Man would disappear forever. I had to get factions more powerful than his protectors to help me hunt him down. Even then, those same factions could just as easily kill me.

The one good thing was that White Shadow left a guard at my guest house. Actually, Comet was in the guesthouse. He was a huge man and sat in the center of the structure and watched TV all day from the time I left to the time I returned. When I did return he gave me a mean look. White Shadow had obviously called him.

I checked my hotel messages remotely, and only one of the many messages was of any interest. It was from Moonbeam.

Comet sat on my favorite chair in the living room, so I made my call from the bedroom. I wondered what bad news

Moonbeam had for me, as he was the one who introduced me to White Shadow in the first place.

"Moonbeam," I greeted as soon as he picked up the vid-phone on his end.

"Cruz, Cruz, Cruz."

"Is it all that bad?"

"You're not making any friends, but that's not what I'm calling you about. That guy, Hip-Hop."

"Yeah, what about him?"

"He called you a few days ago. Didn't know how to get in touch with you. Found out about me. I didn't know he was also one of these conspiracy theorists too."

"A man of many talents."

"He told me some crazy story and wanted me to pass it on to you. First I forgot, then I said it wasn't worth your time, but I remembered I'd heard similar stories when I was on the Moon."

"What story?"

"Hip-Hop said he has a few space watcher types that have all kinds of telescopes pointing at everything in the universe."

"Amateur astronomers," I said.

"Yeah, that. He said that some of his friends said that lights were seen on the far side of the Moon. Every day starting the very same day you arrived on the Moon."

"Well, I can tell you it wasn't me."

"No, you don't understand. There's not supposed to be anyone on the far side of the Moon."

"Don't spaceships or those lunar buggies go there?"

"No, Cruz, no one lives there. The conspiracy nuts are burning up their VR chat rooms that there's a secret lunar colony on the far side of the moon."

"I see why you didn't want to tell me."

"I've heard this story before, but Cruz, something's going on. Ever since you landed there. People, a lot of people, are nervous."

"I have that kind of effect. So what do you want me to do?"

"I'm not finished. Some of Hip-Hop's amateur astronomer friends also have their own satellites."

"You got to be kidding me. Satellites? Real satellites?"

"They pool their money and when legit megacorps are shooting one into space, they have them attach a camera telescope for their own use. Megacorps get a few bucks and a lot of good will. There was a satellite that was supposed to be passing by that area, on the far side of the Moon, and it's gone."

"What do you mean it's gone?"

"Gone."

"Yeah, gone." Comet's voice startled me.

He'd walked into the bedroom and handed me his tablet. I scrolled through the newsfeed and the reports were there.

"What happened to it? Blown up, crashed?"

"No one knows," Moonbeam said. "Cruz, things like this don't happen. It's an expensive satellite. Megacorps don't shoot junk up into space."

"Moonbeam, what does this have to do with me?" I asked.

"Your guy Hip-Hop wanted you to know."

"He wanted me to know because I'm here on the Moon. Why did you want me to know?"

341

"Shadow told me about what you did today," Moonbeam said.

I looked at Comet hovering over me and he shook his head in disapproval.

"Yeah. And?"

"Cruz, Lunas Corp is a shady outfit, but the orbit around the Moon is managed by each major Family and megacorp. The orbit above the far side of the Moon is run by Lunas Corp. Nothing is supposed to be there, which is why the Moon's coalition of Families allowed them to have that area. But maybe there is something there after all."

"What if there was?"

"The other Families would take away their power," Comet said. "Lunas Corp wouldn't let them."

"Moonbeam, I appreciate the info, but even if true this sounds to be beyond me hunting for my killer."

"Your Three-Armed Man may be a mutant."

"Yeah, so?"

"There have been stories of a secret mutant colony there for ages. Maybe it's real. Maybe everyone's so nervous about you being on the Moon because if you find the killer, you may find their colony."

"But I know where he is. Besides, how do you hide a dome colony from everyone?"

"I don't know."

I looked at Comet. "Call Shadow and tell him I do want to meet this Lunas Corp."

"Why would you want to do that?"

"Moonbeam, I think your instincts were right to tell me. Wasn't there a rumor about Lunar Colonists in the past wanting to create other continent colonies on the moon?"

"There were," Moonbeam answered. "The movements never went anywhere. How do you know this?"

"I've been reading."

"One of them did," Comet said. "Lunar Colony Families killed them."

"How do you know that, Comet?" Moonbeam asked him.

"Some of them were my ancestors," Comet said. The tough guy looked like he was tearing up.

"I think I need to call my contact at Interpol," I said. "You need to call Shadow. I don't think we have a lot of time with this. I may have poured a bit too much gas on the fire this time to get my bad guy."

When Mr. 300 called and left a message on my hotel voice mail, I knew why before I called him back.

"Yes, Mr. 300?"

"You know why I'm calling."

"How long ago?"

"Today. Your Three-Armed Man is gone, Mr. Cruz. It's doubtful I'll be able to find him again."

"It's okay, Mr. 300. It's not unexpected, but I have one more card to play."

"Hopefully, it's an ace."

"It is."

"Good luck in your chase. I'm hearing more and more about the Earth detective on Lunar Colony, so however it turns out, I'll read about it in the press."

"Thanks, Mr. 300. You'll read it and much more."

"Yes. But it's the much more that worries me."

CHAPTER 56

Gangsters

Valhalla was a high-class gambling bar-restaurant that looked like a giant planetarium. Above everyone's heads were all of the planets in the solar system, circling endlessly. The air had a sickly-sweet odor that reminded me of cotton candy. My pops gave me cotton candy once. Little did I know his sinister plot was to wean me off sweets. I devoured that stick of cotton candy. Laughing, smiling, then after half of it was sitting at the bottom of my stomach (I'm sure the last of it still hasn't digested) I felt sick for days. It was too sweet, too good, and I never had a speck of cotton candy ever again in my life. This place had the same sickly-sweet smell. Everyone looked high-class, expensive clothes, perfect skin, hair and teeth, to-die-for jewelry, but it was a facade. The people just looked sweet. I'd been in criminal establishments before. This one was just the nicest I'd ever seen.

"My name's Lunas," the tall, dark man said with a slight smile. A man in a suit stood on each side behind him. "Have a seat, Mr. Cruz."

I sat down, with Shadow and Comet sitting too at a table directly behind ours.

"My ancestors started our megacorp," Lunas said. "Not good enough to be a Founding Family, but we fought and died for the Moon the same as they did. I'm the seventh ruling CEO of the company."

"Can I ask you a question, Mr. Lunas?"

"Please do." He took a puff of a cigar, which I instinctively knew to be a weapon of some kind. Shadow warned me that anything in an Up-Top criminal establishment that's not air, can be a weapon—anything.

"My colleague behind me, Mr. Comet, is a descendant of those who wanted to create other Lunar Colonies. I'm just an Earther so I don't know anything about the history or the struggle."

"My family had to struggle against Earth. Your governments and megacorps wanted to take the Moon away from us. We didn't let them. Then the struggle against the Families. My ancestors weren't good enough to be Founders, but enough history. Can't live in the past when you exist in the present."

"You wanted to see me, Mr. Lunas. How can I help?"

He grinned. "You're good at this. Use conversation to disarm a potential adversary. Keep things calm. We've done a lot of checking up on you. You've put down a lot of criminal outfits on Earth, and you're one guy. I need a whole army to do that here."

"May I offer a proposal to keep things calm?"

"Please do, Mr. Cruz."

"Tell me where the Three-Armed Man is, I get him, and I hop on my rocket ship back to Earth and you never see or hear from me again."

Lunas puffed on his cigar again then chuckled. "You want me to give you one of my guys?" He turned to his men behind him. "Do we have a three-armed man working for us?"

"No, Boss," one of them said.

"Sorry, Mr. Cruz, but I have no such employee."

"I was misinformed then. What did you want to talk to me about?"

"Rumors, Mr. Cruz. I'm sure it's the same on Earth. Rumors can cause people trouble, can even get people killed. I'm told that you managed to get not one, but two Founding Families interested in my company. Everyone is asking me about this Three-Armed Man. Threatening me about him, when I have no such employee."

"It's fine."

"It's fine? Why do you say that?"

"I know where he is."

"Then what are you talking to me for? Go get him."

"You shouldn't have let him run though. You should have kept him here. Now, I have to go to the far side of the Moon to get him—literally. Mess up your entire operation."

Lunas put his cigar in his mouth. "Cruz, I—"

I never let him finish his sentence. I was no dummy. I blasted him with my omega-gun, then his two guards. Gunplay was not the Up-Top way, but it was for me. I wished there was normal gravity as I knew how to run fast, but I was on the Moon. Shadow jumped up into the air and Comet pushed me. I flew back, more than ten feet, and fell. The entire establishment erupted in utter pandemonium as people flew like superheroes for the main entrance. I got to my feet. Comet was fighting two thugs with the nastiest laser daggers I'd ever seen.

I screamed so loud that I dropped my omega-gun, something I'd never done before. My jacket was burning up in flame. I saw the one doing it, another thug pointing some device at me. Shadow landed in front of him and sliced off his arm with his own laser dagger. I grabbed my weapon from the ground, flicked the switch, and began firing. The explosive rounds were reducing tables, chairs, everything to nothing. I aimed another near Comet and knocked the growing army he was fighting off their feet.

Suddenly, I felt myself being lifted off the floor. Shadow was flying us out of the place with a sleek jetpack fitted to his chest. Comet had his own and was flying right behind us.

A blast knocked us all out of the air. I was glad I was only thirty pounds because we hit the wall hard. The three of us dropped to the floor.

I sat up slowly and saw the establishment was empty of customers, but filled instead with thugs in suits aiming long guns at us.

Lunas stepped through them to us. I fired. My blast bounced right off him. I'd never seen that before. Did they have personal force fields Up-Top? Then I saw his eyes open wide, really wide, almost if his eyes had grown in size. His teeth clenched. The CEO gangster looked like a monster.

"What's wrong with your face?" I yelled at him.

His eyes were growing in size.

Unfortunately, my omega-gun was lying on the ground instead of resting in my hand. Comet was on the ground unconscious. Shadow was writhing on the ground with a laser spear sticking out of his chest. I flicked my wrist and blew Lunas's face off with my modified pop-gun. Lunas's army of thugs fired their weapons at us, not lasers or bullets but black pellets. The objects became some kind of black barrier between us and them.

I didn't wait. I grabbed Shadow with one hand, Comet with the other and bunny-hopped out the main entrance. Visibly, I'm sure we were the most ridiculous thing to be seen. I stopped.

On one side were Apollo Four, Moon Mother, the Twins and a virtual army of thugs with fezes on their heads. On the other side was another group with their own army of thugs. I recognized Pinwheel, so it was the Artemis Family. Everyone was armed with a long gun. Shadow and Comet sat up conscious on the ground.

We heard an explosion and the Lunas Corp thugs spilled out of the planetarium. The Families trained their guns on them. The thugs pointed their weapons at each other. The three of us were between them; Shadow and Comet glared at me with dirty looks. I knew what they were thinking: You killed us, Cruz! I pointed up.

The first flying saucer appeared. Soon the sky was filled with them.

"This is the interspace police! Drop your weapons and put your hands in the air! Comply or you will be killed!"

I lifted Shadow and Comet to their feet. I raised my hands. They did the same.

"I'm never working with you again," Comet told me.

CHAPTER 57

Seraff

"You have no jurisdiction over us," Moon Mother told Seraff.

Interpol soldiers descended to the ground and arrested everyone in sight. It didn't take long for spectators to start flying or floating to the scene, then the press started arriving.

"We agree completely," a silvery-haired man from the Artemis Family said, Pinwheel standing at his side.

"I do have jurisdiction," Seraff said. "I have the full authorization of the other Founding Families."

"Take our weapons and release us immediately," Apollo Four told him.

"He killed our CEO!" one of the thugs yelled, pointing at me.

"He will be taken into custody too," Seraff said to him. "We're all going to go down to the Interpol Lunar headquarters and we'll sit and talk as long as is needed to clear this up."

The arrested Families and megacorp thugs exploded in a rant of curses and threats. Seraff remained unfazed.

"We don't have time for that," I said to him.

"Why is that, Mr. Cruz?" Seraff asked me.

"We need to go to the Re-You headquarters right now."

"Why?"

"To take Ms. Java into custody."

"Why would Interpol need to do that?" Moon Mother asked. "I sent you to her to help. You want her arrested?"

"Why am I arresting her?" Seraff asked me.

"Re-You created the Three-Armed Man. He works for Lunas."

"That's a lie!" several of the thugs yelled at me.

"Lunas is working with one or more of the other Families?" Seraff asked as he looked at the Monarchs and Artemis Family.

"Aside from being untrue," Mr. Artemis said, "it's not illegal. Release us immediately, Director Seraff. Your career is literally in the balance."

"I don't appreciate being threatened," Seraff said to the man.

"Then do as you're told."

"Mr. Seraff, I think I have what you need to put these Founding Families in their place," I said.

"What would that be, Mr. Cruz?"

"I don't understand all the laws on the Moon, but could someone start a new colony?"

"No, of course not. Any new colony would have to be authorized by the ruling Families."

"I thought so. Mr. Seraff, there's a new colony on the Moon."

To say that one could hear a pin drop was an understatement.

351

"That's impossible," more than one person said.

"The mother dome of Lunar Colony is a city-size colony."

"Yes," Seraff answered, annoyed.

"What is a continental colony?"

"That would be ten times the size."

"Mr. Seraff, release us immediately!" Mr. Artemis commanded.

"There's a continental colony, or the start of one, on the far side of the Moon. Lunas is behind it. Either the Moon Monarchs or the Artemis Family helped, or maybe both of them. Tell the other Founding Families that, and they'll let you keep them under arrest for as long as you need to investigate."

Seraff gave the Family leaders a self-satisfied look.

"It's impossible, Mr. Seraff," Moon Mother said, in a far more respectful tone. "Such a structure could never be built without any of us knowing about it. It's impossible."

"There's one way to find out," I said. "Let's go there."

"Why are we listening to this Earthling?" Apex shouted.

"Do you expect people to fly around randomly on the dark side of the Moon hoping to run into a fictitious colony?" Pinwheel yelled.

"Not at all," I said. "I know exactly where it is. Lights from the colony have been seen from a satellite. That was, until the satellite suddenly stopped transmitting. Did you think I was bluffing?"

No one spoke.

"Seraff, I'm not trying to scare anyone, but you need to get to this Ms. Java because—" I said before I stopped speaking.

I looked around and the press was standing only a few feet from me.

"What, Mr. Cruz?" Seraff said.

"I don't want to cause panic because I don't know what it may mean."

"Say it!" "Tell us!" people in the audience yelled

Seraff gave me his palm device. I typed it in. Seraff looked at it.

"Arrest everyone, including the media!"

As people yelled out in protest, Seraff grabbed me and floated me to his waiting flying saucer transport.

CHAPTER 58

The Far Siders

Seraff was mad. He made the call to send his forces to storm the Re-You headquarters and take Ms. Java into custody.

"Mr. Cruz, what have you uncovered?"

"Why did you want me here? Are you going to tell me?" I asked.

"I'll think about it. I want to talk to this Ms. Java first."

"Did you see their faces?" I said. "The Families knew. None of them were surprised by what I said. They knew."

"That's not exactly going to stand up in court."

Seraff sat me down in the passenger section of the spacecraft. He went to the bridge and directed his crew to take off.

When we arrived at the Re-You headquarters, Seraff marched into the building, while I was hopping around like an idiot. He was wearing special boots that simulated Earth gravity. My micro-rockets in my jacket weren't working anymore after the blast attack in the planetarium.

Interpol soldiers had Ms. Java waiting in a conference room. She saw me and jumped up.

"What is the meaning of this? What has this Earth person been saying?"

"Is there a secret colony on the far side of the Moon?" Seraff asked.

"What? No. How would I know something like that? Is that what he's been saying? This Earth person is not rational. I'm a respected scientist."

"Ms. Java, please listen to me carefully," Seraff said. "I'm going to call my base at Praetoria Station and have them launch tactical missiles at the far side of the Moon."

"Please. Don't," she pleaded.

"Is there a secret colony on the far side of the Moon?"

"Yes."

He directed her to sit. The woman was falling apart before our eyes.

"Who is in the secret colony?" Seraff asked as he sat next to her.

"What is going to happen to me?"

"Is it a violation of the Utopia Bio-Ethics Code?"

"I do not believe that utopian syndrome is a bad thing. Wanting to make humanity better is a noble thing. We are already biologically augmented, genetically modified—even the Earth people are."

"We've been down this road before. That's why the Codes were created."

"They made mistakes. They were trying to create new life forms. We are making existing life better."

"What's the difference? Both lead to the same place. A word of the past was eugenics."

"We are not eugenicists. There is no superior or inferior. We are making all better."

"What's in the secret colony?"

"I refuse to answer."

"I'm sorry to interrupt," I said. "I know what I want is so unimportant to both of you in the grand scheme of things, but I'm a detective and I have a man to catch."

"You did this," Java said with anger.

"No, he did. He came to my planet, killed my client, framed me for it, and the people who sent him conspired to frame me. No, I didn't do this. You all did. I want the Three-Armed Man, then I go home."

"I will not help you."

"Then we'll do what we need to do without your help," Seraff said to her.

"They control the space port. You'll never get in."

"I understand your motives," I said. "You want to create better humans for the environments of off-world. But what about your partners? Lunas wanted to use your superhumans for criminal purposes."

"They are human beings like you and me. I'm not responsible for those who do bad."

"But what about the Families? Why would they do this? They don't care about either of those things. They're already perfect as far as they're concerned and they have plenty of people to do crimes for them. Seraff, do you know?"

"No, I don't, but it's nothing a few missiles couldn't solve."

"No!" Java cried.

"I should go there," I said.

"Go, Mr. Cruz? What makes you think I'll let a civilian anywhere near any secret colony? I know you fashion yourself the bounty hunter-avenger for your dead client, but you're out of this. You'll be going somewhere—home."

He looked at his soldiers.

"I want that Three-Armed Man," I said.

"Get Cruz out of here and find out when the next ship departs for Earth. I want him on it."

Just like that, my case had come to an end. The Three-Armed Man would get away, and I'd never know who sent him.

PART NINE

The Three-Armed Man

CHAPTER 59

Run-Time

Seraff's police soldiers reunited me with my two comrades, then escorted us away from the scene, stuffing us into their spaceship.

"This is your donut boy's show. Go home, Earthling," Comet said to me.

"Donut people? Is that what you Moon people call Space Station Colonists? Donuts?"

"We don't want to talk to you," Comet said.

The officers dumped me at Gist's house. I was told in no uncertain terms to book the next shuttle back to Earth. They took Shadow and Comet to drop off in the center of the Mother Dome.

My best friend gave me the card to call, so I called him.

"Get me out of here," I said as soon as Run-Time's face flashed on the vid-phone screen.

The receptionists answered and connected me immediately. He wasn't back on Earth yet. I could tell from the quality of the line. He was still on one of the Space Station Colonies.

"Finished with your case?" he asked.

"It's finished with me."

"Got your man?"

"He got away."

"Life happens."

"Yeah. Not my first. Won't be my last. I can't believe how much I miss normal gravity. I think I'm getting depressed."

Run-Time grinned. "Nothing's wrong with being homesick."

"I wonder what the family is doing."

"Now that's the right question to ask. I'll send a craft to pick you up. When do you want to leave?"

"As soon as you can get them here? I've been asked by Interpol to vacate the Moon too."

"Making friends wherever you go. I thought he was your friend."

"The spaceman wants me to vacate the Moon. He's arresting all kinds of people that can get him fired, so he's in a bad mood."

"Mr. Seraff is well-connected and well-liked in Up-Top law enforcement circles. I doubt anyone can get him fired. We'll have you off the white rock the day after tomorrow."

"Sounds good. I tried to call Earth but the line's down. I didn't think solar flares affected communication from here anymore."

"If it's bad it can."

"I'll keep trying, then I'll try to get some sleep. Maybe I'll just go to the spaceport and sleep there. Not sure I want to be spending a night here without my bodyguards. But I can't bring my weapons to the terminal, so I guess here I stay."

Run-Time tried to cheer me up, but I didn't like failing at anything, even if it was beyond my control. My desire to set foot on my own planet was growing by the second. I wanted to feel the rain on my face.

Why did the Metro police brass and DA's office set out to crucify me? They were directed behind the scenes by the very powerful Moon Monarchs. I assumed it was them because they truly believed I had something to do with their son's death. More and more the truth seemed to be that they didn't want me to uncover that they were involved in the murder from the start. I'd met lots of psychopathic people who had no problems doing away with a spouse, child, or other family member before. But often said family member was just as evil as they were. Prince— Apollo Five—was such a decent guy. Before I took his case, I couldn't find one speck of dirt on him. A rarity for someone at his level at a megacorp. He escaped from the Moon to be murdered decades later by the very family he escaped from. Or maybe, it wasn't just them. I couldn't help but notice how the Moon Monarchs, the Artemis Family, and the Lunas Corp all looked like the same big family of crooks when I mentioned the secret continent-colony. I wanted to get the Three-Armed Man, but I wanted to get everyone involved in hiring the murderer more. But like I told Run-Time, the case was done with me.

CHAPTER 60

Shadows

Outside of my own bed at home, I never slept on any hotel or strange bed. Being a recovering germophobe didn't mean I'd sleep in any germ-infested blankets. One of my suitcases contained my own travel sleeping bag—hermetically sealed and scented.

I was bundled up in my own cocoon when I heard the door chimes, followed by knocking on the door. I'd seen this movie before, and under no circumstances was I going anywhere near the front door of my guesthouse.

I jumped out of the sleeping bag and had forgotten I was on the Moon, meaning I smashed against the ceiling then floated back down. I hated weighing less than thirty pounds. I was fully dressed, except for my white fedora, with my omega-gun in hand. I had my other weapons strategically placed around the room.

My mobile rang. I answered it. It was White Shadow.

"Open the door," he said. "We know you're in there."

"Why? Why am I answering the door? I'm staying in here until my ride comes to take me back to Earth. I'm not opening the door for anyone. If Seraff and Interpol were to show up, I'm not opening the door."

"Cruz, we're going to the secret colony."

"What? What did you say?"

"We need to go out there."

"Why? Didn't you say that was certifiably insane?"

"We get it. We get that you don't want to let this go because they killed your client."

"Really?"

"But we need to leave the dome."

"Shadow, this isn't about him anymore. In my biz, you don't always win. I'm okay with that."

"There's much more going on here, Cruz. You said so."

"I'm not coming out, Shadow."

"Why would the Monarchs and Artemis be involved with this? You said so. They're Founders. They have more money than entire continents on Earth."

"True."

"We need to scout around this secret colony, but we need you. You know where it is."

"Then what?"

"See what we see and decide from there," Shadow replied.

"Are the dark side of the Moon and the far side of the Moon the same thing?" I asked.

"Dark doesn't mean without light," Comet's voice said in the background. "It means not visible from Earth. Dark side of the Moon and far side mean the same to you Earthers. Means different things to us."

"The exact opposite side of the moon from Lunar Colony," Shadow said.

"The dark side of the Moon gets as much light as our side," Comet added.

"Guys, I'm going home to Earth. You two live here."

"Cruz, the Families are at Lunar PD and Interpol is preoccupied with them."

"There's no way to get outside the dome," I said.

"We'll scout the area and that's it," Shadow said.

"Famous last words," I said. "I'm not coming out."

"We have a spaceship."

"And we put together a team," Comet added.

"There is no way I'm opening that door and coming out."

"The truth is, Cruz, there's an entire illegal smuggling black market outside the domes. There are ways to get out and that's why."

"Smuggling?"

"Smuggling in and out of Lunar Colony, and we don't give the Families a cut. We need you, Cruz, to tell us where the secret colony is. Not only my crew, but everyone has lost contact with their crews outside the domes."

"We've already been out there scouting for the secret colony," Comet said.

"Yeah, we were curious. Curiosity killed the cat. Don't you Moon people have that saying up here too?" I said.

"I need your help, Cruz. We helped you," Shadow pleaded.

"And you never told me why."

"A favor to someone," he revealed.

"Who? Did Quix talk to you?"

"No, I don't know him. It was Tiki."

Tiki was a hood back on Earth. He was also the stepson of my posthumous mentor, Wilford G. We worked together in my AI Confidential Case, a sad case for both of us.

"The fat ninja has contacts on the Moon too?"

"He does."

"Shadow, Moonbeam said they saw the lights near the South Pole—Aitken Basin," I said.

"That's the largest crater on the moon," Comet said. "No one goes there."

"Cruz, I need another gun with me on this one. Everyone knows your rep on Earth."

"You said it yourself. I'm only a detective."

"I have another guy on the team who you know."

"Who?"

"You call him Mr. 300."

"He's Dome Security."

"How do you think we get outside the domes?" Comet said.

"Come on, Cruz," Shadow said. "We have to leave. I need to find my crew out there, Mr. 300 wants to see this secret colony, and you want that Three-Armed Man. We all want something on this one. The more, the merrier."

"How do we know they don't have some kind of death laser out there? We don't know what happened to that satellite."

"Our spaceship has defenses against that," Comet said.

"They won't see us, Cruz. We've been in the smuggling game a long time. Interpol has never caught us, neither have the Families. We'll be like shadows moving in the night."

I sat in my chair marveling at my uniform. From head to toe, I was clothed in a real white spacesuit. The only thing missing was my helmet, which was tucked in a large pouch on the side of my chair. I was in a real spacesuit!

"The average Earther would be terrified," Mr. 300 said to me, seated beside me. "You're rolling around the surface of the Moon, outside the protective dome into danger, and you sit there as if it's a vacation adventure."

Now that I knew Mr. 300 was a government bureaucrat and criminal on the side, my admiration for him had waned. But I'd keep that to myself.

"I'm not in danger yet. I choose to enjoy the situation," I said.

The spaceship cabinet wasn't cramped at all. The exterior reminded me of a lizard without legs. An elongated craft with a passenger cabin to seat six comfortably, but more if needed on the floor. The cargo area wrapped around the command cabin with the propulsion engines in the tail.

Shadow sat in the cockpit in the immediate front with another guy, whom I'd never seen before and wasn't introduced to. In the seats behind us were Comet and a bunch of other guys. A dozen more sat on the deck, gripping its handholds.

"You said they didn't care," 300 said to me, continuing.

"These Families have risked everything. The Monarchs don't care that we suspect they killed their own heir-apparent."

"Seraff already told you. They joined together to create a veto bloc on the government. No one can touch them. Not Interpol, nor the other Founding Families. No one."

"They did this because Apollo Five might find out they had a secret colony? Why would he care? He wouldn't."

"A race of genetic super-people inside?" 300 said.

"He wouldn't care about that either. No, there's more."

"Possibly. None of us should let speculation get ahead of the facts. It's also possible this is a wild goose chase. The secret colony may not actually exist. If it does, it may be nothing more than people, other smugglers, and not genetic super-people."

"Our crews are missing," Comet interjected. "That's a fact."

"Yes, it is. The explanation may merely be they don't like trespassers. It may be more as Mr. Cruz is suggesting. We'll know soon. Hopefully, this all won't end with my body floating lifeless in the void of space above the Moon."

"How long has this secret smuggling network existed?" I asked 300.

"Forever," he answered.

"How could a secret colony exist without any of you knowing?"

300 didn't immediately answer me. I glanced back at Comet.

"We don't know," Comet answered. "We can't explain it."

"The logical answer is cloaking tech that we didn't know existed," 300 said.

"That exists?" I asked.

"It does. We use it against you Earthers."

I laughed. "I'm not offended at all. I expect you Up-Toppers to do such things. Why are we moving so slow?" I asked.

"So no one knows we're coming," 300 replied. "Our moon-runner has its own cloaking shield, but it has limitations. The faster we move, the less effective it is."

"They wouldn't see the ship, but they'd see the dust and dirt cloud," I said.

"You are IQ club material."

Earth was a world of analog hi-tech. Up-Top was all about digital. As the moon-runner craft continued its flight to the far side of the Moon, I had a chance to observe and note more of its construction. Earth vehicles had physical knobs, buttons, switches, dials, indicators. Shadow and the main pilot sat in front of a screen where every single interface was digital. They both had bulky headsets on, which I assumed were giving them audio reports of any nearby spacecraft.

We were two hours into the trip and no one really talked. None of us wanted to sleep either. There was no mistaking that what we were doing was extremely dangerous. However, I was the only one in the craft that had never done this before. All of them, including Mr. 300, were smugglers. I thought to myself, what other private detective in Metropolis, or any place on Earth, went to the Moon to wrap up a case? From a psychological standpoint, I kept reminding myself that I would be returning to Earth, hopefully aboard a Let It Ride spaceship.

The moon-runner rolled to a stop. Everyone looked up to see what was going on in the cockpit. The pilot was focused on what he was hearing in his headphones. Shadow swiveled around to face us and said, "There's a craft nearby. We'll wait here until it flies off."

"Who is it?" Comet asked. The same question others were going to ask.

"Looks like Surface Security."

He turned back to his console.

"You Moon people have security this far out from Lunar Colony?" I asked.

"Of course, we do," 300 said. "We wouldn't want you Earthers, or anyone else, landing and illegally setting up their own base or colony on our territory."

"Has that happened before?"

300 looked at me with amusement. "You're asking me that honestly? Yes, it's happened before and will continue to happen. It's a constant threat that neither Earth, the Space Colonies, nor Mars has to deal with."

"I'm sorry to hear that," I said. "You have to watch out for space invaders on your own planetoid."

"Meteor swarm!" the pilot yelled.

To my ear, it sounded like hail falling. I couldn't get a good look outside the craft because the only main window was in the cockpit. All the other windows were closed.

I observed the others. They all were unconcerned. Meteors seemed to be another thing they were all used to. If they weren't worried, I wasn't.

"Did it fly off?" Comet asked the cockpit.

"Still hovering out there," Shadow answered.

I looked at 300. "Do you think the Families know we're here?" I asked.

"The Families know about the illegal smuggling. They don't care. It's too small for them to be bothered with."

"What's the plan?" I asked.

"Plan?" 300 asked me.

"You've already lost other crews. Maybe this craft sees us and is calling in backup. What's our plan if that's true?"

"They can't see us," Comet said. "We've been doing this for years."

"So were your other crews, but they're gone. I like to be prepared, so I'm going to ask a third time: what's the plan? If they've seen us, they're calling in backup and they're readying to attack us."

"Shadow, he has a point," Comet yelled to the cockpit.

"Suit up then," Shadow answered.

"Suit up?" That was not the answer I expected or wanted.

Mr. 300, Comet, and the other guys were on their feet, checking their suits and putting on their helmets.

"Get moving, Cruz," Comet said to me. "It was your idea."

I reluctantly stood and put on my helmet too. It was idiot-proof. Place it on your head and it auto-sealed. In my field of view, all kinds of indicators turned on. The audios turned on, so I could hear. There was even a blast of fresh air to equalize the inner atmosphere and keep the faceplate from fogging up.

I smiled. "I'm a real-life astronaut now. All I need is to hop around outside with my national flag and make it official."

That's when the craft blew up.

CHAPTER 61

The Cabal

When I said the craft blew up, it exploded in a way I'd never seen before. It exploded and disintegrated at the same time, leaving all of us floating and bouncing around the surface of the Moon, disoriented. I was about to get my bearings when my suit shut off. It was exactly why we Earthers didn't trust digital tech. No power, not a thing you could do. My face-plate indicators were gone and my arm controls were completely off.

High above us, I saw them begin to land all around us. We were in our white astronaut suits; our captors were in sleek black ones. Shadow and the pilot were dragged away by black astro-suits. They tossed us all together in a pile, disarmed us of our long guns, and encircled us with their own long guns. I couldn't tell if the weapons were projectile shooting or laser shooters, but I didn't want to find out. I slowly looked up and there was nothing. No dome, no atmosphere. The vastness of endless space, and it was a reality that was terrifying for a true Earth-born. One of the captors could grab one of us and throw us into that void, and there'd be nothing we could do about it. I remembered a story I heard on Earth where they found a rock supposedly from another galaxy, and they said it had been floating for at least a million years before entering our solar system. That was exactly the kind of story I didn't need to be thinking about at the moment.

Something was going on, but it was difficult to tell with a helmet with no power. However, my audio was working, but barely. Shadow stood to his feet and was yelling at the captors in their black astro-suits. Not a smart move, but he wanted to know where his crew was. We all now knew what happened to his crew's spaceships. Two of our captors slammed him back down to the ground. Some of us grabbed him to keep him from bouncing, and to make sure he stayed down.

Another spaceship of an unknown configuration glided to a stop next to us and the rear opened. Our captors pulled us off the ground and pushed us in. When we were all loaded in, the rear door closed. None of the captors got in with us, but we still were helpless to do anything. It was a windowless compartment with barely any illumination. We felt the craft rise up and jet forward. All of us were bouncing against the walls and ground. It stopped.

When the door opened, there were a lot more of them waiting. They ran in and grabbed us. Others kept their long guns trained on us. We saw one huge dome in the shadowed area of a mountain. Then I realized it wasn't a mountain, but the edge of a giant crater. Then I saw another dome. By the time we reached the entrance of the dome they were taking us to, I counted at least six large domes, but there could have been more not visible in the darkness.

We were pushed through a large door, it closed, and we heard alarms. Through another door, it closed, and more alarms. We went through about a dozen other bay doors before we stopped in a large open area where even more of the people waited, but they weren't wearing helmets. I felt myself rise up in the air as my helmet was turned and pulled off. I looked around and other black astro-suits were taking the helmets off the others.

"Where's my crew?" I heard Shadow yell at them.

A thug without his helmet looked like he was going to butt Shadow in the face with his long gun.

"Do it," Shadow yelled.

"Stop," one of the captors said. "Throw them all in the hold with their friends. Let the Selenites occupy their time."

They pushed us ahead again, following a few of the captors in the lead. Our destination was literally a black hole in the ground. They pushed and kicked us in. Again, I was glad in this instance, I weighed less than thirty pounds. We fell into the pitch black, and finally crashed to the ground.

I heard voices call out Shadow's and Comet's names.

I sat up on the ground. We were in some cavern-like dungeon. Shadow's crew was found, but we had joined them. I got to my feet and joined the crowd. Shadow's crew went through the exact same thing we did. Their ships were blown apart, they were captured, and they were tossed into the pit as prisoners.

Their astro-suits were worn a bit, but they looked okay. Then I noticed the large rocks in some of their hands.

"What are the rocks for?" I asked.

Everyone looked at me.

"Who's he?" someone asked.

"A client," Shadow asked.

"He asked a question," Comet spoke up for me.

The looks on the faces of Shadow's missing crew made all of us scared. I was waiting for it. Mr. 300 asked.

"They said Selenites would occupy our time," he said. "What is a Selenite?"

"Don't panic when we tell you," one of them said. "You have to keep calm or more of them will come."

"What will come?" Comet pressed.

"The creatures."

"What creatures?" Shadow asked.

"Keep your voices down," another man said.

I was a recovered germophobe. It was far worse than that when I was a child. Doctors were going to commit me to a Bubble Boy colony at one of the space stations for those with severe germophobia of an untreatable nature. My parents told those doctors where to shove their diagnosis, but it was a lot of work on both of our parts to overcome it. I still had more than a few quirks, but I'd beaten it. However, that didn't mean I could tolerate any kind of nastiness. It didn't mean there weren't situations or things that could bring on a full-blown germophobic attack—more like a psychotic fit. Isopods, the aquatic world's version of a rat, were my Achilles' heel.

The bloodsucking crustaceans with their roly-poly, segmented exoskeletons, antennae, and multi-jointed legs were the terror of my nightmares. Even non-germophobic citizens were horrified by them. We were terrified of the tiny ones, but even on Earth larger ones the size of a cat had been seen. What was crawling to me was larger than a flat elephant. A Selenite was an isopod—an isopod the size of a hovercar, and with a lot more legs. I lost it.

I don't even clearly remember all that I did, other than it involved yelling, running, jumping, shooting, and explosions. There wasn't just one giant isopod—a product of evil genetic modifications; there were hundreds of them!

I had gone mad. I jumped and ran up the wall of the pit. When I reached the surface, I crashed into three black astro-suits. I threw two of them into the pit, grabbed the long gun from the last one and kicked him into a fourth captor. My madness was far from over. I was running, shooting, and jumping. The long guns shot black pellets that liquified inorganic matter.

Black pellets flew past me. I turned. Dozens of black astro-suits ran at me, firing a shower of black pellets in my direction.

"I will not be infested!" I yelled.

I'd been hit so many times, my suit was gone. Above me, two mini-spaceships aimed their turrets at me. A laser blast struck a few feet from me. I ran, but not away. I ran to the attacking spaceship. How he missed me, I didn't know? How I jumped onto the moving craft, I didn't know? However, I did and fired my long gun at the cockpit. The black pellets weren't working for me. I used the long gun as a bat and, with one swing, cracked the glass and knocked out the pilot. I grabbed him and tossed him out. I hit every weapons button there was. Lasers fired everywhere. Explosions. Things catching fire. A missile fired! The missile curved upwards to the roof. I dove out of the craft.

That's when the roof of the dome blew up.

The two dome spaceships were sucked out first. "Evacuation" was the technical term. All the air within the dome rushed out into the vastness of space. Black astro-suits, weapons, furniture, food, water, cargo containers, everything flew out the hole. The hole itself grew in size as more pieces of the dome were ripped apart. Then I saw what I didn't want to see. Giant isopods, masses of them, were sucked out of the pit into space. Sirens flashed and a barrier closed over the opening. I'd been holding on to a handhold on the ground. The breach sealed, and I could feel and hear the rush of oxygen back into the dome from the generators.

I knew there were lots more giant isopods in the pit than I saw. My rampage continued. I ran through the dome and shot every last person and robot left that I caught sight of. With that done, I gathered every long gun I could find like a hoarder, pushed the pile in front of the pit, and prepared to shoot any giant isopod that crawled up to the ground level. In fact, I didn't wait to see one. I started firing into the darkness.

"Stop shooting!" I heard someone below yell out.

"Where are the giant isopods?" I yelled back.

"Cruz, is that you?" Shadow yelled.

"Where are the giant isopods?"

I saw a face appear and almost blew his head off. Shadow winced and ducked down for a moment. He reappeared and stared at me.

"Cruz, can you lower your guns?"

"Where are the giant isopods?"

"Cruz, they're gone. Did you do all this damage up here?" He glanced up to see the big hole in the dome roof.

"Where are the giant isopods?"

"I'm guessing you really don't like isopods."

"Who is this Earth guy?" one of Shadow's guys said.

"I thought I knew. I was told he was some street detective. I didn't know we had a superhero among us," Shadow said.

"He's not even genetically engineered," Comet said as he walked to me and patted me on the shoulder. "You saved our butts, Earth man."

The dome we were in was a cargo receiving spaceport and hangar, with a warehouse and its own dungeon prison. As of now, it was under Shadow's control. His men were armed and had taken strategic positions. As for the many black astro-suits I'd shot, we had them lying on their chests, face down, with their hands interlaced behind their heads. I was counting all the captors I'd shot; it was over a hundred of them and I was still counting. But I had no memory of it because of my panic attack.

Those not on sentry duty sat in the dome's port command center. Mr. 300 was typing, hacking into the systems. I sat on the ground quietly, my heart racing. I hadn't had such an attack in a long time. But at least all the remaining Selenites in the pit were dealt with by Shadow's men.

"I'm in," 300 said. "This is one of two spaceports. There is a larger living dome. A power dome. A fifth and final primary defense dome. Also, there are other dome clusters. I'm not clear as to how many in total, but we are connected to two others."

"How many in the living dome?" Shadow asked.

"Unknown. Not listed from what I can tell."

"We need to grab one of their spaceships to get out of here," the pilot said.

"Are we sure we can log in?" Shadow asked.

"Do we have a choice?" the pilot asked.

"We have another problem," Mr. 300 said. "We're being surrounded."

"How many?" Comet asked.

"Not able to get a count, but a lot. They're gathering at the main port entrance and multiple spacecraft have taken positions around the dome."

"There's one craft inside here left, but it's damaged," another man said.

"Get it repaired and ready to go," Shadow said to them.

Two of the men ran off.

"They'll shoot us out of the air," the pilot said.

"We need a plan," Shadow said.

"The only plan needed is to keep them from getting in," Mr. 300 said.

"We have men, but not enough to keep them all out," Shadow said.

"Mr. Cruz has his tracking bracelet and I have an embedded chip device. We keep them out and wait till Interpol arrives."

"How can you be a smuggler with a chip?" I asked.

"I know how to turn it off when I need to," he said.

"Waiting is the plan?" Comet asked.

"Yes," 300 said.

"I don't like it," Comet said.

I walked to Mr. 300's console and looked at the monitors. "Call the main dome."

Everyone looked at me.

"Why?" Shadow asked.

"Maybe they'll pick up," I said.

"I wouldn't," 300 said.

"Shadow is the only one here who's got what he came for. You and I are still waiting for our presents. You want to see what's in the living dome, and you know what I want. What do you think we can say to them to make them talk to us?"

300 leaned forward and tapped a few buttons on the digital screen. "That's easy."

We waited until the pilot and his men repaired the spaceship, damaged from being lifted up and slammed to the ground after almost being sucked out of the dome. They drove it closer to the office and kept it powered, ready to fly or fire weapons.

"Main dome, please respond," Mr. 300 said into the console audio-mic. "We know you're monitoring us and your forces are surrounding us. Please respond, or I'll call my superiors and give them the go-code to initiate a full laser barrage and destroy everything within this crater valley."

A virtual screen popped up, then another, and so on. The first screen was of Apex and Nadir. The twins appeared to be sitting on the bridge of a spaceship. On another screen were Pinwheel, the Artemis elder, and a third man. The people on the other screens I'd never seen before. One of the screens had Apollo Four and the Moon Mother.

"All transmissions are being blocked," Apex said. "Exit the dome or we'll be the ones initiating a full laser barrage to destroy everyone in your dome."

"If that were true, you'd have done it by now," Mr. 300 said. "What is it that you want? We're all smugglers here. What can we negotiate so everyone walks away happy?"

"We were about to ask you the same thing," Mr. Artemis said.

"You kidnapped my men," Shadow yelled.

"You trespassed into the forbidden area," one of the men on another screen said. "We've allowed you smugglers to operate. All you had to do was follow that one simple rule."

I looked at Shadow. "How long has this rule been in place?"

"A long time. Years," Shadow said.

"Decades," Mr. 300 corrected.

"We were wrong again," I said. "It wasn't only the Moon Monarchs and the Artemis Families. The people on the other screens are the other Founder Families."

"Yes," 300 replied.

"This wasn't about the Moon Monarchs and Artemis. All of them were involved from the start. You killed my client—all of you!" I yelled at them. "Apollo Five was never coming back to the

Moon. He had a happy life. He was never coming back to discover your plot."

"What plot?" Shadow asked.

"Where's the Three-Armed Man?" I asked. "That's who I want. Is he outside the dome now? Where is he?"

"You have a singular sickness, Mr. Cruz," said another man on another screen. "If he was, what would you do about it?"

"Tell me, and I'll show you."

"Can we negotiate?" 300 asked.

"What kind of mother are you?" I yelled at the Moon Mother. "They killed your son and you sit there."

"You don't know anything," she said.

"You're right. I don't. You are all a sick and twisted lot. I see why he ran away from all of you."

"Shut up!" the Moon Mother shouted, almost crying.

"Interpol will destroy these domes," Mr. 300 said. "We are all expendable."

"If any such act of aggression is taken against our Children, we will destroy everyone responsible," another Founder said. "Lunar Colony maintains its own space fleet."

"Children?" 300 asked.

"We will never allow you to capture our Children in the other domes," Mr. Artemis said.

"The Selenites were only the first test. We've progressed far beyond that to create the perfect race. Our Children," a founder said. "We will fight to the death to protect them, or avenge them."

"What's this button?" I asked.

"Don't touch that," Mr. 300 said. "That will disconnect this call."

I pressed the button. All the virtual screens turned off. Everyone jumped up and looked at me.

"Why did you do that?" Shadow yelled at me.

I looked at Mr. 300. "You already know too, don't you?"

"How do you know?" he asked.

"What are you two talking about?" Comet and the others asked.

"The life-sign readings," I said to Mr. 300. "I guess the symbol is universal."

"What are you two talking about?" Shadow asked.

"There are no life-signs in the other domes," 300 told them.

"What does that mean?" Shadow asked.

"It's a ruse. There are no Children, no mutants, or super-people in the domes. What do you think they have in them, Mr. 300? Weapons? A space armada."

"I'm in," Mr. 300 said.

On the screen, he'd hacked into the camera system of the other domes. The feed was promptly cut off. But we'd seen it already. The domes housed a space fleet larger than we'd ever seen. The black craft were of a design we were sure no one had ever seen before either, on Earth or off-world.

"If we blew up the domes, they'd claim they contained their Children and still use it as an excuse to attack whoever they wanted—the Space Colonies and Earth," Mr. 300 said.

"Then call Interpol now," Shadow said.

"Too late," Mr. 300 said. "They're jamming everything."

"I need a new spacesuit!" I said.

They were jamming transmissions, cut the digital camera feed to the other domes, but not the camera of our own dome. I'd been watching our adversaries in their black astro-suits gathering outside. One of them immediately caught my attention.

"Why? What are you going to do?" Shadow asked.

I looked at 300. "You can figure out a way to contact Seraff and tell him to get into those domes first to get the evidence. He can destroy them after. You're a genius, so I know you can do it."

"No mutants? But the Selenites," Comet said.

"Don't remind me. That's not the only mutant thing they created."

"Where are you going then?" Shadow asked again.

"My Three-Armed Man. He's right outside the dome!"

CHAPTER 62

Moon Shot

I'd read a lot about the Founders—the different Families that created the space colonies, built the first permanent human habitats on the Moon, and colonized Mars. The Families started out as idealistic pioneers, builders, scientists, and terra-formers. They were visionaries wanting to create a new utopia for humanity, a true utopia to leave behind the dystopia they felt Earth had become. The history began with great promise and hope, but not unlike many of humanity's epic journeys, devolved into a kind of horror. Both Earth's governments and megacorps tried to take the "new worlds" the Founders had created from them. It was centuries ago, but those wide-eyed Founding Families transformed into human beings so inhuman that Earth surrendered and withdrew to our planet, never to cross the Founders again. We had our own problems on Earth with the Fall—regressing from our own digital tech to a new analog tech regime. Then Up-Top began to war amongst themselves, just as we had done, but the Founders restored order. Earth also got its act together with our careful balance between our super governments and the megacorporations, with the crime world in between.

When I burst through the main entrance, I fired my new weapon at the Three-Armed Man first. He let loose with a double-barreled laser rifle, which blackened and disrupted a good section of the wall behind me; I'd side-stepped the blast. My shot landed and blasted him back. Was his black astro-suit laser-proof or laser-resistant? I meant to find out. He ran. I flew after him.

Obviously, he wasn't alone. The army of Founders had encircled our dome. But I wasn't alone either. Shadow's men spilled out of the domes and occupied them with heavy laser fire.

Before he fled, the Three-Armed Man made a crude gesture at me with his third arm. Multiple jet nozzles lit up his back as he blasted away. My suit had the same, and with my arm controls, I followed after him. We were one rocket man chasing another across the surface of the Moon.

He was never going to lose me, but he was too far away for me to get a clean shot with my weapon. But I was patient. I aimed and simply waited for my shot. However, I had to fight the growing awe that was overtaking me. I was flying across the white surface of the Moon. It wasn't a virtual or augmented reality simulation. It was real. The void of space above us; I could see stars, and even, I think, a flickering comet. The sights were mesmerizing.

On the other hand, I was in a suit. Yes, it was comfortable, roomy, climate-controlled, but I still viewed it as being wrapped in a body bag of a sort. The digital viewscreen was impressive. The effect made your helmet and suit invisible to the eye. You had an obstructed view of everything around you, but it was too perfect. It didn't allow your mind to truly grasp the enormous danger that surrounded you. In my case, the danger was a thousand-fold. If anything happened to me, as I'd been warned by many others, there'd be no one to come to my rescue. My body would bounce off the surface into the void of space and never be seen again. I was fighting the beauty of my surrounds and the perfection of my gear to focus on my target—the Three-Armed Man. One of us was going to die at the end of this chase. We both knew it.

A fleet of flying saucer spaceships zipped over us in the direction of the secret colony. We both kept a steady direction away from that battle. Unlike a hovercar race on Metropolis, there was no going faster. We Earthers liked speed. When in space, these Up-Toppers liked their senior citizen speeds. I kept my arms locked, maintaining my aim on him. He was about twenty feet ahead of me. A spaceship appeared above us. I ignored it.

The Three-Armed Man dove for a crater. I followed and as I came over the ridge, with my advanced optics, I saw a piece of him in the distance lying on the surface, aiming at me. But I was already prepared. My volley of lasers showered him before he could get off one shot. Then he was distracted by a sudden spotlight on him from the spaceship above us. He panicked and tried to blast off again. All he did was give me a bigger target as I drew closer. I shot him apart with my volley—his suit, then his body. I set down on the surface and watched. The Three-Armed Man's corpse floated off. Any blood that spilled out of him had frozen solid and moved with him on the same trajectory. Another casualty of another failed crime plot. The Families wanted me to think he was one of their many super-human mutants. I'd built him up in my mind too, but he was just an average hood and a lousy shot with a third arm protruding from his chest. There was nothing special about him at all. My "great" anticlimactic showdown was over. Framing me wasn't personal; they probably never knew who I really was—just some fake-famous private detective. If they'd known, they'd never have set this all in motion.

The flying saucer shadowing us was still above. It trained its light on me. I'd known it was the space police. I let my gun fall, and held my hands up.

Was I finally going home to Earth? I'd had my fill of the White Rock.

I'd learned in my Blade Gunner and Alien cases that Up-Toppers had an unhealthy fear of lasers. Earth was crawling with laser gun-toting crooks, cops, and citizens. On the Space Station and Lunar Colonies, and Mars, a simple laser blast could potentially rupture a barrier or dome and kill every last man, woman and child. They had more safeguards against that and other threats like meteors, but mentally every off-worlder was terrified of lasers, like I was scared of isopods. It made them crazy. Only space authorities with every authorization imaginable could use them, and it had to be in response to an "immediate threat to the population."

I looked back at the secret colony, and the space above it was lit up by a lightshow of lasers. The Founders were shooting lasers at the space police, but the police had the superior firepower. A fierce battle between the Lunar Founders and Interpol happened at the site of the oldest, largest, and deepest impact crater on the Moon. But it was a battle that the Founders could never win. They did surrender. To live was to survive. Founders were survivors. I only wished that Mr. Prince, Apollo Four, had been so lucky on his adopted home planet called Earth.

CHAPTER 63

Fight Club

Was it over? It was over for me.

I left Lunar Colony on a Let It Ride shuttle the next day. Interpol had taken me into custody briefly, but I was released an hour later. All my belongings were returned, and this time I went to the Lunar spaceport and stayed there until my departure.

From the spaceport, I did call Shadow and Comet to give my thanks and say my goodbyes. There was a complete media blackout about the Lunar Founders, their secret colony, and the space battle that occurred. I also learned that Interpol never did destroy the secret colony of the Moon's Founders as Seraff said he would. In the near future, I expected to see Up-Top news reports of the Spacies and Martians fighting for control of them. Or maybe, Interpol would keep the whole thing for themselves.

I did receive an official commendation from Interpol, courtesy of Seraff, for my assistance in their investigation, but he never called me. In fact, no one could tell me what happened to the Moon Monarchs, Artemis, or any of the Families. It was as if nothing ever happened. There was only one piece of news months later: Apollo Four had died of natural causes. I wouldn't be surprised at all if he "accidentally" found himself outside the mother dome without a spacesuit.

Gist ended up selling his lunar house and returned to Earth. He bought a hover mansion in one of the residential animal sanctuaries in Africa, with giraffes, rhinos, and elephants right outside his porch. He told me he had a guesthouse there too, if I ever wanted to visit. Not sure if I wanted to visit him and wake up to monkeys jumping up and down on me; Cruz Jr. did that already.

Months later, my curiosity had gotten the better of me and I found myself on one of those conspiracy Net sites Moonbeam had told me about. I wanted to see what the chatter was about regarding my Moon "visit." They did a better job of reporting it all than the media. And surprisingly, it was all accurate, including one item I would never have guessed or found out on my own in a million years for obvious germophobic reasons. The Selenites were the Founders' new race. The creatures were to be the pilots for the Founders' space armada and whatever conquests these Lunar Families had in mind. Intelligent isopods that could fly spaceships? The crazy Up-Toppers were making real space invaders!

But I realized something else. I recalled a line that I'd read about the Founders. The ultimate allegiance of all Founder members was to the Family, not one's own family. I had reasoned that the Lunar Founding Families had thought Mr. Prince, or Apollo Five, posed a perceived threat to their conquest plans, whatever it was. Then it was decided as a group to eliminate him. From the Moon Mother's face, she'd voted against the action, but was overruled and that was the end of it. Founders over family. Apollo Five was heir apparent to the Moon Monarchs, but by leaving the Family, he was no longer considered a true member. Once he was discovered his fate was sealed.

I was wrong. Not that the Lunar Founders weren't capable of cold homicide when it came to a royal member, but I suspected there was more, even if it seemed a trivial motivation to me. I'd thought they had found him. The truth was that they always knew where and who he was on Earth. He wasn't the threat. Cookie was. Prince was killed to prevent him from marrying his girlfriend, Cookie. Such a marriage would have made her—an Earth commoner—a royal member of the Family. That's what they couldn't allow. The revelation made me angry, and I was glad I helped end their mad plot—the Moon Monarchs, Artemis, Lunas, and all their fellow co-conspirators. If they'd left him alone, I would've never known about them. I would never have set foot on the Moon. Who told me? An unlikely source called me weeks later after his own return from the White Rock: Mr. Hip-Hop. Apparently, the entertainer, musical inventor, and street hustler also had a very large young fan base on the Moon, including among the Founding Families. Adults would take their secrets to the grave, but their kids? They'd reveal all to their favorite celebrity for an autograph.

When I touched down at Metro International, I literally dropped and kissed the ground.

"Love you, Earth!"

I was told by customs that I hadn't been the first Earther to visit the Moon or Mars, return, and do that. Just as I'd been warned, I felt weird walking; I wasn't thirty pounds anymore. Instead, I felt as if I were six hundred pounds.

All I wanted to see was the family. Dot waited outside the customs area with Kat in one arm, and Cruz Jr. holding her other hand. Cruzie burst away when he saw me, ran to me, and jumped into my arms, smiling. I was so happy. I kissed my wife, my daughter, and my son. We went home to the beautiful Concrete Mama. When we exited the terminal, I had to stand under the rain for a while. My ma and pops were there too. And the Hellspawn were there as well—well, it couldn't all be perfect.

PJ and Phishy had held down the business. PJ actually already added news photos from what she was calling my Moon Case. There was only one thing left to do for me to close the books on the case.

There were lots of illegal mixed-martial arts rings in Metropolis. Sometimes the ones for normals were more popular than the cyborg fights. The fights always went much longer, so spectators and bettors felt they got more show for their money.

This amateur MMA ring was huge. Any one of the spectators, including the women and children, could beat the Average Joe to a pulp. They were a blood-thirsty bunch and craved their violent nights of bouts.

"Undefeated in the blood red corner is the Masked Nightmare!" the announcer yelled.

The bruiser came into the ring wearing a blue Mexican wrestling mask, tights and skintight boots. His chest was covered in filthy tattoos. He cracked the knuckles of his right hand, then left fist. It was a very good disguise. No one would have guessed he was really a Metro PD detective.

"I could beat you to death!" he yelled to the crowd, and they responded back to him in anticipation.

"We have a new challenger in the brown vomit corner. His name is Fedora!"

I was in a mask too, but the second Detective Dent saw my tan fedora...

Well, he didn't say "holy crap." He said "holy" something else. I'll leave it to your imagination as to what he said, and what colors of the dark rainbow he ended up being when my fists and feet were finished with him. He tried to jump out of the ring, but spectators threw him back in. I never forgot a thing, and Dent never should have cracked his knuckles that way in that first interrogation. I knew it looked familiar. When the fight bell rang, the first thing I did was kick him in the head, to loud cheers of the crowds.

It's supposed to be a nice island getaway for Cruz and the family. Instead it's *Write Me a Murder on Jules Verne's Island: A Liquid Cool Cozy Murder Mystery (Book 9)!* What does a private detective have to do around here to get a quiet vacation?

THANK YOU FOR READING!

Dear Reader,

I hope you enjoyed my **Liquid Cool** cyberpunk detective novel, *The Moon Is A Great Place to Die.*

Can You Write Me a Review?

I'd greatly appreciate an honest review on one or more of the following sites:

Reviews are the best way for readers to discover good books. My writer's motto is simple: "Readers Rule!" Thanks so much.

Always writing,

Austin Dragon

CONTINUE THE ADVENTURE

Get Your Next *Liquid Cool* Books!

These Mean Streets, Darkly (Liquid Cool Prequel Short)
Liquid Cool (Liquid Cool: The Cyberpunk Detective Series, Book 1)
Blade Gunner (Liquid Cool, Book 2)
NeuroDancer (Liquid Cool, Book 3)
The Electric Sheep Massacre (Liquid Cool, Book 4)
I, Alien Hunter (Liquid Cool, Book 5)
A.I. Confidential (Liquid Cool, Book 6)
Biopunk Blues (Liquid Cool, Book 7)
The Moon Is A Good Place to Die (Liquid Cool, Book 8)
Write Me a Murder on Jules Verne's Island: A Liquid Cool Cozy Murder Mystery (Book 9)

Liquid Cool Box Set (Liquid Cool Prequel and Books 1-3)
Liquid Cool Box Set 2 (Liquid Cool: Books 4-6)
Liquid Cool Box Set 3 (Liquid Cool: Books 7-9)

Liquid Cool: From the Crazy Maniac Files mini-series

Classic Cyborg (Book One)
Digital Samurai (Book Two)

Also by Austin Dragon

See all my books in science fiction, horror, and fantasy at:
http://www.austindragon.com/books

ABOUT THE AUTHOR

Austin Dragon is the author of the *After Eden* **Series**, including the *After Eden: Tek-Fall* mini-series, the classic *Sleepy Hollow Horrors*, the new epic fantasy adventure *Fabled Quest Chronicles*, and cyberpunk detective series, *Liquid Cool*. He is a native New Yorker, but has called Los Angeles, California home for the last twenty years. Words to describe him, in no particular order: U.S. Army, English teacher, one-time resident of Paris, political junkie, movie buff, Fortune 500 corporate recruiter, renaissance man, dreamer.

He is currently working on new books and series in science fiction, fantasy, and classic horror!

Connect with Austin on social media at:

Website and blog: http://www.austindragon.com

Pinterest: http://www.pinterest.com/austindragon

Goodreads: https://www.goodreads.com/ADragon

Other books by Austin:

See all my books at: http://www.austindragon.com/books